Flying over water | Volar damunt l'aigua

PETER GREENAWAY

Fundació Joan Miró
Barcelona

MERRELL HOLBERTON
PUBLISHERS LONDON

"WHO KILLED COCK-ROBIN?"

17.

sp

Wardour   raspberry 7.4.7

Nightingale Lane blackberry 2.9.11

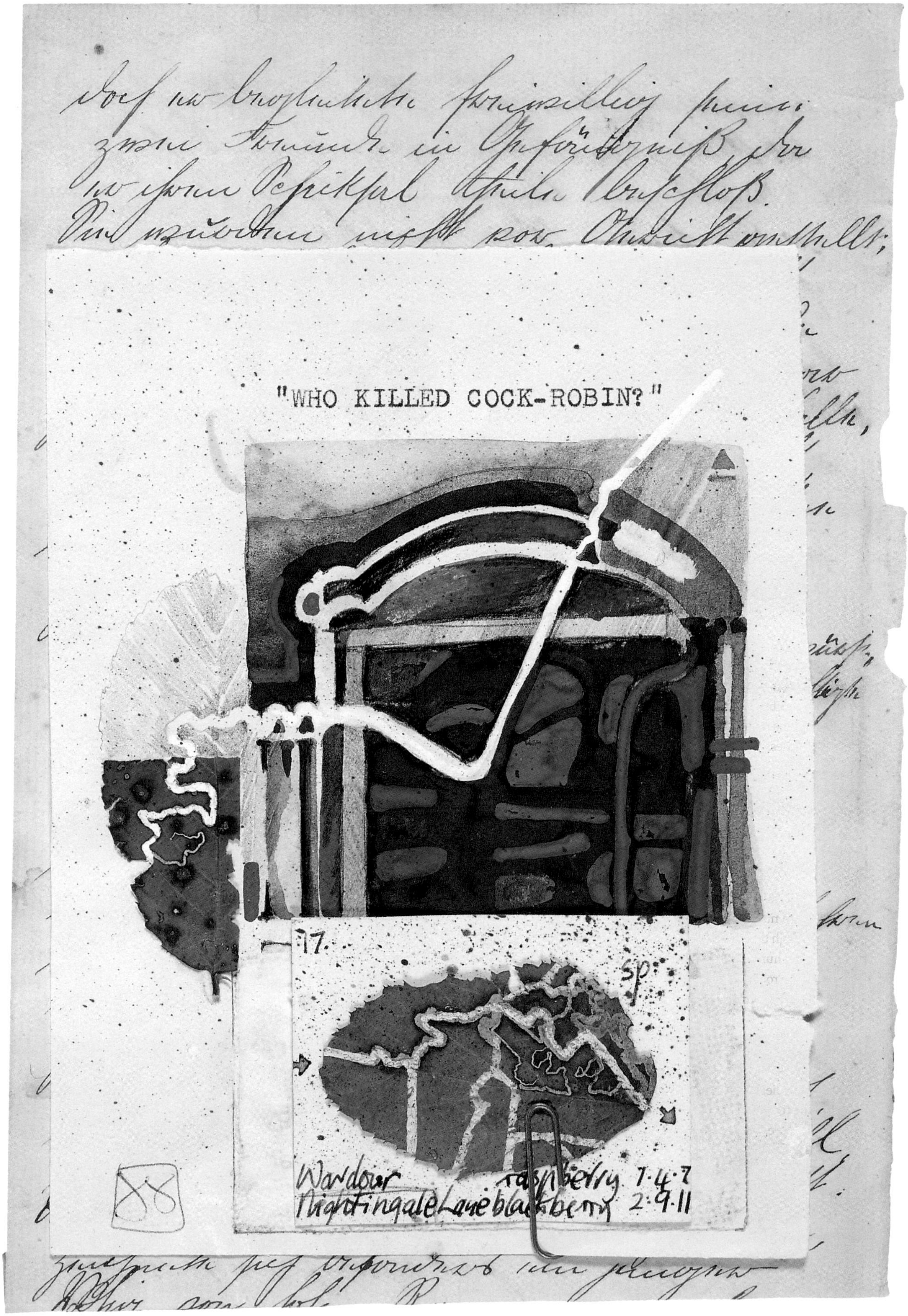

Flying over water

Volar damunt l'aigua

PETER GREENAWAY

This is a map from the film *A Wall Through H*. In fact it's several maps – a composite – and the most important element is the bramble leaf mined by a gall-wasp grub. As the grub fattens up on the leaf, eating a tunnel within the leaf's thickness, so the tunnel gets wider and larger in proportion to the grub's growing body, until the grub is satisfied, pupates, de-chrysalizes and flies away to lay eggs elsewhere to start the cycle again. The labyrinthian windings of such a tunnel of such a voracious eater, whose appetite wondrously dictates both a map and its own body size, must be significant.

The legend "Who Killed Cock Robin" is the title of a tragic sentimental English nursery rhyme that lugubriously works its way through the animal kingdom – anthropomorphic crows and humanoid rooks, all declaring the last rites on the robin's existence.

> "Who killed Cock Robin?"
> "I", said the sparrow,
> "With my bow and arrow,
> I killed Cock Robin".
> "Who saw him die?"
> "I said the fly,
> With my little eye."

No wonder English children learn cruelty to animals in the nursery. The robin is sometimes called the redbreast, for the blood that dripped from the cross stained the bird's feathers. Such a pedigree is bound to make the bird an excuse for tragedy. In this map from the film *A Walk Through H* are many elements of the Icarus story – the labyrinth, the hopeful growth of the child, the tragic bird, free flight, a death, the grand funeral, and the ominous taint of sacrifice. No wonder the *H* in the title *A Walk-Through H* can stand for Heaven or Hell.

And one day the paper clip in the picture will rust and improve the image.

Això és un mapa de la pel·lícula *A Walk Through H*. De fet és una combinació de diversos mapes, i el seu element més important és la fulla d'esbarzer minada per la larva d'un insecte parasitari. La larva es va engreixant a mesura que va obrint un túnel dins el gruix de la fulla, i el túnel s'engrandeix i s'eixampla de manera proporcional a l'augment del cos de la larva, fins que la larva queda satisfeta, es converteix en crisàlide, després es descrisalitza i se'n va volant a pondre els ous en algun altre lloc i així tornar a iniciar el cicle. Els meandres laberíntics d'un túnel construït per un devorador tan voraç, l'apetit del qual configura un mapa extraordinari i alhora determina la grandària del seu propi cos, han de ser significatius.

La frase "Who Killed Cock Robin?" (Qui ha matat el pit-roig?) és el títol d'uns versos infantils anglesos sentimentals i tràgics, que recorren lúgubrement el regne animal: corbs antropomòrfics i gralles humanoides declaren els ritus finals de l'existència del pit-roig:

> "Qui ha matat el pit-roig?"
> "Jo", va dir el pardal,
> "amb el meu arc i la meva fletxa,
> jo he matat el pit-roig".
> "Qui l'ha vist morir?"
> "Jo", va dir la mosca,
> "amb el meu ullet."

No és estrany que els nens anglesos aprenguin a ser cruels amb els animals des del parvulari. El pit-roig s'anomena així perquè la sang que va degotar de la creu li va tacar les plomes. Un pedigrí d'aquest tipus ha de convertir necessàriament aquest ocell en una excusa per a una tragèdia. En aquest mapa de la pel·lícula *A Walk Through H* hi ha molts elements de la història d'Ícar: el laberint, l'esperançat creixement de la criatura, l'ocell tràgic, el vol lliure, una mort, el solemne funeral i la màcula ominosa del sacrifici. No és estrany que la H del títol *A Walk Through H* tant pugui ser la inicial de Heaven (Cel) com de Hell (Infern).

I, un dia o un altre, el clip de la il·lustració es rovellarà i millorarà la imatge.

This book accompanies the exhibition
Flying over water
at the Fundació Joan Miró
6th March 1997–25th May 1997

Aquest llibre accompanya l'exposició "Volar
damunt l'aigua" de la Fundació Joan Miró
6 de març–25 de maig de 1997

Translation/Traducció
Joan Sellent

Copyright ©1997 Peter Greenaway

First published in 1997, in association with the
Fundació Joan Miró,
by Merrell Holberton Publishers Ltd,
Axe and Bottle Court, 70 Newcomen Street,
London SE1 1YT

All rights reserved

ISBN 1 85894 033 8

Produced by Merrell Holberton
Designed by Stephen Coates
Printed and bound in Italy

The Joan Miró Foundation wishes to thank the
following for loans/La Fundació Joan Miró vol
agrair els préstecs de:

Arxiu Capitular de la Catedral de Barcelona
Arxiu Històric de la Ciutat Barcelona
Biblioteca Artur Martorell
Biblioteca de Catalunya
Biblioteca del Col·legi d'Arquitectes de Catalunya
Biblioteca de la Universitat de Barcelona
Calcografía Nacional
Canaletes, S.A.
F. Museu d'Història de la Medicina de Catalunya
Herrera, J., S.A.
Josep Mañà
Museo Arqueológico de Sevilla
Museo Provincial de Ourense
Museu d'Arqueologia de Catalunya
Museu Episcopal de Vic
Museu de Zoologia
Òscar Pujol
Manel Sánchez Damián

The Joan Miró Foundation also wishes to thank/
La Fundació Joan Miró vol expressar el seu
agraïment a:
Josep Bancells
Ricard Batista
Ricard Alcojor
Agustí Argelic
Rosma Barnils
Josep Bosch
Miquel Bruguera
Martí Bonet
Teresa Carreras
Juan Carrete Parrondo
Felip Cid
Victòria Colomé
Eric De Visscher
Francisco Fariña
Fernando Fernández Gómez
David Ferrer
Enric Figols
Francesc Fontbona
Eulàlia García
Miquel S. Gros
Javier Herrera
Maria Àngels Iglesias
Manuel Jorba
Dolors Lamarca
Juan Loeck
Ramon Mas
Glòria Massó
Rosa Mut
Josep M. Olivé
Manuel Rovira
Jordi Torra
Francesc Uribe
Maria Josep Virgos

Cerabella
Soler & Palau
Pujol Muntalà, S.A.
Observatori Fabra
Fundació Barcelona Olímpica

and particularly Maria Carme Farré/i, d'una
manera molt especial, a Maria Carme Farré

We are also grateful for help from/També vol
agrair la col·laboració de

The British Council
IRCAM, Centre Georges Pompidou

Frontispiece: *Peter Greenaway*, Who killed
Cock Robin. *A map from the film* A Walk
through H. *In it are many elements of the
Icarus story,– the labyrinth, the hopeful
growth of the child, the tragic bird, free
flight, a death, the grand funeral, and the
ominous taint of sacrifice.*
Cover illustration: clockwise – *Anthony
Oliver*, photo; *A Second World War pilot;
Sue Fox*, Open Hand (*detail*), 1995, photo;
Rembrandt, The Abduction of Ganymede
(*detail*), Paris, Musée du Louvre.

Frontispici: *Peter Greenaway*, Who Killed Cock
Robin (*Qui va matar el pit-roig*). Un mapa de la
pel·lícula A Walk Through H, *on apareixen molts
elements de la història d'Ícar: el laberint,
l'esperançat creixement de la criatura, l'ocell
tràgic, el vol lliure, una mort, el solemne funeral i
la màcula ominosa del sacrifici.*
Il·lustració de la coberta (*en el sentit de les agulles
del rellotge*): Anthony Oliver, Ploma, *foto; un pilot
de la Segona Guerra Mundial; Sue Fox*, Mà
oberta (*detall*), 1995, *foto; Rembrandt*, El rapte
de Ganimedes (*detall*), *París, Musée du Louvre.*

CONTENTS ÍNDEX

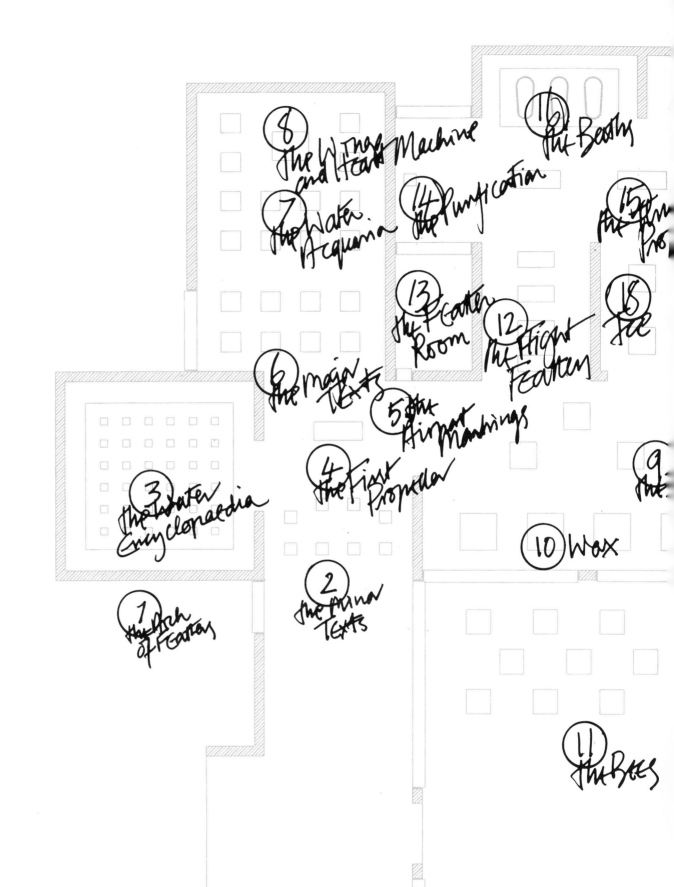

Plan for the exhibition
Flying over water, *1997,*
Barcelona, Joan Miró Foundation
Plànol de l'exposició
"Volar damunt l'aigua", *1997,*
Barcelona, Fundació Joan Miró

26 The Bird Bones

27 The Wine Spill

29 The Big Splash

25 The Autopsy Room

22 The Coffin

23 The Stairs

30 The Candles

21 The Firestone

24 The Beating Wings

28 The Last Leg

30 The Welcoming Frame.

P e t e r
Greenaway is a film-maker
trained as a painter. He has long been

sceptical about the restricted boundaries of cinema and you could not say that his films were obsessive about the traditional characteristics of cinema – the cinema that we have arrived at after a hundred years based on plot, narrative, story-telling, the demands for an emotional involvement between audience and screen, psychologically drawn characters, and a cinema that can justifiably be described for the most part as illustrated text. **Some commentators have said that his films are anti-cinema, and that he is not a film-maker at all. He might not disagree with that.** He is disquieted by the inability of the cinema that we now have to give us all the rich possibilities and make all the innumerable connections and engender all the potential excitements of the late twentieth-century world. **No touch, no smell, no temperature, short duration, passive, sedentary audiences, no real audience dialogue, overloaded technical specifications in set-piece High Street architecture, limited to a single frame at a time visible from only one direction, excessive desire for reality, temporary sets, actors trained to pretend, flat illusions, little comprehension of the screen as a screen, omnipotent financial vested interests, and the tyrannies of the frame, the** actor and text, and most disturbing of all, subject to **the tyranny of the camera.**

The list of disenchantments is long. He is far from being alone in holding these views. His present particular strategy to investigate and change these shortcomings, as he sees them, is to invest much time in extra-cinema activities if only in the hope of bringing those activities back into cinema to find ways to reinvent it – for reinvention of the cinema is surely long overdue, and very very necessary. **A medium without constant reinvention is doomed to perish. Many say now that there are no great inventors working in cinema any more. They have gone elsewhere.**
Perhaps they are right.

Greenaway might say that all cinema is a form of exhibition – demonstrably showing you things, objects, images, events, ideas; but, he might argue, not showing you enough, or for long enough, or in sufficient depth, or from contradictory points of view, or giving you, the audience, the chance and opportunity to make up your mind or exhaust your pleasure or interest with an event or object or idea for as long as both you and he would wish. In *A Walk through H* and *The Belly of an Architect*, the central theme is an exhibition – the first in a picture gallery where the painted maps become the film's substance, the second in the account of an architect obsessed with arranging an exhibition of a favoured architectural hero in Rome. Greenaway has curated exhibitions of paintings – his own and the paintings of others – into which are introduced the possibilities of cinematic vocabulary. He has used cinematic ideas of sequence and narrative and filmic perception in exhibitions of drawings at the Louvre, of paintings in Vienna, of historical artefacts in Geneva, of industrial archaeology in Swansea, of

He has used the EXHIBITION as a filmic device

1. Caravaggio, Amor Victorious, 1600, oil on canvas, Berlin, Staatliche Museum. This is Cupid not Icarus, but the winged image of the flying boy-hero intent on causing ecstasy with infinite invention, has parallels, not least in the danger and fatal fall from love that his exuberance unleashes.
1. Caravaggio, Amor victoriós, 1600, oli sobre tela, Berlín, Staatliche Museum. El personatge no és Ícar, sinó Cupido, però la imatge alada del nen-heroi volador decidit a proporcionar èxtasi amb una inventiva infinita té diversos paral·lelismes, entre ells el perill i la caiguda fatal de l'amor que la seva exuberància desencadena.

Peter Greenaway és un cineasta amb formació pictòrica. Sempre ha estat escèptic respecte als límits restringits del cinema, i no es pot dir que les seves pel·lícules mostrin una obsessió per les característiques tradicionals d'aquest art –un art que és el resultat de cent anys basats en l'argument, en la narració d'històries, en la necessitat d'una implicació emocional entre el públic i la pantalla, en uns personatges de perfil psicològic… un cinema que, majoritàriament, es pot descriure com la il·lustració d'uns textos. Alguns comentaristes han dit que les seves pel·lícules són l'anticinema, i que Greenaway no és pas cap cineasta. Pot ser que ell mateix subscrigui aquesta opinió, perquè l'inquieta la incapacitat del cinema actual per oferir-nos tota la riquesa de possibilitats, per establir totes les innombrables connexions i per engendrar totes les emocions potencials del món de final del segle XX. Absència de tacte, d'olor, de temperatura, durada curta, públics passius i sedentaris, absència d'un autèntic diàleg amb el públic, instruccions tècniques sobrecarregades en una arquitectura artificiosa i efectista, limitada a un sol enquadrament només visible en una direcció, desig excessiu de realisme, escenaris efímers, actors ensinistrats per fingir, il·lusions anodines, una escassa comprensió de la pantalla com a tal, subjecció als interessos econòmics d'uns inversors omnipotents, a les tiranies del fotograma, de l'actor i del text, a la tirania de la càmera (la més inquietant de totes)…, la llista de desencisos és molt llarga. Greenaway no està sol i menys encara, en aquests punts de vista. La seva estratègia actual, per investigar i corregir això que ell veu com a defectes, consisteix a dedicar molt de temps a activitats extracinematogràfiques, encara que només sigui amb l'esperança d'incorporar aquestes activitats al cinema i trobar noves maneres de reinventar-lo, perquè la reinvenció del cinema és sens dubte una tasca pendent des de fa molt de temps, i enormement necessària. Un mitjà que no es reinventi constantment està condemnat a morir. Molts diuen que el cinema actual ja no té grans inventors, perquè han emigrat a altres camps; i potser tenen raó.

Greenaway podria dir que tot producte cinematogràfic és una forma d'exhibició, que ens exhibeix coses, objectes, imatges, fets, idees. Però podria argüir que no ens mostra prou coses, o que no ens les mostra durant prou estona, o en suficient profunditat, o des de punts de vista prou contraposats, o que no ens dóna, com a públic, l'oportunitat de decidir o d'exhaurir el nostre plaer o el nostre interès per un fet, un objecte o una idea durant tot el temps que tant nosaltres com ell voldríem.

Peter Greenaway ha utilitzat l'exposició com un recurs cinematogràfic. Tant *A Walk Through H* ('*Un passeig per H*') com *The Belly of an Architect* ('*El ventre d'un arquitecte*') se centren en el tema d'una exposició: en el primer cas, es tracta d'una sala d'exposicions on els mapes pintats constitueixen la substància del film; en el segon, de la història d'un arquitecte obsessionat per muntar una exposició d'un popular heroi arquitectònic a Roma. Greenaway ha estat comissari d'unes exposicions de pintura –d'obra seva i d'altres pintors– on han estat incorporades les possibilitats del vocabulari cinematogràfic. Ha utilitzat

portrait photography in Cardiff, and the manufacture of light in Venice. He has initiated a series of ten exhibitions called The Stairs to use wide city spaces, starting in Geneva and Munich, to contemplate ten different aspects of cinema vocabulary –

location,
    light,
        frame,
            audience,
                properties,
                    actors,
                        text,
                            time,
                                scale,
                                    illusion.

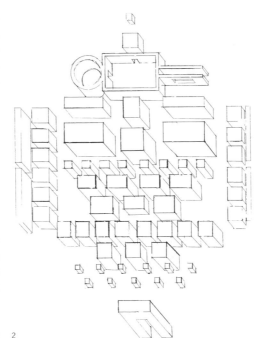

He has cinematically lit architectural spaces like the Piazza del Popolo in Rome to utilize the given *genius loci* of a space to emphasize its history and public usage.

This present exhibition, FLYING OVER WATER, builds on these experiences and is, in a way, a new departure, for this exhibition-installation is a dramatic consideration of a fiction; it is an exhibition about a fiction, a mythological narrative whose many intriguing parts have been deconstructed to be examined and contemplated variously as real objects, prepared objects and as illusions. The audience is invited to compare and collate and ruminate on all the parts that go together to make an exhibition which might conceivably be the preparation for a film, or be an exhibition on the reconstruction of an historical event, or be an exhibition of the relics of a piece of history, or be a combination of all three. This exhibition shows the real and the imagined, the found and the reconstructed, with objects, sets, actors, props, texts, diagrams, projections and research references, to offer a multifaceted

2. Prototype plan for the exhibition Flying Over water. *This ground-plan gathers all the basic elements of the exhibition in one single space.*

3. Caravaggio. St Matthew and the Angel, *1602, oil on canvas, Rome, San Luigi dei Francesi. This is St Matthew being instructed by the angel. The image reflects ideas of the intimate familiarity of a father and son, of the exuberant doer and the cautious thinker, and in Caravaggio's dramatic light, of a Daedalus-Icarus relationship of aged wisdom and flying youth set against the blackness of night and death.*

4. William Blake, Elohim creating Adam. *ca. 1805, watercolour, London, Tate Gallery. Christian theology may interpret the Daedalus-Icarus mythology as God the father-inventor giving spiritual wings to his invented Adam before Adam's fall through not heeding parental warning.*

idees cinematogràfiques de seqüència, narració i percepció fílmiques en exposicions de dibuixos al Louvre, de pintures a Viena, d'artefactes històrics a Ginebra, d'arqueologia industrial a Swansea, de retrats fotogràfics a Cardiff i de luminotècnia a Venècia. Ha iniciat una sèrie de deu exposicions, anomenada "The Stairs" ('Les escales'), que utilitzen amplis espais urbans –començant per Ginebra i Munic– cada una de les quals abastarà un aspecte diferent del vocabulari cinematogràfic: localització, il·luminació, enquadrament, públic, accessoris, actors, text, so, escala i il·lusió. Ha il·luminat cinematogràficament espais arquitectònics com la Piazza del Popolo de Roma, utilitzant el *genius loci* d'un espai determinat per realçar-ne la història i l'ús públic.

Aquesta exposició-instal·lació, "Volar damunt l'aigua", es basa en aquestes experiències i en certa manera constitueix un nou punt de partida, perquè és una consideració dramàtica d'una ficció; és una exposició sobre una ficció, una narració mitològica amb molts components intrigants que han estat descompostos per ser examinats i contemplats com a objectes reals, com a objectes preparats o com a il·lusions. Es convida el públic a comparar, confrontar i considerar totes les parts que s'ajunten per compondre una exposició que tant podria ser la preparació d'una pel·lícula com una exposició sobre la reconstrucció d'un fet històric o de les relíquies d'un període de la història, o una combinació de totes tres coses. Aquesta exposició mostra el real i l'imaginari, coses trobades i coses reconstruïdes, amb objectes, escenaris, actors, attrezzo, textos, diagrames, projeccions i documentació, per oferir una experiència de facetes múltiples que, de fet, s'emparenta amb la manera com la nostra vida transcorre per aquest món: absorbint i aprenent a través de l'observació casual, incidental o concreta, amb la recerca conscient, a través de les opinions dels altres, a través de la memòria estimulada. de l'acceptació i del rebuig d'informació rebuda i prejudicis desenvolupats, i a través de la reinterpretació imaginativa i dels somnis aparentment intranscendents duts fins als límits de l'exhaustió.

El tema de l'exposició és la dualitat vol/ofegament, o aire/aigua, o cel/mar. Aquests dos àmbits imaginatius són, des de fa molt de temps, una característica dels interessos de Greenaway. Les seves primeres pel·lícules, com *Windows* ('Finestres'), *A Walk Through H* i *The Falls* ('Les caigudes'), contenen referències obsessives a la caiguda, als vols, als ocells, al saber popular sobre vols, a la tradició dels vols, a la història dels vols, al misteri dels vols i al mite dels vols. La seva filmografia és plena de títols com *Making a Splash* ('Fer un capbussó'), *Water-Wrackets* ('Monstres d'aigua'), *26 Bathrooms* ('26 cambres de bany'), *Drowning by Numbers* ('Ofegaments numerats', estrenada a Espanya amb el títol *Conspiración de mujeres*) i *Death in the Seine* ('Mort al Sena'). Les seves exposicions porten títols com «Watching Water» ('Observar l'aigua') o «Flying Out of This World» ('Fugir volant d'aquest món'), i un dels seus llibres d'autocomentari es titula *Fear of Drowning* ('Por d'ofegar-se'). Els seus protagonistes sovint moren a l'aigua, es tiren o cauen daltabaix d'una finestra, fan l'amor a l'aigua, intenten suïcidar-se a l'aigua, es pengen d'un arbre, són trets de dins de rius, es creuen que són peixos, somien el rai de la Medusa, naufraguen a les Bermudes o s'identifiquen amb Marat, Leda, Ofèlia, Neptú o Hero i Leandre.

2. Plànol prototip per a l'exposició "Volar sobre l'aigua". Aquesta planta reuneix tots els elements bàsics de l'exposició en un sol espai.
3. Caravaggio, Sant Mateu i l'àngel, 1602, oli sobre tela, Roma, San Luigi dei Francesi. Sant Mateu és instruït per l'àngel. La imatge reflecteix la idea de l'íntima familiaritat entre un pare i un fill, de l'exuberància de l'acció i de la prudència de la meditació, i, en la llum dramàtica de Caravaggio, d'una relació Dèdal-Ícar (maduresa assenyada-joventut voladora) sobre el fons negre de la nit i de la mort.
4. William Blake, Elohim creant Adam, ca. 1805, aquarel·la, Londres, Tate Gallery. La teologia cristiana pot interpretar la mitologia Dèdal-Ícar com el Déu pare-inventor que dóna ales espirituals al seu Adam inventat, abans de la caiguda d'Adam, ocasionada per no haver fet cas de l'advertiment patern.

experience that is akin in fact to the way we go about the world – absorbing and learning through casual, incidental and focussed observation, through conscious research, through the opinions of others, through jogged memory, through accepting and rejecting received information and developed prejudices, and through imaginative reinterpretation and apparently non-consequential dreaming taken to the point of exhaustion.

The subject of the exhibition is Flight and Drowning, or Air and Water, or the Sky and the Sea. These two areas of imagery have long been a characteristic of Greenaway's interests. His early films, like *Windows*, *A Walk through H* and *The Falls*, were obsessively referenced with falling, flying, birds, flight-lore, flight tradition, flying history, flying mystery and flying myth. His filmography is scattered with titles like *Making a Splash*, *Water-Wrackets*, *26 Bathrooms*, *Drowning by Numbers* and *Death in the Seine*. His exhibitions have titles like *Watching Water* or *Flying out of this World*, and his books of self-commentary have titles like *Fear of Drowning*. His protagonists often die in water, jump from windows, make love in water, fall from windows, try to commit suicide in water, hang their bodies from trees, are pulled from rivers, liken themselves to fish, dream of the Raft of the Medusa, are shipwrecked in the Bermudas, or identify with Marat, Leda, Ophelia, Neptune or Hero and Leander.

For this exhibition, the nexus that pulls these pairings of air and water, flying and swimming, the sky and the sea together is ICARUS – mythological hero who was both the first pilot and the first flying disaster. The man who first flew and then drowned, fell straight from the sky into the sea.

The most authoritative account of the story of Icarus comes from Ovid's *Metamorphoses*. Painters from Giulio Romano to Rubens, Bruegel to Rembrandt have directly used this source. But there are many variations on the story. The basic narrative material tells of Icarus, attempting, with his father, to escape the tyranny of King Minos on the island of Crete, achieving lift-off on wings made of feathers cemented with wax. So exuberant was Icarus in his newfound freedom and pleasure that, against his father's best advice, he flew too near the sun. The wax melted, the wings collapsed and Icarus fell to his death in the sea that still bears his name. It is a tale of hubris, over-reaching ambition that ends in a tragedy of three parts – **the death of a young man, the loss of a son, the collapse of an ideal.**

Myths so readily sustain universal wish-fulfilments, and are so likely to embody deeply held aspirations and desires at different times and in

Per a aquesta exposició, el nexe que aparella l'aire i l'aigua, el vol i la natació, el cel i el mar, és Ícar, l'heroi mitològic que simbolitza el primer pilot i alhora el primer accident aeri. El primer home que va volar i que després es va ofegar, caient directament del cel al mar. La crònica més autoritzada de la història d'Ícar prové de les *Metamorfosis* d'Ovidi. Pintors com Giulio Romano, Rubens, Bruegel o Rembrandt s'hi han basat directament. Hi ha, però, moltes variants d'aquesta història. El material narratiu bàsic ens diu que Ícar i el seu pare volien fugir de la tirania del rei Minos, a l'illa de Creta, i van aconseguir alçar el vol amb unes ales fetes de plomes enganxades amb cera. Entusiasmat amb aquesta llibertat i aquest plaer acabats de descobrir, Ícar, contra el consell del seu pare, es va acostar massa al sol. La cera es va fondre, les ales es van desprendre i Ícar va caure i es va ofegar en el mar que encara porta el seu nom. És la història d'una arrogància, d'una ambició excessiva que acaba amb una tragèdia en tres parts: la mort d'un home jove, la pèrdua d'un fill i l'esfondrament d'un ideal.

Els mites propicien tan fàcilment la realització de desigs universals, i són tan proclius a encarnar aspiracions i desigs profunds en èpoques i llocs diferents, que la figura d'Ícar, directament o indirectament, representa moltes variants del tema i emergeix en molts sistemes que s'allunyen del cànon clàssic. Altres tradicions mitològiques anteriors i posteriors, amb diferents perspectives i graus de sofisticació, també es pot dir que contenen figures semblants a Ícar en el nucli de les seves diverses recerques d'elevació física o espiritual, o en la seva representació de cels ideals, o en el seu desig de comunió amb el cel, o en el seu afany d'assolir diverses manifestacions del més enllà. Els teòlegs cristians poden veure, en l'al·legoria del Dèdal-pare i de l'Ícar-fill, un paral·lelisme amb el Déu-pare-inventor que dóna ales espirituals al seu Adam inventat, abans de la caiguda d'Adam, ocasionada perquè no va fer cas de l'advertiment paternal. O com una variant de l'intent Abraham de sacrificar Isaac, o com un tast profètic de la relació entre el Déu Pare i el Déu Fill que abasta amb detall el mite de la resurrecció. El material pare-fill, inventor-inventat, mestre-alumne, home savi-fill inconscient, és constantment reprès amb variants que de vegades decanten les nostres simpaties cap a Dèdal i de vegades cap a Ícar.

Quins són els múltiples components d'aquest mite? Poden ser analitzats en relació amb els nostres superiors coneixements actuals sobre sistemes de volar amb l'ajuda de màquines, sobre enginyeria, anatomia humana, meteorologia, ornitologia, entomologia i física? Fins a quin punt no és frívola la nostra ironia quan pensem en la cera d'abella i en el vol d'Ícar cap al sol? En relació amb la nostra idea contemporània de l'infant i de l'adolescent, és interessant especular sobre l'edat d'Ícar? Quants anys tenia? Tres, sis, dotze, divuit, vint-i-un? Tant l'oreneta com l'albatros són magnífics voladors; tenint en compte la nostra experiència actual en el camp de l'atletisme, i l'estatus, l'ús i l'exhibicionisme dels jocs olímpics, si haguéssim de fabricar unes ales personalitzades, com les construiríem? I, quin seria el cos ideal que hauria de tenir el millor volador: el físic d'un velocista, d'un corredor de fons, d'un saltador, d'un bus, d'un nedador? Imaginem una medalla d'or olímpica per a l'especialitat de volar. Si parlem de mites-au, ens serveix el de Leda i el Cigne? Ícar va morir a causa de l'impacte amb l'aigua en caure

different places, that directly and indirectly, the Icarus-figure stands in for many variations of the theme, surfacing in many systems other than the classical canon. Older and younger mythological traditions, with different perspectives and different degrees of sophistication, can be said to have Icarus figures at the heart of their various quests **for physical or spiritual elevation, or their depiction of ideal heavens, or their wish to obtain a unity with the sky, or their desire to reach various manifestations of the after-life.** Christian theologians can see the Daedalus-father and Icarus-son allegory as a parallel to God-the-inventor-father giving spiritual wings to his invented Adam before Adam's fall through not heeding paternal warning. Or as a variation of Abraham's intended sacrifice of Isaac, or as prophetic foretaste of God the Father–God the Son relationship, embracing in detail the Resurrection myth. The father and son, inventor and invented, teacher and taught, wise man and foolish son material is constantly reprised with variations that sometimes manoeuvre our sympathies to Daedalus and sometimes to Icarus.

What are the many components of this MYTH; can they be examined against our current superior knowledge of machine-assisted flying, of engineering and human anatomy, of meteorology and ornithology and entomology and physics?

How deep would our irony be to present beeswax and think of Icarus's flight towards the sun? Up against our contemporary notions of the child and the teenager, is it interesting to speculate on Icarus's age – was he three, six, twelve, eighteen, twenty-one years old? A swallow and an albatross are both superb flyers; up against our present experience of athletics and the status and use and exhibitionism of the Olympics, if we were to develop personalized wings, how would they be constructed and what sort of athletic body would you ideally need to possess to make the best flyer – the physique of a short- or long-distance athlete, a jumper, a diver, a swimmer? Imagine an Olympic gold medal for flying. If we are talking bird-myth, are Leda and the Swan relevant? Did Icarus die concussed as he hit the water after falling 25,000 metres, 60,000 metres, 120,000 metres? Or did he drown, in 10 metres, 100 metres, 250 metres of salt water? If he drowned, is this not an irony? **After failing to fly, did Icarus fail to swim?** Flying and swimming – both defying the normal pull of gravity on the human frame – can they be seen as analogous? Would we first have to learn to swim before we could learn to fly, in the same way as it is sensible to learn to drive a car before learning to pilot a plane?

And what if Icarus had not FALLEN, but had accompanied Daedalus to Italy and to Naples? **Supposing Icarus had merely got LOST?** Was there not a great deal of sky to get lost in? Daedalus could perhaps have misjudged the evidence of the feathers lying on the water? **What if there were to be built a landing platform for the still-returning Icarus, and a frame to section up the sky to anticipate his final flying in to land?**

Because the questions are of the shifting ground of fiction, the speculation is endless. And entertainingly so. And probably there are more questions and more speculations than we have space for in one exhibition; indeed this exhibition has seen, in the planning stages at least, more than one manifestation. It is hoped that there may be other versions of this exhibition in other places, so Greenaway, in this catalogue, **invents a form of ideal exhibition on the theme of Flying over Water, and provides it with a second title in A DESCRIPTION OF AN EXHIBITION,** which also gives him the opportunity to discuss exhibition-experience in general, and to make connections with other media, prime of which of course is cinema. He has not made it a secret that he has both an opera and at least one film-script in some form of pre-production, utilizing the same or similar subject-matter. This Description of an Exhibition, The Icarus Adventure, is a prologue to certainly much further investigation on the theme of Flying over Water.

5. Peter Greenaway, Leda from 100 Allegories to Represent the World. *Leda mated with a swan to produce two pairs of twins from two eggs, which might be one way of producing offspring with wings. Here are the eggs and the double sets of twins, Castor and Pollux and Helen and Clytemnestra. Here also is a recipe for omelettes.*
6. Herbert Draper, The Lament for Icarus, 1898, oil on canvas, London, Tate Gallery. *The first painting on the subject of Icarus to attempt some realistic appraisal of mass of feathers relative to human body weight, which though arising from the scientific reasoning of a nineteenth-century English gentleman painter, also underlines the impossibilities of the adventure in terms of muscle power and human balance. But if we can believe in the water-mermaids, then we ought to believe in Icarus.*
5. Peter Greenaway, Leda, de "100 al·legories per a representar el món". *Leda es va acoblar amb un cigne i va produir dues parelles de bessons a partir de dos ous, la qual cosa podria ser una manera de tenir fills amb ales. Aquí hi ha els ous i les dues parelles de bessons, Càstor i Pòl·lux i Helena i Clitemnestra. També hi ha una recepta per a fer truites.*
6. Herbert Draper, El lament per Ícar, 1898, oli sobre tela, Londres, Tate Gallery. *És la primera pintura sobre el tema d'Ícar que intenta avaluar amb realisme la relació entre una massa de plomes i el pes del cos humà, una avaluació que, si bé provè del raonament científic d'un pintor anglès del segle XIX, també subratlla la impossibilitat de l'aventura d'Ícar des del punt de vista de la potència muscular i de l'equilibri humà. Però si podem creure en sirenes, aleshores també hauríem de creure en Ícar.*

d'una alçada de 25.000 m, de 60.000, de 120.000? O potser es va ofegar en una profunditat de 10, de 100 o de 250 m d'aigua salada? No és una ironia que s'ofegués? Després d'intentar volar i no sortir-se'n, tampoc no va ser capaç de nedar? Volar i nedar –dues maneres de desafiar la força de la gravetat sobre el cos humà– poden considerar-se dues coses anàlogues? Hauríem d'aprendre a nedar abans de poder aprendre a volar, de la mateixa manera que és més sensat aprendre a conduir un cotxe abans d'aprendre a pilotar un avió?

I si Ícar no hagués caigut, sinó que hagués acompanyat Dèdal a Itàlia i a Nàpols? I si, senzillament, s'hagués perdut? No hi havia cel de sobres per perdre-s'hi? I si Dèdal hagués jutjat erròniament la prova de les plomes flotant sobre l'aigua? I si resulta que el que calia fer era construir una plataforma d'aterratge per a l'Ícar que encara havia de tornar, i un marc per seccionar el cel i anticipar l'últim tram del seu vol abans d'aterrar?

Com que aquests interrogants pertanyen al terreny movedís de la ficció, les possibilitats d'especular són infinites, i al mateix temps molt divertides. I segurament hi ha més interrogants i més especulacions que no ens permet l'espai d'una sola exposició; sens dubte, aquesta exposició, com a projecte, ha vist, almenys en les fases de planificació, més d'una manifestació. Esperem que pugui haver-n'hi altres versions en altres llocs, per això Greenaway, en aquest catàleg, inventa una forma d'exposició ideal sobre el tema de "Volar sobre l'aigua", i li proporciona un segon títol, "Descripció d'una exposició", que també li dóna l'oportunitat de debatre l'experiència de les exposicions en general, i d'establir connexions amb altres mitjans, el principal dels quals

és, naturalment, el cinema. No és cap secret que Greenaway té en cartera una òpera i com a mínim un guió de pel·lícula en alguna forma de preproducció que utilitzen el mateix tema, o un de semblant. Potser aquesta «Descripció d'una exposició. L'aventura d'Ícar» és un pròleg per a posteriors recerques sobre el tema de "Volar damunt l'aigua".

A description of an exhibition

Descripció d'una exposició

El desig de volar és universal. Volar com un ocell, volar com un esperit, pujar fins al cel, vèncer la gravetat, és una aspiració humana antiga i d'un immens atractiu. És una ambició que es pot traduir en coses ornitològiques, espirituals, poètiques, religioses i pràctiques. Totes les cultures de tots els temps, tard o d'hora, obertament o de manera encoberta, expressen aquest desig. Fins i tot els troglodites senten el desig de volar. I, tanmateix, és un somni impossible. Individualment i sense cap ajuda, nosaltres no podrem mai enlairar-nos, flotar per l'aire i volar. La gravetat ha conformat la nostra anatomia perquè tinguem els peus ancorats a terra.

KALA WAS AVENGED. TARZAN TURNED HOMEWARD TOWARD THE TRIBE OF KERCHAK, STOPPING ONLY TO RETRIEVE KULONGA'S BOW AND ARROWS FROM THE TREE TOP IN WHICH HE HAD HIDDEN THEM.

1. *Peter Greenaway,* Icarus *from 100 Allegories to Represent the World. Here is a contemporary presentation of Icarus before, during and after his flight, with a six-frame "cell-animation" of his fall, wings containing the Ovid text, and a body that acknowledges a literary torso, blue sky thighs and watery shins.*
2. *Edgar Rice Burroughs,* Tarzan. *Tarzan did not have wings but that did not stop him from prodigious leaps and bounds that simulated flight. His models were not birds but apes. His propulsion was no more than a muscular body and a network of convenient lianas.*

1. *Peter Greenaway, Ícar, de "100 al·legories per a representar el món". Això és una representació contemporània d'Ícar abans, durant i després del vol, amb sis imatges representant la seva caiguda, unes ales que contenen el text d'Ovidi i un cos que consta d'un tors literari, unes cuixes blau cel i unes canelles aquoses.*
2. *Edgar Rice Burroughs, Tarzan. Tarzan no tenia ales, però això no li impedia de fer uns salts prodigiosos que simulaven l'acció de volar. El seu model no eren els ocells, sinó els micos. El mecanisme de propulsió no era altra cosa que un cos musculós i una xarxa de lianes convenientment situades.*

The desire to fly is universal. To fly as a bird, to fly as a spirit, to ascend to the Heavens, to escape gravity, is a human aspiration of long standing and wide appeal.

It is an ambition that can be translated into things ornithological, spiritual, poetic, religious and practical. Every culture in every age sooner or later, covertly or openly, expresses such a desire. **And yet it is an impossible dream.** We, as unassisted individuals, are never going to be able to lift off and float and fly. Gravity has fashioned our bodies to keep our feet on the earth.

Leonardo's flying wings, Montgolfier's balloon, the Wright brothers' aeroplanes, helicopters, parachutes, Concorde, the Apollo Mission, hang-gliding are not the answer. These are all machines condemned ultimately to fall to Earth. They are temporary, artificially powered machineries. All limited, all specialized. **No human is going to be able to fly like a swallow. No one can fly like an albatross or a buzzard, a butterfly, a bee or a hummingbird.** So the highest dream is impossible. We invent angels. We invent Heaven. **We are so good at inventing what cannot come to pass.**

EVEN TROGLODYTES WISH TO FLY

European culture has been excessive in its embroidered invention of the flying myth – Perseus, Pegasus, the Sphinx, Cupid, Hermes, Phaethon, angels, putti, and Christ's Ascension. Prime among these myths is **Icarus – the first pilot, the first flyer, the first air disaster.** And into the experiences of Icarus and his father Daedalus, we can read Blériot, Lindbergh, Gagarin, Amy Johnson. The list is long. We could add the failures ... Glenn Miller, Buddy Holly. This exhibition is about the hopes, ambitions, brief apocryphal

Ni les ales de Leonardo, ni el globus dels Montgolfier, ni els aeroplans dels germans Wright, ni l'helicòpter, ni el paracaigudes, ni el Concorde, ni la missió espacial Apol·lo ni el vol delta són la solució. Són màquines que, tard o d'hora, estan condemnades a tornar a la Terra; màquines temporals que s'alimenten d'una energia artificial, totes limitades i especialitzades. Cap humà no podrà volar com una oreneta. Ningú no pot volar com un albatros, com un aguilot, com una papallona, com una abella o com un colibrí. El somni més elevat, per tant, és impossible. Hem inventat els àngels. Hem inventat el cel. Sempre ens ha estat molt fàcil inventar coses irrealitzables.

La cultura europea ha mostrat una inventiva exuberant a l'hora de crear mites voladors: Perseu, Pegàs, l'Esfinx, Cupido, Hermes, Faetont, els àngels, els querubins, l'ascensió de Crist... Entre tots aquests mites es destaca Ícar, el primer pilot, el primer volador, el primer accident aeri. En ell, i en el seu pare Dèdal, hi podem veure reflectits Blériot, Lindbergh, Gagarin, Amy Johnson..., la llista és llarga, i podríem afegir-hi molts fracassos: Glenn Miller, Buddy Holly...

Aquesta exposició tracta de les esperances, de les ambicions, dels breus èxits apòcrifs i del fracàs ubic i definitiu del somni impossible de volar, aplegats al voltant d'Ícar, el primer pilot i el primer accident aeri.

És una investigació sobre el mite d'Ícar i el seu somni de volar. Examinem els diversos candidats a Ícar per veure qui compleix els requisits més desitjables per poder volar, examinem les plomes d'Ícar, la cera que soldava aquestes plomes, els ous postos pels cignes que van proporcionar les plomes, la seva estratègia d'enlairament, la substància de l'aire en què va volar, les condicions meteorològiques, l'aigua on va caure, els sistemes alternatius que haurien pogut fer que el seu vol tingués més èxit... Analitzem la seva caiguda, l'impacte sobre l'aigua que va assenyalar la seva mort. Tenim curiositat per saber el pes del seu cos quan va caure al fons del mar, i els trets d'arqueòpterix dels seus ossos en descomposició, petrificats sota l'aigua. Observem altres aspectes del mite per entendre per què era necessària una ambició

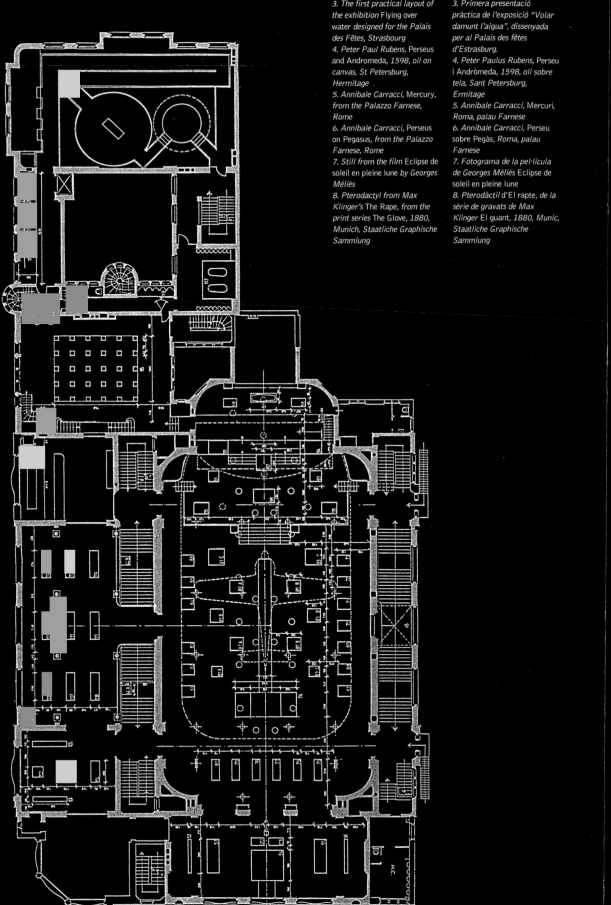

3. The first practical layout of the exhibition Flying over water *designed for the Palais des Fêtes, Strasbourg*
4. *Peter Paul Rubens,* Perseus and Andromeda, *1598, oil on canvas, St Petersburg, Hermitage*
5. *Annibale Carracci,* Mercury, *from the Palazzo Farnese, Rome*
6. *Annibale Carracci,* Perseus on Pegasus, *from the Palazzo Farnese, Rome*
7. *Still from the film* Eclipse de soleil en pleine lune *by Georges Méliès*
8. *Pterodactyl from Max Klinger's* The Rape, *from the print series* The Glove, *1880, Munich, Staatliche Graphische Sammlung*

3. *Primera presentació pràctica de l'exposició "Volar damunt l'aigua", dissenyada per al Palais des fêtes d'Estrasburg.*
4. *Peter Paulus Rubens,* Perseu i Andròmeda, *1598, oli sobre tela, Sant Petersburg, Ermitage*
5. *Annibale Carracci,* Mercuri, *Roma, palau Farnese*
6. *Annibale Carracci,* Perseu sobre Pegàs, *Roma, palau Farnese*
7. *Fotograma de la pel·lícula de Georges Méliès* Eclipse de soleil en pleine lune
8. *Pterodàctil* d'El rapte, *de la sèrie de gravats de Max Klinger* El guant, *1880, Munic, Staatliche Graphische Sammlung*

successes, and the ultimate ubiquitous failure of the impossible dream of flying – all gathered together around Icarus the first pilot and the first flying disaster.

This exhibition is an investigation into Icarus and his dream of flying. We **audition**[9] Icarus candidates to see who might best incorporate those features most desirable for a man to fly, we examine Icarus's **feathers**[10], the **wax**[10] that held those feathers together, the **eggs**[2] that made the swans that made the feathers, the **take-off strategy**, the substance of the **air**[4] that he flew in, the **meteorological conditions**[15,17], the **water**[7] he fell into, the alternate ways he might have chosen to make his flight more successful. We examine his fall and the **splash**[29] that indicated his death. We are curious about the weight of his body as it fell to the sea-bed, and the **archaeopteryx**[26] features of his mouldering bones, petrified beneath the water. We look at other parts of his myth to see why such an ambition was necessary, why such hubris was inevitable, and to see what other dreams and myths it might have engendered. And against our better judgement we build a **frame of the sky**[30] and tiers of welcoming seats and a landing platform in hope of his ultimate safe return.

We examine all these questions and curiosities from a contemporary perspective, and perhaps most pertinently from the perspective of contemporary technologies we associate with the manufacture and enjoyment of cinema. **You are not asked to sit, but it is familiarly dark. You can expect constructed drama but it is not necessarily of a narrative kind. There is, in bountiful measure, a pursuit of sequence in every direction.**

Our expectations of cinema probably encourage us – in this exhibition – to be just a little anxious. Knowing cinema's usual preoccupations, we probably expect to confront **sex, danger, blood, some violence. Perhaps some moral dilemma. Perhaps humour** – though that is always incalculable. We will find most of cinema's preoccupations and characteristics; there is obvious artifice, the familiar obligation to

d'aquest tipus, per què era inevitable aquesta pretensió arrogant, i per veure quins altres somnis i quins altres mites podria haver engendrat.

I, des de la perspectiva de la nostra superior capacitat de judici, construïm un marc del cel i graderies de benvinguda i una plataforma d'aterratge, tot esperant el seu retorn definitiu i estalvi.

Totes aquestes qüestions i curiositats les analitzem des d'una perspectiva contemporània, i potser, més pertinentment, des de la perspectiva de les tecnologies contemporànies que associem amb la producció i gaudi del cinema. No se'ns demana que ens asseguem, però la foscor ens resulta familiar. Ens en podem esperar una acció dramàtica, si bé no necessàriament de tipus narratiu. Hi trobarem, en generosa compensació, una evolució seqüencial en totes direccions. És probable que, en aquesta exposició, allò que esperem del cinema ens provoqui una certa inquietud. Coneixent la temàtica habitual del cinema, pot ser que esperem trobar-hi sexe, perill, sang, alguna dosi de violència i potser algun dilema moral; o fins i tot humor (si bé això sempre és incalculable). Hi trobarem la majoria de temes i característiques del cinema: un artifici evident, la típica obligació de deixar la incredulitat en suspens, canvis d'escala sobtats i impossibles, espectacle, una barreja de realitat i ficció, canvis de ritme, uns canvis ràpids d'escena, uns plans visuals canviants... i el concepte de muntatge, entès com l'acte de construir idees a partir d'unes imatges dispars unides tan estretament que semblen indivisibles. I hi trobarem també una cosa que, desgraciadament, rares vegades aconsegueix proporcionar-nos el cinema: la simultaneïtat. En aquesta exposició, l'acció simultània hi és tan present que sembla que tot passi al mateix temps. Sens dubte,

4

5

6

7

8

suspend disbelief, sudden and impossible changes of scale, spectacle, the mingling of the real and the fake, changes of pace, rapid changes of location, a changing eye-level. And montage – if montage is the act of constructing ideas from disparate images butted so close to one another that they feel indivisible. What we will also find, and what is – sadly – seldom successfully experienced in the cinema – is

S I M U L T A N E I T Y.

There is indeed so much simultaneous action in this exhibition that everything could be said to happen at once. **Certainly the Past and the Present are contained together along with the Post-mortem – and also the Process by which these tenses are constantly intermingled.**

This exhibition can make several easy victories over cinema. We will certainly be able to experience smell and touch. We can directly experience dampness and draughts, sensations which are not, you might think, always advantageous, but in an exhibition about sea-martyrdom, the insidious creep of dampness and the presence of sea-wrack, mist and fog are power-ful factors to **a ready suspension of disbelief.** Since the use of space and the time-frame of this particular 'three-dimensional film in the dark' belong to the visitor and not the director, the visitor or spectator can be selective. Com-mitted to watch a film in the cinema, a viewer has no choice in the re-empha-sis of events, he has no opportunity to re-experience an incident, or immedi-ately revisit an occurrence for another look or a more thorough investigation. **In an exhibition, the visitor's attentions are variable, infinitely repeatable and his own.**

AND THERE IS TEXT. Cinema has never been able – despite anyone who might wish it otherwise – to exist without a text – as origin, as method, as critique, as criticism, as description, even as title. Like almost all painting, the **cinema is a slave to text** to the point of reducing imagery to the role of illustra-tion. There is certainly text in this exhibition, and text that performs all the above functions.

All of this, I have supposed, supports current particular preoccupations to investigate a notion of expanded cinema ... **that puts live action with dead film, that puts live sound with dead film, that relates live actors to dead film, that uses theatre with cinema, that uses real time, that investigates simultaneity, that performs an opportunity for an interactivity with an audience as far as it is possible to get without alienating the director's choice, that makes an audience much more than passive spectators, that is curious to mix media, that believes that cinema is indeed the highly imaginative tool the early twentieth century has believed it to be,** that wants to believe certainly in the huge potential of the new Guten-berg Revolution and in the visual literacy that the new visual technolo-gies are unleashing. To explore cinema as an exhibition and to expand the exhibition with cinema language and cinema expectancy is to empower both to new reinvented heights in preparation for the next century. **Perhaps with this enthusiasm and ambition Icarus can indeed**

LEARN TO FLY.

el passat i el present hi conviuen juntament amb el *post mortem*, i amb el procés que fa que aquests diversos estadis temporals puguin entremesclar-se.

Aquesta exposició pot apuntar-se fàcilment diverses victòries sobre el cinema. Hi podrem, sens dubte, experimentar amb l'olfacte i amb el tacte. Hi podrem experimentar directament humitats i corrents d'aire, sensacions que podríem pensar que no sempre són avantatjoses; però, en una exposició sobre el martiri al mar, el lliscament insidiós de la humitat i la presència de varec, boirina i boira baixa, són factors poderosos per deixar fàcilment la incredulitat en suspens. Com que l'ús de l'espai –i del marc temporal d'aquest «film tridimensional en la foscor»– pertany al visitant i no al director, el visitant o espectador pot ser selectiu. En presenciar una pel·lícula al cinema, un espectador no té capacitat de decisió per reemfasitzar els esdeveniments, no té l'oportunitat de reexperimentar un incident o de reviure immediatament un fet per mirar-se'l des d'una altra perspectiva o investigar-lo més a fons. En una exposició, l'atenció del visitant és variable i infinitament repetible, i li pertany a ell.

I també hi ha el text. El cinema no ha pogut existir mai –a pesar dels qui voldrien que fos d'una altra manera– sense un text; un text com a origen, com a mètode, com a crítica, com a descripció, fins i tot com a títol. Com gairebé tota la pintura, el cinema és esclau del text fins al punt de reduir la imatgeria al paper d'il·lustració. Sens dubte hi ha text en aquesta exposició, i un text que realitza totes les funcions que acabo d'esmentar.

Totes les quals, he suposat, donen suport a les preocupacions actuals per investigar una idea ampliada del cinema... que incorpora acció viva en un film mort, que incorpora so viu en un film mort, que relaciona actors vius amb un film mort, que combina teatre i cinema, que utilitza temps real, que investiga la simultaneïtat, que permet una interacció amb el públic, en la mesura en què sigui possible aconseguir-la sense alienar la capacitat d'elecció del director, que converteix el públic en alguna cosa més que espectadors passius, que té curiositat per la barreja de mitjans, que creu que el cinema és certament l'eina altament imaginativa que es va creure que era a principi del segle XX, que certament vol creure en el potencial enorme de la nova revolució Gutenberg i en l'educació visual que les noves tecnologies van desencadenant. Explorar el cinema com una exposició i ampliar l'exposició amb el llenguatge del cinema i les expectatives del cinema és permetre a l'un i a l'altra d'assolir altures noves i reinventades en aquesta avantsala del segle vinent. Potser, amb aquest entusiasme i amb aquesta ambició, Ícar podrà certament aprendre a volar.

Los dos proyectiles perforaron la placa. Como ocurrió en la prueba anterior, el proyectil simplemente al cromo rompió en muchos pedazos, de los que 10, con un peso de 33 kgs., fueron recogidos. El proyectil al cromoníquel fué intacto a una distancia de

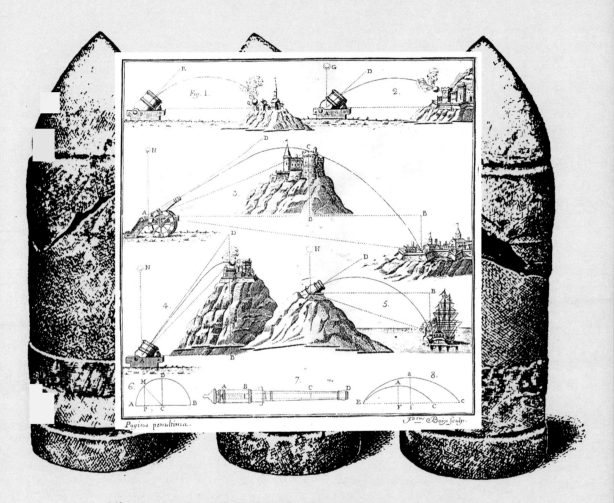

Fig. 127. — Proyectiles perforantes de Ac. Cr. y Ni

2460 a 2700 m. La ojiva sufrió una ligera fractura cocoidal, según se ve en la figura 126. En vista de la gran energía remanente de este proyectil se efectuaron ensayos con menores velocidades de impacto.

Esta quedó a 569 m. y la energía a 872 tonelámetros.

Los proyectiles atravesaron la placa pero a estas bajas velocidades los proyectiles al cromoníquel rompieron, pero en·con-

The arch of feathers
1
L'arc de plomes

THE EXHIBITION BEGINS with an arch of feathers to celebrate Icarus's potential success. In very necessary optimism, memorials, like tombs and obituaries, can often be prepared before the event. There should be several arches erected in the surrounding streets, in the city's main square, on the city's most important bridge, at the entrance to the town, and certainly at the airport, the official and appropriate site for an Icarine descent back to Earth. These arches should be made of glass stuffed full with pure white feathers, accompanied by the sound of the sea. At night, they should be illuminated with watery blue light that shimmers and sparkles.

The arch is a traditional architectural symbol that declares entry with a loud public gesture. Walled towns, fortresses and places of worship display and maintain them. Most freestanding, triumphal arches were temporary, erected for the event and taken down soon after – arches for the Queen of the May, for visiting dignitaries, returning heroes, and variously made of wood, painted cloth, tree branches, flowers. The permanent models are famous – the Arch of Septimius Severus is the Northern Gate to the Roman Forum, the Arch of Constantine fronts the Colosseum, the Arc de Triomphe is the gateway to the Champs Elysées, heavy, ponderous, massive, momentous, manufactured of costly sculptured stone dragged great distances, covered with graphic symbolism of heroism, sacrifice, nationalism, death and power – and with portentous promises no man or nation can keep.

To pass through a ceremonial arch is like making a committal, like passing through a doorway into an official building, like crossing the threshold of a house into a marriage, like passing through a lych-gate for a funeral, like daring to pass under a ladder and risk

bad luck, like passing under a yoke as an agreement.

If, by repute, the grand architectural arch is a Gateway of Triumph, like the Paris Arc de Triomphe, like the Berlin Brandenburg Gate, it is also the traditional memorial to the dead. For Icarus it can indeed be both – it is an arch of triumph, for Icarus was indeed the second man to fly; and it is an arch memorial to the dead. For Icarus was the first airman to crash.

However, as in the Roman Forum and at L'Etoile, it is possible to bypass the arch, to go around its formality – though such a timid bypass is not going to ring with the same architectural experience.

To parody the heavy stone ceremonial and triumphal and monumental arches of Rome, Paris and Berlin, our ceremonial, memorial arch for Icarus is made of glass so that we can easily see its contents, which are feathers, the most ephemeral and insubstantial of materials. This arch is in effect stuffed full of flying material. There is no inscription, no ponderous symbolic decoration, the feathers are enough. The conceit is deliberate, for who could build a monument out of feathers? It is an entry to the presence of a flying mystery associated with Icarus. A poignant entry.

1

L'EXPOSICIÓ COMENÇA amb un arc de plomes per celebrar l'èxit potencial d'Ícar. Amb un optimisme molt necessari, els monuments als difunts, com també les tombes i les necrològiques, sovint es poden preparar abans de l'esdeveniment. Hi hauria d'haver diversos arcs erigits en els carrers circumdants, a la plaça principal de la ciutat, en el pont més important de la ciutat, a l'entrada de la ciutat i sens dubte a l'aeroport, el lloc oficial i apropiat per al descens d'Ícar en el seu retorn a la Terra. Aquests arcs haurien de ser de vidre i totalment farcits de plomes d'un blanc pur, acompanyades del so del mar. De nit, s'haurien d'il·luminar amb una llum d'un color blau aquós que refulgís i guspiregés.

L'arc és un símbol arquitectònic tradicional que assenyala una entrada amb estridents lletres públiques. Les ciutats emmurallades, les fortaleses, els llocs de culte, n'exhibeixen i en sostenen. La majoria d'arcs de triomf erigits aïlladament eren efímers, es construïen per a una ocasió concreta i s'enderrocaven poc després: arcs per a la Reina del Primer de Maig, per a visites de dignataris, per al retorn d'un heroi, construïts amb materials diversos, com ara fusta, tela pintada, branques d'arbres, flors... Els models permanents són famosos: l'arc de Septimi Sever és la porta nord d'accés al fòrum romà, l'arc de Constantí és davant del Colosseu, l'arc de Triomf de París és la porta d'entrada als Camps Elisis, pesant, feixuc, massiu, transcendental, fet amb costosa pedra esculpida arrossegada des de grans distàncies, cobert amb símbols

gràfics d'heroisme, sacrifici, nacionalisme, mort i poder... i promeses portentoses que cap home ni cap nació no poden complir.

Passar per sota d'un arc cerimonial és com adquirir un compromís, com franquejar la porta d'accés a un edifici oficial, com passar el llindar d'una casa per a un casament, com accedir a un recinte funerari, com atrevir-se a passar per sota d'una escala i temptar la mala sort, com passar per sota d'un jou per segellar un acord.

Si el gran arc arquitectònic és una porta triomfal –com l'arc de Triomf de París, com la porta de Brandenburg de Berlín–, també és el monument tradicional als morts. Per a Ícar, sens dubte, pot ser totes dues coses: un arc de triomf –perquè Ícar és el segon home que va volar– i un arc commemoratiu de la seva mort, perquè Ícar és també el primer aviador que es va estavellar. Però, com en el cas del fòrum romà i de l'Étoile, és possible no passar per sota de l'arc, esquivar la seva formalitat –si bé un desviament tan tímid com aquest no ens permetrà de viure amb plenitud la mateixa experiència arquitectònica.

Parodiant els pesants arcs cerimonials, triomfals i monumentals de pedra de Roma, París, Berlín i Londres, el nostre arc de triomf, cerimonial i commemoratiu de la mort d'Ícar, és fet de vidre perquè puguem veure'n fàcilment el contingut, que consisteix en plomes, el material més efímer i més insubstancial, i que és l'essència d'aquesta exposició. Aquest arc, en efecte, és totalment farcit de material volador. No hi ha cap inscripció, cap feixuc ornament simbòlic: amb les plomes ja n'hi ha prou. La presumpció irònica és deliberada, perquè, qui pot edificar un monument a base de plomes? És una entrada a la presència del misteri del vol associat a Ícar. Una entrada punyent.

2

1. The Arch of Titus, Rome
2. The Arch built for the Universal Exhibition, 1888, Barcelona
1. Arc de Titus, Roma
2. Arc de triomf construït per a l'Exposició Universal de Barcelona, 1888

3

it is an arch of triumph, for Icarus was indeed the second man to fly, and it is an arch memorial to his death. For Icarus was the first airman to crash.

un arc de triomf –perquè Ícar és el segon home que va volar– i un arc commemoratiu de la seva mort, perquè Ícar és també el primer aviador que es va estavellar.

4

5,6,7

9

8. The Arch of Constantine,
Rome
9. The Arch built for the
Universal Exhibition, 1888,
Barcelona
8. Arc de Constantí, Roma
9. Arc de triomf construït per a
l'Exposició Universal de
Barcelona, 1888

The first flying texts: the minor texts

Els primers textos sobre vols: els textos menors

ON PASSING THROUGH the arch of feathers, we are at once confronted with a set of texts, a first set of texts called the Minor Texts, which are half illuminated in the daylight of our entrance and half concealed in the shadow that is to come. This first set of texts is an ironic introduction to our general subject-matter. We should stop and read. So much visual material in our literate Western world is first a question of text, second a question of image. We should acknowledge this equivocal state of affairs. This, for example, is the way cinema is made.

These first texts are cased in vitrines arranged in a regular grouping, like a small troop of soldiers protecting what lies beyond. The important status of these texts as an introduction to this exhibition is confirmed by their presence in glass cases lifted up to reading-height. Each text is lit from beneath with a warm green, moving light that suggests shallow fresh water, as though we might be walking in the flooded basement of a cool building, perhaps even the basement of the Palace of Knossos on Crete, anteroom to the Cretan labyrinth that Daedalus constructed for King Minos to house the Minotaur. And, foretaste of the future, two of the texts, the last two, are under water. They could be said to be submarine. The words of these texts must be read through water. You could say that these two texts drowned.

The texts may perhaps be taken from the following:
1. A newspaper telling of a Spanish aeroplane crash in 1959.
2. A text in an open book of how to fly a kite.
3. A page of diagrams from an in-flight magazine showing the plan of Medina Sidonia airport.
4. A page of a novel about flying twins.
5. A page of instructions from a flight manual.
6. A pilot's log.
7. A description of a large pelagic bird.
8. A child's description of how to make a paper aeroplane.
9. Manuals of swimming, swimming feats, swimming-pool architecture.
10. An account of a suicide by jumping from the top of Gaudí's cathedral.

DESPRÉS DE TRAVESSAR l'arc de plomes, ens trobem de seguida davant d'un conjunt de textos, un primer conjunt de textos anomenats Textos Menors, mig il·luminats per la claror diürna de la nostra entrada i mig ocults en l'ombra que vindrà.

Aquest primer conjunt de textos és una introducció irònica al nostre tema general. Convé que els llegim. En el nostre món literari occidental hi ha molt material visual que en primer lloc és una qüestió de text, i en segon lloc una qüestió d'imatge. Hauríem de reconèixer aquest estat de coses. Així és, per exemple, com es fa el cinema.

Aquests primers textos estan tancats en vitrines agrupades de manera regular, com una petita tropa de soldats que protegeixen el que hi ha més enllà. L'important estatus d'aquests textos com a introducció a aquesta exposició, és confirmat per la seva presència en vitrines col·locades a l'altura adequada per poder-los llegir.

Cada text està il·luminat des de sota per una càl·lida llum mòbil de color verd que recorda aigües dolces i poc profundes, com si caminéssim pel soterrani inundat d'un fresc edifici, potser fins i tot pel soterrani del palau de Cnossos, avantcambra del laberint de Creta, que Dèdal va construir per al rei Minos amb la finalitat d'allotjar el minotaure. I –un tast del futur– dos dels textos, els dos últims, es troben sota l'aigua. Es podria dir que són submarins. Les paraules d'aquests textos s'han de llegir a través de l'aigua. Podríem dir que aquests dos textos estan ofegats.

Els textos poden consistir en el següent:
1. Un diari amb la notícia d'un accident aeri a Espanya, l'any 1959.
2. Un text en un llibre obert que expliqui com es fa volar un estel.
3. Una pàgina de diagrames d'una revista d'unes línies aèries que mostrin el plànol de l'aeroport de Medina Sidonia.
4. Una pàgina d'una novel·la sobre bessons voladors.
5. Una pàgina d'instruccions d'un manual de vol.
6. El diari de vol d'un pilot.
7. Una descripció d'un gran ocell pelàgic.
8. Una descripció, feta per un nen, de com es fa un avló de paper.
9. Manuals de natació, proeses natatòries, construcció de piscines.
10. La crònica d'un suïcida que es va tirar des de dalt de la Sagrada Família.

1. French bi-plane pilot. Uniform obligatory
2. French bent-wing flying prototype
3. The Airplane and its Engine. Competent design, confident text
1. Pilot de biplà francès. Uniforme obligatori
2. Prototip d'aeroplà francès d'ales còncaves
3. The Airplane and its Engine (L'aeroplà i el seu motor). Disseny competent, text fiable

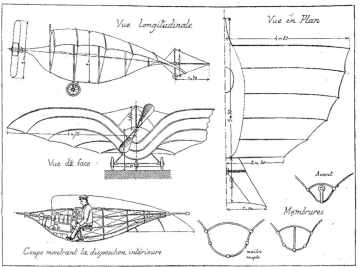

is said to have *dihedral*, and the *dihedral angle* is that between the surface of the wing and the horizontal, as seen from the front. *Sweepback* is the angle, if any, between the wings and a perpendicular to the longitudinal center line of the airplane, as seen from

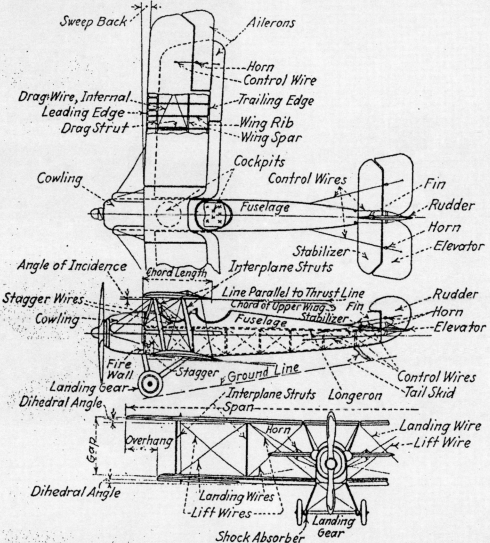

FIG. 4.—Nomenclature of airplane parts. (*Courtesy National Advisory Committee for Aeronautics.*)

above. Figure 4 illustrates these and other terms in airplane nomenclature.

The Power Plant.—The most conspicuous parts of the power plant, the next essential of the complete airplane, are the *engine* and the *propeller*, though there must be also a fuel-supply system,

AFTER THE FIRST texts, and set in a brighter light, that sparks and glints like sunlight on a grey sea, are some thirty stoppered glass jars each containing water. Just water. For the most part, the water is very clean and very clear. So clean and clear in fact that unless you stepped very close, you might think that at least some of the stoppered glass jars were empty. The jars are spaced equally one from another and all are numbered and labelled. And the labels state where the water in the jar was found and collected and at what time. Water from a certain stream. Water from a nearby river. Water from a wash-tub in a certain village. Water from a certain waterfall, a certain lake, pond, puddle, well, cistern, underground cave, river, stream, ditch.

We are, as visitors, certainly a little surprised at first that there should be so many places where you can find water. But then after a while, when the repetition of the containers becomes mesmeric, we realize the truism. After all there is a great deal of water in the world, and it has to reside somewhere. And Icarus had to fall, according to the myth, into water somewhere. Water is volatile, constantly changing its state – ice, snow, rain, steam, condensation, spray, fresh water, salt water, warm, hot, cold, frozen. And water as water is constantly moving. In with the tide, out with the tide. Up the coast, down the coast. Rising up from the sea-bed, falling back to the sea-bed. Rushing into the Mediterranean from the Aegean. Swirling into the Mediterranean from the Atlantic through the Straits of Gibraltar. Scooped up by the wind, blown into clouds, precipitated over mountains, gathered in streams, trickled down into the rocks, remaining sullen in the ground, sucked into the sponge of the water-table. New water? Old water? Can water be old? It is said that the same water passes through the Queen of England at least two times a year. The water in which Icarus drowned can now be in any place on Earth.

> **And Icarus had to fall, according to the myth, into water somewhere.**

> **I Ícar havia de caure, segons el mite, en algun lloc on hi hagués aigua.**

1. *Ingres,* La source, ca. *1854, oil on canvas, Paris, Musée d'Orsay*
1. *Ingres,* La font, ca. *1854, oli damunt tela, París, Musée d'Orsay*

DESPRÉS DELS PRIMERS textos, i instal·lats en una llum més brillant, centellejants i espurnejants com la llum del sol sobre una mar grisa, hi ha uns trenta pots de vidre tapats, cada un dels quals conté aigua. Només aigua. En general, l'aigua hi és molt neta i molt clara. Tan neta i clara, de fet, que si no ens hi acostem gaire podem pensar que almenys alguns dels pots tapats són buits. Els pots estan col·locats a una mateixa distància l'un de l'altre, i van tots numerats i etiquetats. Les etiquetes indiquen el lloc i el moment en què va ser trobada i recollida l'aigua de cada pot: aigua d'un cert rierol proper, aigua d'un riu proper, aigua d'una banyera d'un poble determinat, aigua d'una certa cascada, d'un cert llac, estany, bassal, pou, cisterna, gruta subterrània, riu, rierol o rec.

Sens dubte, com a visitants, al principi ens sorprèn una mica que hi hagi tants llocs on es pugui trobar aigua. Però, al cap d'una estona, quan la repetició dels recipients esdevé hipnotitzant, ens adonem del truisme. Al capdavall, al món hi ha una gran quantitat d'aigua, i en un lloc o un altre ha de ser. I Ícar havia de caure, segons el mite, en algun lloc on hi hagués aigua. L'aigua és volàtil, i el seu estat canvia constantment: gel, neu, pluja, vapor, condensació, ruixim, aigua dolça, aigua salada, tèbia, calenta, freda, glaçada. I l'aigua, com a tal, es mou constantment.

Avança i recula amb les marees. Va costa amunt i costa avall. S'alça del fons del mar i torna cap al fons del mar. Es precipita en el Mediterrani des de la mar Egea. Entra arremolinada en el Mediterrani des de l'Atlàntic, a través de l'estret de Gibraltar. Arrossegada pel vent, convertida en núvols, precipitada sobre les muntanyes, aplegada en corrents, caient gota a gota sobre les roques, romanent cavernosa sota terra, xuclada per l'esponja de la capa freàtica. Aigua nova? Aigua vella? Pot ser vella, l'aigua? Diuen que una mateixa aigua entra i surt de l'organisme de la reina d'Anglaterra dos cops l'any com a mínim. L'aigua on va caure Ícar pot ser actualment a qualsevol lloc de la terra.

4
The first propeller
La primera hèlice

ONCE HAVING PASSED by the introductory first texts, we can approach a tall glass case, containing a vertically standing, rotating propeller, the sort of propeller that drives a plane through air, that, working on the same principle but with a different design and configuration, drives a boat through water.

We have almost always been aware of this propeller because its rotating blade has been casting a dangerous-looking shadow that spills and flickers and rotates across the exhibition space. The propeller makes a noise, now perhaps a drone and then perhaps a purr. Sometimes it sounds like a summer buzz of bees, sometimes like a child's spinning top, sometimes like the whine of a dentist's drill, sometimes like the zzzzzzz written in a cartoon to indicate the monotony of sleep. You can just feel, through your feet, the vibration of this propeller's turning. If only Icarus had had a propeller. Perhaps he did. Perhaps the theory of wings made of feathers and wax is wrong. This rotating blade is intimidating, for we have been told many times and have seen the evidence on film, that such an item can slice a man in half, knock off his head and send it spinning into space across the tarmac, across the fields, into the water.

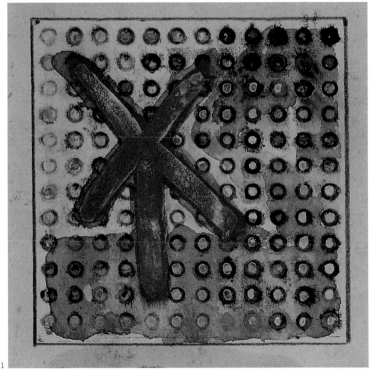

1

1. *Peter Greenaway*,
Windmills: Number 33
From the series of 100
Windmills, *1978, mixed
media on paper*
1. *Peter Greenaway*, Molins de
vent: número 33
De la sèrie 100 molins de vent,
*1978, tècnica mixta sobre
paper*

THE WEST WIND
Perhaps this is the propeller of the West wind, blowing Daedalus and Icarus away from the persecutions on the island of Crete
EL VENT DE PONENT
Potser aquesta és l'hèlice del vent de ponent, que ajuda Dèdal i Ícar a fugir de l'illa de Creta

DESPRÉS D'HAVER PASSAT pels primers textos introductoris, ara podem acostar-nos a una alta vitrina que conté una hèlice que gira en posició vertical, el tipus d'hèlice que mou un avió per l'aire; el mateix que, basant-se en el mateix principi però amb un disseny i una configuració diferents, fa que un vaixell avanci per l'aigua.

Gairebé tota l'estona hem estat conscients de la presència d'aquesta hèlice perquè la seva ala rotatòria ha anat projectant una ombra d'aspecte perillós, que sobreïx i centelleja i gira a través de l'espai de l'exposició. L'hèlice fa un soroll que de vegades és com un brunzit i de vegades com un ronc felí. De vegades recorda un zumzeig d'abelles a l'estiu, de vegades una baldufa, de vegades el grinyol d'una fresa de dentista, de vegades el "zzzzzzzz" que surt a les historietes per indicar la monotonia del son. Amb els peus podem notar la vibració del moviment rotatori d'aquesta hèlice. Si Ícar hagués tingut una hèlice... Potser la tenia; potser la teoria de les ales fetes de plomes i de cera és errònia. Aquesta ala que gira és intimidant, perquè ens han explicat moltes vegades –ho hem vist demostrat a les pel·lícules– que un objecte com aquest pot partir un home pel mig, arrencar-li el cap i llançar-lo giravoltant per l'aire, per sobre de l'asfalt i per sobre dels camps, fins a anar a parar a l'aigua.

Second World War flying men and their machines.
2. German pilot bales out of burning Focke-Wulf 190
3. Crew of US B-24 Liberator returns to base
4. USA 8th Air Force bombers and fighter escort
5. Crew of a B-24 Liberator prepare for bombing raid over Germany
6. US B-24 Liberator upturned on runway after braking incident during take-off

Aviadors de la Segona Guerra Mundial i les seves màquines.
2. Pilot alemany llançant-se en paracaigudes d'un Focke-Wulf 190 incendiat
3. Tripulació d'un B-24 Liberator nord-americà tornant a la base
4. Bombarders de la 8ª Força Aèria dels EUA i escorta de combat
5. Tripulació d'un B-24 Liberator preparant-se per a un bombardeig sobre Alemanya
6. Un Liberator B-24 nord-americà bolcat a la pista a causa d'una avaria dels frens durant l'enlairament

If only Icarus had had a propeller. Perhaps he did. Perhaps the theory of wings made of feathers and wax is wrong.

Si Ícar hagués tingut una hèlice... Potser la tenia; potser la teoria de les ales fetes de plomes i de cera és errònia

6

5

The airport markings
Les marques d'un aeroport

THERE ARE TWO new phenomena that should be noted. Both of them start at our feet, but stretch away forward left and right into the distance; and they are related. The first concerns a plethora of markings on the floor and the associations are not unfamiliar. The markings suggest that we are walking on the tarmac of an airport, not necessarily on a major runway, but on an airport forecourt or parking-ground. These could be our guide lines. It may be that the persistent frontality of all the glass cases we have experienced so far is not relevant to these markings – for at this moment they appear to run at an angle to the central axis of our present progress. The markings of this hypothetical airport floor are therefore considered to be off-centre, which may of course be a relevant metaphor.

Most of the markings are not necessarily new. Some indeed are fragmentary as though manufactured by a hesitant eye and hand, unsure of how airport tarmac directions should operate. Undoubtedly the maker has understood that they must be comprehended from a considerable height – to be seen certainly at a distance from above by a moving aircraft.

Also, the lines make us aware of the suggestion of a major flight path up ahead, but there are distractions – secondary flight paths with no-go significances, blunted arrows, barely perceived fragmentary figures and numbers. Because of the gloom, these floor instructions are not necessarily easy to see or easy to read. Certain sections are bright and clean as though newly painted, others have been worn and distressed by passing feet, by the repeated abrasion of wheels, by areas of spilt liquid that could well be acid, or is it something that has been burnt, or are the marks suggestive of something that has perhaps decayed – a large animal maybe, that died eighteen months ago and quietly rotted on the floor across the linear instructions, and was finally swept brusquely, but not too cleanly, away? There are also marks that do not satisfy any easy explanation – as though their manufacturer has suddenly decided not to fly at all, or that flying was too dangerous, or too absurd, or much too stupid to contemplate.

As to the second phenomenon – there are lights in the floor. They are dim – sometimes we doubt whether they are there at all. They trace several fragmentary paths in thin lines – like

També hi ha dos nous fenòmens que caldria assenyalar. Tots dos comencen als nostres peus, però s'estenen cap endavant, a dreta i esquerra, en la distància; i es relacionen entre ells. El primer té a veure amb una plètora de marques a terra, i les associacions no ens són estranyes. Les marques suggereixen que caminem sobre la pista d'un aeroport, no necessàriament una pista d'aterratge principal, sinó més aviat una pista d'entrada o un aparcament. Això podrien ser les nostres línies orientadores. Pot ser que la frontalitat persistent de totes les vitrines que hem experimentat fins ara no tingui cap relació directa amb aquestes marques, perquè sembla que avancen angularment respecte a l'eix central de l'evolució que seguim en aquest moment. Es considera, per tant, que les marques d'aquesta hipotètica pista d'aeroport estan descentrades, cosa que, per descomptat, pot resultar una metàfora pertinent.

La majoria de les marques no són necessàriament noves. Algunes, certament, són fragmentàries, com si haguessin estat traçades per un ull i una mà vacil·lants, insegurs de com han de funcionar les instruccions de la pista de l'aeroport. Sens dubte, l'autor d'aquestes marques ha entès que s'han de poder veure des d'una altura considerable, la d'un avió en moviment.

Les línies també ens suggereixen una pista d'enlairament principal més enllà, però també hi ha desviaments, pistes d'enlairament secundàries amb indicacions d'entrada restringida, fletxes esmussades, figures i xifres a penes perceptibles. A causa de la foscor, aquestes instruccions a terra no són necessàriament fàcils de veure ni de llegir. Certs segments són brillants i clars com si fossin acabats de pintar, altres estan mig esborrats i desgastats pel trepig continu de la gent i l'abrasió constant de les rodes, hi ha zones on s'han vessat líquids que podrien ser perfectament àcids... o potser és alguna cosa que s'ha cremat, o és que les marques suggereixen alguna cosa que potser s'ha descompost, qui sap si un animal de grans dimensions que va morir fa un any i mig i s'ha anat podrint a poc a poc

sobre les instruccions lineals, i finalment ha estat retirat de manera brusca però no gaire pulcra? També hi ha marques que no resulten fàcils d'explicar, com si de cop i volta el seu autor s'hagués desdit de volar, o hagués pensat que la pretensió de volar era massa perillosa, o massa absurda, o massa estúpida.

Pel que fa al segon fenomen, hi ha llums a terra. Fan una claror somorta, i de vegades arribem a dubtar que hi siguin. Tracen un trajecte de diversos camins fragmentaris en línies primes –com un solc–, que és com un rastre de llum no pas més gruixut que una corda. De vegades es repeteixen i transcorren paral·leles durant curtes distàncies, o fins i tot en diagonal, i s'entrecreuen com si dubtessin abans d'arrencar definitivament. Sens dubte no transcorren en simpatia amb les altres marques de la pista que hem descrit. Aquestes línies de terra són d'un color blau fosc –gairebé negre–, però més enllà ja podem veure com el color blau de la línia es va fent més clar i més brillant, i adopta

1. Real, repaired and fake bomb craters on a German airfield to confuse further Allied Forces bombing
2. Plan for the floor-markings of the exhibition Flying over water at the Joan Miró Foundation, Barcelona
1. Cràters de bomba reals, reparats i fingits en un aeròdrom alemany per despistar els bombarders de les forces aliades
2. Plànol de les marques a terra per a l'exposició "Volar damunt l'aigua" de la Fundació Joan Miró, Barcelona

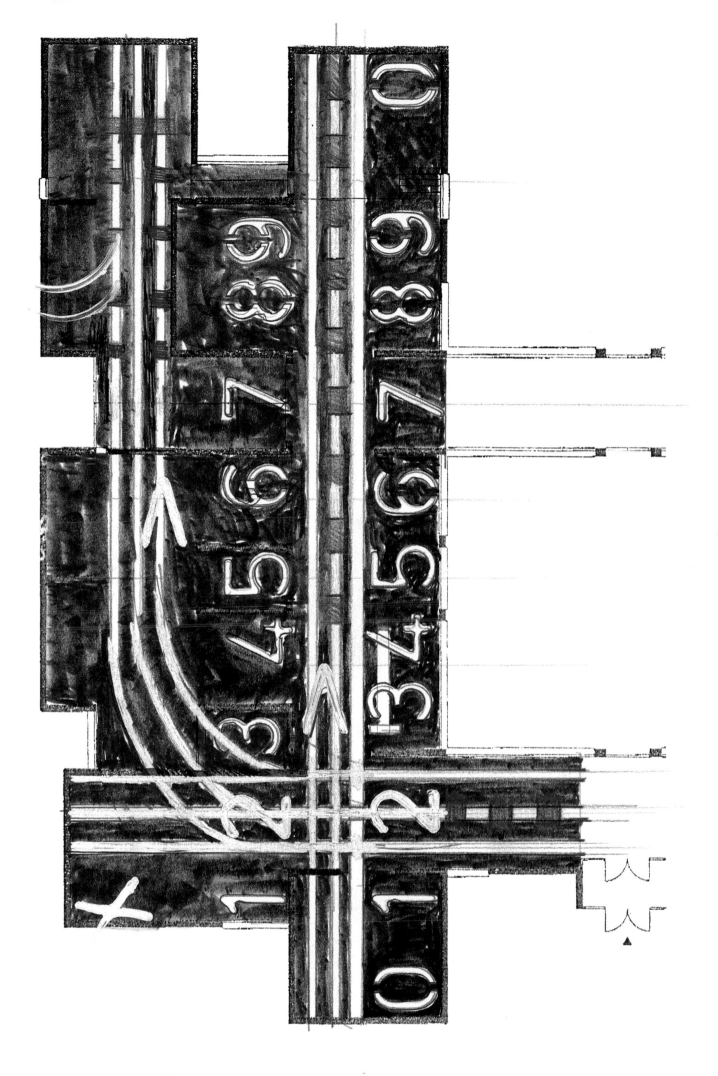

trails which are each no wider than a rope's width. Sometimes the trails repeat themselves, running parallel for short distances, crossing over one another as though hesitant to make a definite start. They certainly do not run in sympathy with the other tarmac marks we have described. Up ahead we can already see the blue of the line getting lighter and brighter, taking on a purple, even a mauve, colouring. These lines of light could well be offering a special path through the maze of glass cases. However, at present there is no particular desire or urgency to follow these markings. They may well be no more than a suggestion of Ariadne's thread through the Cretan maze as devised by Daedalus.

There are dark figures walking about on the floor. Are they silent and shadowy airport ground staff, complete with earphone headpieces that give their heads the look of the eyes of a giant fly? And do they wear white overalls smudged with oil and do they carry illuminated flight-bats and wear reflective panels on their elbows and across their chests and in the centre of their backs?

When these shadowy figures approach us, we can hear the slightest sound of voices – garbled messages indistinctly heard through their headphones – instructions no doubt interfered with by the airwaves – destinations perhaps we are familiar with and places we have never heard of – inaccessible places – utopias, on and off known maps, inside the body, under the earth that is under the sea – and there is plenty of earth under the sea. We live in a well watered planet.

But these shadowy figures move away from us as we approach them – they have been instructed to keep a safe distance from visitors – they should only be interested in looking up into the sky to look for incoming planes, flying creatures, dirigibles, falling men, floating feathers.

The floor markings – such as we see them in the half-dark – are now more clearly drawn or stencilled. They are now associated with large letters and large numbers. Perhaps we are standing at the beginning of a runway, the very start of an old airport launching pad whose far distant finish is four kilometres away. This is where the unseen dirigibles once taxied to begin their ground-rush to attempt flight.

We can hear voices. They are reading and whispering the second set of texts. There is no particular concern for complete comprehension of every word of these texts – just sufficient evidence that in fact the texts are being read. We can hear Latin and Greek and certainly English and certainly Catalan – these Western-world languages that have, at one time or another, been obliged to perform international services in diplomacy, art discourse, astronomy, physics, and indeed for our present purposes, those necessary instructions from airport watch-tower to airport watch-tower.

We can be certain that every word relevant to us from the exhibited texts has been recorded on the sound tapes. Yet the full tape is not very long – just ten minutes. If a visitor is very patient, although he cannot decipher every word, he can be confident that every word of our texts is indeed there.

una coloració porpra, o fins i tot malva. Podria ser perfectament que aquestes línies de llum oferissin un camí especial a través del laberint de vitrines. En aquest moment, però, no hi ha cap desig ni cap urgència particular de seguir aquestes marques. És possible que no siguin més que una al·lusió al fil d'Ariadna a través del laberint de Creta, tal com va ser ideat per Dèdal.

Hi ha unes figures fosques que caminen per damunt del terra. Són empleats obscurs i silenciosos de l'aeroport, amb uns auriculars que fan que els seus caps semblin els ulls d'una mosca gegantina? I, porten granotes tacades de petroli i cascs il·luminats i franges reflectores als colzes, i sobre el pit, i al mig de l'esquena?

Quan aquestes figures fosques se'ns acosten, podem sentir un lleugeríssim soroll de veus: missatges fragmentaris rebuts confusament pels seus auriculars, instruccions sens dubte plenes d'interferències de les ones aèries, destinacions que potser ens són familiars i llocs dels quals no hem sentit parlar mai,

llocs inaccessibles, utopies, mapes de vegades coneguts i de vegades desconeguts, a l'interior del cos, sota la terra que hi ha sota el mar... i sota el mar hi ha una gran quantitat de terra. Vivim en un planeta molt ben proveït d'aigua.

Però aquestes figures fosques se'ns allunyen a mesura que ens hi anem acostant: les han instruïdes per mantenir-se a una distància prudent dels visitants, i només els interessa mirar el cel per buscar-hi avions que s'acostin, criatures voladores, dirigibles, homes caient, plomes que floten.

Les marques del terra –tal com les veiem en la mitja penombra– ara estan dibuixades o estergides amb més nitidesa. Ara estan associades amb lletres i xifres de grans dimensions. Potser ens trobem al principi d'una pista d'aterratge, al començament mateix d'una plataforma de llançament d'un vell aeroport, el final de la qual és a quatre quilòmetres de distància. És aquí on, en altres temps, els dirigibles ocults feien la seva cursa prèvia a l'intent d'enlairar-se.

Se senten veus. Veus que llegeixen, xiuxiuejants, el segon grup de textos. No hi ha cap interès especial perquè entenguem totalment totes i cada una de les paraules d'aquests textos: només hi ha la constatació suficient que algú els llegeix. Sentim paraules en llatí i en grec, i sens dubte en anglès i en català: aquestes llengües del món occidental que, en un moment o un altre, s'han vist obligades a fer serveis internacionals en la diplomàcia, discursos sobre l'art, l'astronomia, la física, i certament, per al nostre propòsit actual, a transmetre les instruccions necessàries entre torres de control de diferents aeroports.

Podem estar segurs que cada paraula dels textos exposats que ens pugui resultar pertinent ha estat gravada a les cintes magnetofòniques. Però la cinta total no és gaire llarga: només dura deu minuts. Un visitant amb molta paciència, encara que no en pugui desxifrar totes les paraules, podrà estar segur que cada paraula dels nostres textos es troba allà.

3. R.B. Kitaj, Aureolin, *1964, oil on canvas*
4. Design for the costume of Icarus as a grounded pilot in the opera Flying over water. *Costume Designer: Cathy Strub*
3. R.B. Kitaj, Aureolin, *1964, oli sobre tela*
4. Disseny del vestit de pilot d'Ícar per a l'òpera Volar damunt l'aigua. *Dissenyadora: Cathy Strub*

3

només els interessa mirar el cel per buscar-hi avions que s'acostin, criatures voladores, dirigibles, homes caient, plomes que floten

they should only be interested in looking up into the sky to look for incoming planes, flying creatures, dirigibles, falling men, floating feathers.

4

7
The water aquaria
Els aquaris

drinking, washing, lubricating, urinating, cleaning, cleansing, thirst requited and drowning confirmed.

l'acció de beure, de rentar-se, la lubricació, l'orina, la neteja, la set sadollada i l'ofegament confirmat.

BY PASSING THROUGH the Arch of Feathers, reading the Minor and the Major Texts, viewing the types of water available, acknowledging the signs and maps of the ground beneath his feet, the visitor has made a committal and now meets water – for its own sake – water, the enemy and the balm.

Water. Just water. Encased in a rank of large glass acquaria which are lifted up to eye-level and lit with an exhilarating programme of controlled light is ... water.

We are reminded of sunlight on the sea, of drowning, of respite from the hot sun, of lurking dangerous fish, of corpses floating down to the sea-bottom.

Water covers four-fifths of the Earth. Water makes up nine-tenths of the human body. Water is life on Earth. Any animal or plant that does not live in water, is obliged to carry water with it wherever it goes. Water represents drinking, washing, lubricating, urinating, cleaning, cleansing, thirst requited and drowning confirmed. You could easily submerge a man's head in each of these twelve water-filled glass tanks. The water is clean and clear and cold. Light is conducted through these tanks and is made solid in these cold cubic blocks of water.

We know water is heavy, and to have water lifted up into the air like this is a little worrying. If the tanks should burst – we should be struck down with flying glass and a rush of cold water.

There is no doubt whatsoever that this water could very well be the possible medium of disaster.

PASSANT A TRAVÉS de l'Arc de Plomes, llegint els textos Menors i Majors, contemplant els diferents tipus d'aigua, reconeixent els senyals i mapes del terra sota els seus peus, el visitant ha adquirit un compromís i ara s'enfronta a l'aigua en estat pur: l'aigua, l'enemiga i el bàlsam.

Aigua. Només aigua. Aigua reclosa en un rengle de grans aquaris de vidre situats per sobre del nivell dels ulls i il·luminats amb un estimulant programa de llum controlada... simplement, aigua.

Se'ns recorda l'efecte de la llum del sol sobre l'aigua, de l'ofegament, de la treva de l'escalfor del sol, de l'amenaça de peixos perillosos, de cadàvers que suren i s'enfonsen en el mar.

L'aigua ocupa les quatre cinquenes parts de la terra i constitueix les nou desenes parts del cos humà. L'aigua és la vida de la terra. Qualsevol animal o planta que no visqui a l'aigua està obligat a transportar aigua en el seu interior arreu on vagi. L'aigua representa l'acció de beure, de rentar-se, la lubricació, l'orina, la neteja, la set sadollada i l'ofegament confirmat. Podem submergir fàcilment el cap d'un home en cada un d'aquests recipients plens d'aigua. L'aigua és neta, clara i freda. La llum és conduïda a través d'aquests aquaris i se solidifica en aquests blocs d'aigua freds i cúbics.

Sabem que l'aigua és pesant, i veure l'aigua en aquesta posició elevada, sobre aquesta mena de podis, resulta preocupant. Si els aquaris es rebentessin, seríem sepultats per una pluja de vidres i una allau d'aigua freda.

No hi ha cap mena de dubte que aquesta aigua podria ser perfectament el medi possible d'un desastre.

1

1. 100 Objects to Represent the World, *Vienna, 1992 Item 3. Water. An exhibition for the close of the Millennium*
1. "100 objectes per a representar el món", *Viena, 1992*
Peça 3. Aigua. Una exposició per al final del mil·leni

The wings and the heart machine **8**
Les ales i el cor mecànic

AFTER HAVING READ the texts and been intimidated by the rotating propeller and pondered the ambiguity of the floor markings and the disturbing presence of the air-watchers with their headphones, this exhibition of evidence of Icarus's first and final flying adventure is particularized and focussed.

We are presented with two new items. The first, the smaller of the two, is a submerged machine. It is winking with concealed lights that illuminate the surrounding cold water. It is a machine that has experienced a disaster. It is a squash of metal. It has curled and destroyed parts, sliced-off metal limbs, fractured short pipes. It may be described anthropomorphically as a metal heart. It has traces of aorta and ventricle. Perhaps it slowly pumps. It is a relic, a metal machine of a long-gone aeronautical, archaeological disaster, but its power, crypton-like, is causing it still to glow, like volcanic evidence at the bottom of a deep sea.

The second item is a pair of battered wings. At the very least, these objects are wing-shaped, prototype enough to be generic. They almost certainly once flew. There is no doubt that the machine-heart and the machine-wing could have been related. Indeed, they act now in some sort of unison. The wing has lights, port and starboard, winking rhythmically, and winking in concert with the pulsing machine-heart. The relationship is not simple. Perhaps five beats of the flickering of the metal heart are concomitant to two light pulsations of the proto-wings. It is a curiosity that the water of the wing's submersion may be protective. Like a foetus taken out of amniotic liquid, if the machine is taken out of its surrounding water, its life might die. Perhaps the water is not water, but a conductive spirit of some sort, alcohol, alkali, acid, water of aloes, almond water – important fluids all initialled with the letter A.

Perhaps the heart and the wings are the power centre of the exhibition. They are a reminder that anything new is probably modelled on something very old, archaeologically old. Perhaps they are relics of a golden age of flying that make them revered artefacts which have inspired the present endeavour.

DESPRÉS D'HAVER llegit els textos, d'haver estat intimidats per l'hèlice rotatòria i d'haver ponderat l'ambigüitat dels senyals del terra i la presència inquietant dels observadors de l'aire amb els seus auriculars, aquesta exposició de proves de la primera, última i definitiva aventura aèria d'Ícar és particularitzada i centrada temàticament.

Immediatament davant nostre hi ha dos objectes. El primer, el més petit, és una màquina submergida que parpelleja a causa d'uns llums ocults que il·luminen l'aigua freda del seu voltant. És una màquina que ha tingut un accident. És un amuntegament de metall. Té els components retorçats i destruïts, els seus membres metàl·lics han estat tallats en rodó, les seves canonades han estat fracturades. Es pot descriure antropomòrficament com un cor de metall. Presenta rastres d'una aorta i d'un ventricle. Potser bomba lentament. És una relíquia, una màquina metàl·lica d'un antic accident areonàutic, un accident arqueològic, però la seva potència, com si fos criptonita, fa que encara brilli, com un vestigi volcànic al fons d'un mar profund.

Al seu costat hi ha una ala masegada. És, com a mínim, un objecte en forma d'ala, prou prototípic per ser genèric. És gairebé

1. Aircraft destroyed by hailstones
1. Avió destruït per una pedregada

cert que havia volat, que havia volat arqueològicament. No hi ha dubte que el cor-màquina i el cor-ala podrien estar relacionats. I és evident que ara, en certa manera, funcionen a l'uníson. L'ala té uns llums a babord i a estribord que centellegen rítmicament, i compassats amb les pulsacions del cor-màquina. La relació no és senzilla. Potser cinc batecs del centelleig del cor de metall es corresponen amb dues pulsacions de llum de la protoala. És curiós que l'aigua de la submersió de l'ala pugui ser protectora. Com un fetus separat del líquid amniòtic, si la màquina se separa de l'aigua que l'envolta, la seva vida es pot extingir. Potser l'aigua no és realment aigua, sinó algun tipus d'esperit conductor, com ara alcohol, àlcali, àcid, aigua d'àloes, aigua d'ametlles... tots fluids importants, i que comencen amb la lletra a.

Potser aquest cor i aquestes ales són el centre de poder de l'exposició. Ens recorden que qualsevol cosa nova és probablement feta a imatge d'alguna altra de molt antiga, arqueològicament antiga. Potser són relíquies d'una edat d'or dels vols, i això les converteix en artefactes venerats que han inspirat aquesta temptativa.

The Icarus auditions 9
Els aspirants a Ícar

THERE ARE A NUMBER of glass cases containing contenders for the rôle of Icarus. We do not know how old Icarus was on his maiden flight. The younger the child, the less weight to be carried on the air, but the less strength available in his arms to manoeuvre the wings. If Ovid is our source of information, then the suggestion is that Icarus was not much older than a child, say ten or eleven years old, of an age to listen to his father's warning not to fly too close to the sun, but impetuous or forgetful enough not to heed it. Other sources, visual as well as literary, make Icarus older. These young men, auditioning for the role of Icarus, are broadly divided into two categories. The first set of contenders are six young men who feel that stringiness of frame and angularity of anatomy are suitable characteristics for long-haul flight. They sit awaiting the visitor's appraisal, they are the contenders who demonstrate their ability to play Icarus as an athlete of long-distance abilities. Here is a hypothetical list of candidates.

1. The first young man is nervous. He is a thin youth in nondescript clothes, perhaps a white open-neck shirt and a pair of dirty white trousers. He sits with his hands between his knees, his boots pressed tightly together.
2. The second candidate is so eager to impress on us his ability to play the rôle, he has stripped naked, and his white body looks unhealthy in the bright top-light. With his shoulders hunched, he looks like a featherless chicken, for nakedness is not an easy rôle for him to play in public.

3. The third young man, thinking to copy his neighbour, has also taken off all his clothes, but only to his white underpants. He has a moustache. Did Icarus have a moustache? In the Second World War in England it was traditional for airmen to wear moustaches. Could the moustaches, combed out right and left above the lips, have been a symbol or emblem of wings?
4. The fourth young man is a soldier. He is dressed in camouflage fatigues and he has taken off his socks and boots as though he is prepared only to paddle in the sea and not to drown in it.
5. The fifth candidate wears blue bathing-trunks that he knows advertise and boast his sex. He is sort of prepared, but he is cold and wears a short black T-shirt that exposes his navel. His toenails need cutting.
6. The sixth has stripped himself to the waist and wears red

HI HA UNA SÈRIE de vitrines que contenen els aspirants a assumir el paper d'Ícar. No sabem quants anys tenia Ícar quan va fer el seu vol iniciàtic. Com més jovenet hagués estat, més lleuger hauria estat i menys li hauria costat aguantar-se suspès en l'aire, però d'altra banda també hauria tingut menys força als braços per maniobrar les ales. Si Ovidi és la nostra font d'informació, aleshores ens podem decantar per la hipòtesi que Ícar encara era un nen, diguem que d'uns deu o onze anys, prou jove per fer cas de l'advertiment del seu pare de no acostar-se massa al sol, però també prou impetuós i oblidadís per no fer-ne cas. Altres fonts, tant visuals com literàries, presenten un Ícar més gran. Aquests homes joves que es presenten per al paper d'Ícar es divideixen bàsicament en dos grups. El primer grup de candidats són sis joves que pensen que una complexió fibrosa i una anatomia angular són característiques idònies per a un vol de llarg recorregut. Seuen mentre esperen ser avaluats pels visitants, i són els candidats que mostren més capacitat d'assumir el paper d'Ícar com a atleta capaç de cobrir llargues distàncies. Això és una llista hipotètica de candidats:
1. El primer és un jove nerviós. És prim i va vestit amb una roba indefinida, potser una camisa blanca de coll obert i uns pantalons blancs bruts. Porta botes. Seu amb les mans entre els genolls i amb els peus junts.

2. El segon candidat té tantes ganes de convèncer-nos de la seva aptitud per al paper, que va completament despullat i el seu cos blanc té un aspecte poc saludable sota la llum intensa que l'il·lumina des de dalt. Carregat d'espatlles, sembla un pollastre sense plomes, perquè no li resulta fàcil exhibir-se en públic totalment nu.
3. El tercer jove, amb la intenció de copiar el seu veí, també s'ha tret tota la roba, però s'ha deixat posats uns calçotets blancs. Porta bigotis. Portava bigotis, Ícar? Durant la Segona Guerra Mundial, a Anglaterra, era tradicional que els aviadors portessin bigotis. És possible que els bigotis, pentinats a dreta i esquerra per sobre el llavi, fossin un símbol o emblema de les ales?
4. El quart jove és un soldat. Porta un uniforme de camuflatge i s'ha tret els mitjons i les botes, com si estigués disposat a caure al mar però no a ofegar-s'hi.
5. El cinquè candidat porta un banyador blau, conscient que li accentua i realça el sexe. Se'l veu ben disposat, però té fred i du una samarreta curta de color negre que li deixa el melic al descobert. Li convindria tallar-se les ungles dels peus.
6. El sisè va despullat de cintura en amunt, i porta uns elàstics vermells que li aguanten uns pantalons de xeviot amb mostra d'espiga; té una cintura insignificant. Potser pensa que els elàstics són una ajuda per a la propulsió. També va descalç.

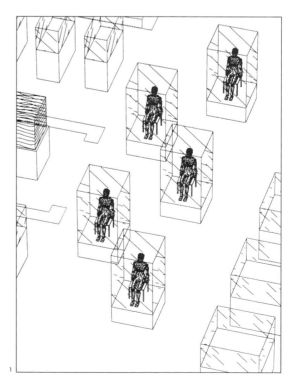

1. Computer plan of Section 9 featuring the vitrines of the candidates to audition for the part of Icarus
2. Opposite. Is swimming a useful template for flying? Conrad Witz, The Miraculous Draught of Fishes *(detail), 1442, oil on wood, Geneva, Musée d'art et d'histoire*
3. Swimmer from The Technique of Competitive Swimming
4. Caravaggio, Amor Victorious, *1600, oil on canvas, Berlin, Staatliche Museen*
5. Overleaf. Eugène Delacroix, Dante and Virgil in Hell, *(detail), 1822, oil on canvas, Paris, Musée du Louvre*

6. Antonio da Crevalcore, angel from Madonna and Child, *1485, oil on wood, private collection*
7. Egyptian long-distance swimmer Abo-Heif finishing a 60-mile, 35-hour swim on Lake Michigan
8. Gentile Bellini, The Miracle of the Cross on San Lorchzo Bridge *(detail), Venice, Galleria dell'Accademia*
1. Plànol informàtic de la Secció 9, amb les vitrines dels candidats al paper d'Ícar
2. La natació, és un possible patró per a l'acció de volar? Conrad Witz, La pesca miraculosa *(detall), 1442, oli sobre fusta, Ginebra, Musée d'art et d'histoire*

3. Nedador de The Technique of Competitive Swimming
4. Caravaggio, Amor victoriós, *1600, oli sobre tela, Berlín, Staatliche Museen*
5. Eugène Delacroix, Dante i Virgili a l'infern *(detall), 1822, oli sobre tela, París, Musée du Louvre*
6. Antonio da Crevalcore, àngel de Verge i infant *(detall), 1485, oli sobre fusta, col·lecció particular*
7. El nedador de fons egipci Abo-Heif després de fer una travessia de 60 milles en 35 hores al llac Michigan
8. Gentile Bellini, El miracle de la Creu al pont de San Lorenzo *(detall), Venècia, Galleria dell'Accademia*

THE STO
to dispr
that the
greater
insepara
Would D
of heat?
enquiry
ever scal
cold incr

Here
for each
water slc
a little v
ice-block
melting
dripping
zinc tub
sentinels
niscent
pole, or c
or of hyp
extreme
that melt
as destru
becomes
releases i

4

1. Peter Gree
the ice, 1995
2. 100 Objec
the World,
item 64. Ice
for the close c
Millennium
3. Caspar Da
Arctic shipw
on canvas, H
Kunsthalle
1. Peter Gree
gel, 1995, ac
2. "100 objec
representar el
1992
Peça 64. Gel.
per al final de
3. Caspar Dav
Naufragi àrti
sobre tela, Hä
Kunsthalle

THERE IS A GROUPING of three domestic cast-iron baths. They are supplied with running water from metal taps. The water in all three baths is controlled by an inflow and an outflow that perform an ever-running balancing act. The noise of water so comfortably running into the baths is amplified. It fills the local space. It conjures up domestic comforts, warm water for the naked body, peaceful submersion. But in this gloomy public space, there is uncertainty, for who would stand naked here to take a bath? Perhaps several portents are at stake. Perhaps there cannot be any soporific lazing, no lounging in warm water here. Just a quick naked dip to clean the body before flight – a purification.

There are other resonances. Perhaps at one time the baths contained diluted wax or warm grease. Swimmers swimming great distances are known to coat their bodies with grease to keep the body temperature constant and to stop the chafing of the sea.

Perhaps it was in a warm bath that Daedalus thought his inventive thoughts. They say that ideas come to those who lie and dream in their baths. Think of Archimedes. "When a body is wholly or partly immersed in a fluid, the fluid exerts on the body an upthrust which is equal to the weight of water displaced."

Why three baths? Was there to be a third flyer? Perhaps it was to be the disappointed Ariadne abandoned by Theseus after successfully guiding him through the maze to kill the Minotaur? Ariadne was seduced and abandoned by Theseus, and then taken up later by Bacchus. But what of the time in between these two lovers? Did she consider flight from

2

HI HA UN GRUP de tres banyeres domèstiques de ferro fos, totes amb aigua corrent que surt d'unes aixetes metàl·liques. El nivell de l'aigua, a totes tres banyeres, és sempre el mateix: es manté constant gràcies a un moviment d'afluència i desguàs que proporciona un equilibri hidràulic. El soroll de l'aigua que entra i surt tan còmodament de les banyeres és amplificat, omple l'espai circumdant i conjura les incomoditats domèstiques. Àigua tèbia per al cos nu. Submersió plàcida. Aquí, però, en aquest fosc espai públic, hi ha un ambient d'incertesa: qui entraria aquí despullat per banyar-se? Potser hi ha en joc diversos presagis. Potser aquí, en aquesta aigua, no és possible el relaxament soporífer, el ganduleig en aigua tèbia: només una ràpida immersió del cos nu, per rentar-lo abans d'emprendre el vol. Com el bany d'aigua freda que potser van prendre Ícar i Dèdal abans del vol, per purificar-se.

També hi ha altres ressonàncies. Potser, en altres temps, les banyeres havien contingut cera diluïda o greix tebi. Sabem que els nedadors de llarga distància es cobreixen el cos amb greix per mantenir la temperatura corporal i combatre la irritació que provoca l'aigua del mar.

Potser va ser en un bany d'aigua calenta on Dèdal va forjar les seves idees inventives. Diuen que les idees sobrevenen a aquells qui s'ajeuen i somien a dins d'una banyera. Pensem, per exemple, en Arquimedes: "Un cos totalment o parcialment submergit en un fluid és afectat per una força ascensional igual al pes del fluid desallotjat."

I per què tres banyeres? Hi havia un tercer volador? Era potser la decebuda Ariadna, abandonada per Teseu després d'haver-lo guiat amb èxit a través del laberint per poder matar el minotaure? Ariadna va ser seduïda i posteriorment abandonada per Teseu, i finalment va ser recollida per Bacus. Però, i durant el temps que va transcórrer entremig? Pot ser que Ariadna pensés en la possibilitat de fugir volant de Creta i de tota la seva infelicitat? O potser la tercera banyera estava destinada a la mare d'Ícar, l'esposa de Dèdal, a qui la mitologia grega no assigna cap nom? Si una dona hagués previst acompanyar Dèdal i Ícar, li hauria resultat més difícil volar que a un home? Potser tenia menys força, però també un cos més lleuger. Estableix cap diferència l'anatomia femenina? La redistribució del pes a les natges, a les cuixes i als pits, justifica un càlcul diferent? És potser una qüestió de reequilibri? Els nedadors contemporanis s'afaiten el cos per augmentar el rendiment aquanàutic: això, almenys, seria una prioritat menor per a una dona.

I encara cal fer una altra consideració. Hi havia el rumor que Dèdal havia matat el seu cap tirànic, el rei Minos, en una banyera d'aigua bullent. Potser una d'aquestes banyeres és l'arma homicida.

3

Crete and all its miseries?

Or was the third bath intended for Icarus's mother, Daedalus's wife, who has no name in Greek mythology. If a woman had planned to accompany Daedalus and Icarus, would flight be any more difficult for a woman than for a man? Less strength perhaps but a lighter body. Does the female anatomy make a difference? Is the redistributed weight of buttock, thigh and breast a consideration important enough to make a recalculation? Is it a question of rebalance? Contemporary swimmers shave their bodies for greater aquanautical success. This at least would be a low priority for the female.

There is yet one more consideration. There was a rumour that Daedalus killed his tyrannical boss, King Minos, in a bath of scalding water. Perhaps one of these three baths is the murder weapon.

1. Jacques Louis David,
Dying Marat, 1793, oil on
canvas, Brussels, Musées
Royaux des Beaux-Arts
2. 100 Objects to Represent
the World, 1992, Vienna
Item 49. Water. An
exhibition for the close of the
Millennium
3. The Belly of an Architect,
1985, film, The architect
Stourley Kracklite takes a
Roman bath
1. Jacques Louis David, La
mort de Marat, 1793, oli
sobre tela, Brussel·les, Musées
royaux des Beaux-Arts
2. "100 objectes per a
representar el món", Viena,
1992
Peça 49. Aigua. Una
exposició per al final del
mil·lenni
3. El ventre d'un arquitecte,
1985, pel·lícula
L'arquitecte Stourley
Kracklite pren un bany romà

IF YOU HAVE A DESIRE for flight and you wish to remain associated with birds, and you want to stay away from hitching a ride on a flying horse or the probably grounded Sphinx, there are three possible mythological paths to follow. First make your own feathered wings like Daedalus. Second hitch a ride with an eagle like Ganymede. Or third mate with a swan, be patient and wait for the eggs. Like Leda.

Perhaps Daedalus considered the last option. He was no stranger to curiously inappropriate sexual congress, consider his ingenious assistance to Pasiphaë. How many eggs would he need to breed how many birds to produce how many feathers? His years of Cretan captivity would easily have given him time to make the calculations and become a chicken-farmer. His silver tongue could have convinced Minos that he was developing some research programme for universal Cretan benefit, possibly in the military department.

In anticipation that Daedalus considered the possibility of eggs as a solution to his problem, and in honour of Leda who dropped two white eggs in her lying-in bed, here are one thousand white eggs – white for purity. All are carefully arranged in formation in two large vitrines. Five hundred to the left, five hundred to the right. Five hundred white eggs lying on their rounded long side, each its length's length from its neighbour, five hundred white eggs standing on their rounded short side – Columbus-style – each again a safe distance from its fellow.

Two curiosities arise here. Can eggs be sexed before hatching? Perhaps Daedalus insisted on using the feathers from one gender only. And secondly, look how difficult it is to describe the geometry of an egg.

SI TENIU EL DESIG de volar i que se us associï amb els ocells, i no voleu haver de dependre d'un cavall volador o de l'Esfinx, probablement subjectada a terra, hi ha tres potents camins mitològics que podeu seguir. Fabriqueu-vos unes ales amb plomes, igual que Dèdal. Munteu damunt d'una àguila, com Ganimedes. O acobleu-vos amb un cigne, tingueu paciència i espereu els ous. Igual que Leda.

Potser Dèdal va considerar aquesta última opció. No era aliè a les unions sexuals atípiques, si tenim en compte la seva enginyosa assistència a Pasífae. Quants ous li haurien calgut per criar el nombre d'aus necessari per produir la quantitat adequada de plomes? Els anys de captivitat a Creta li haurien pogut donar temps suficient per fer els càlculs necessaris i convertir-se en criador de pollastres. La seva habilitat verbal hauria convençut Minos que duia a terme un cert programa de recerca a benefici de tot Creta, possiblement en l'àmbit militar.

Preveient que Dèdal hauria pogut considerar la possibilitat d'utilitzar els ous com a solució del seu problema, i en honor de Leda, que va pondre dos ous blancs en el seu jaç, aquí hi ha mil ous de color blanc (el color de la puresa, el color de les ales de cigne, si bé és dubtós, naturalment, que això siguin ous de cigne). Estan tots acuradament arrenglerats en dues grans vitrines. Cinc-cents a l'esquerra, cinc-cents

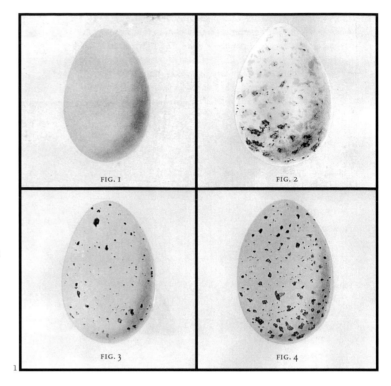

FIG. 1   FIG. 2   FIG. 3   FIG. 4

3. Piero della Francesca, The Brera Madonna, *ca. 1475, tempera on panel, Milan, Brera*
3. Piero della Francesca, La Verge de Brera, *ca. 1475, pintura al temp sobre taula, Milà, Pinacoteca di Brera*

a la dreta. Cinc-cents ous blancs que s'aguanten sobre la part arrodonida més llarga, cada un a la mateixa distància del seu veí, cinc-cents ous blancs que s'aguanten sobre la part arrodonida més curta –a l'estil de l'ou de Colom– i també cada un a la mateixa distància del seu veí. Això planteja dos interrogants. L'un és si es pot determinar el sexe dels ous abans de ser incubats, suposant que els ous que Dèdal volia utilitzar haguessin de ser tots d'un mateix sexe. I l'altre interrogant el planteja la dificultat de descriure la geometria d'un ou.

Perhaps Daedalus should have been more patient. He should have taken a feather from Leda's cap and arranged to mate with a swan – perhaps that way he might have had progeny with wings, for if a human female can mate with a male swan to produce humans out of an egg, perhaps a human male can mate with a female swan to produce birds out of an egg, The snag seems, however, to be a mighty proliferation of twins.
Potser Dèdal hauria d'haver tingut més paciència. Hauria d'haver agafat una ploma del capell de Leda i haver-se acoblat amb un cigne: potser així hauria tingut fills amb ales. Perquè, si una dona pot acoblar-se amb un cigne mascle per produir éssers humans a partir d'un ou, potser un home pot acoblar-se amb un cigne femella per produir ocells. Sembla, però, que hi ha un problema: que això comportaria una enorme proliferació de bessons.

The suspended egg in this Piero della Francesca *sacra conversazione* is a mystery. Is it a symbol of fertility, some prophetic image of a spermatozoa about to fertilise the cockleshell ovum behind it? Why is the egg upside down, hanging from its broader end? Is it a masonic emblem? Is it sheer virtuosity, plumb-lining a weight into a shadowy void to demonstrate skill?

Is it a commentary on complex mathematical symmetry? Is it a Leda reference identifying God with Zeus? Is it a reference to Immaculate conception and virginal birth – the fertilised egg transplanted into the Virgin's womb, thereby bypassing carnal fertilisation?

L'ou suspès d'aquesta *sacra conversazione* de Piero della Francesca és un misteri. Es tracta d'un símbol de la fertilitat, d'una imatge profètica d'un espermatozoide a punt de fertilitzar l'òvul en forma de closca de nou que hi ha darrere seu? Per què està penjat de cap per avall, per l'extrem més ample? És un emblema maçònic? És el simple virtuosisme d'introduir un pes a plom en un buit tenebrós per fer una exhibició de destresa? És un comentari sobre la complexitat de la simetria matemàtica? És una referència a Leda que identifica Déu amb Zeus? És una referència a la Immaculada Concepció i al part virginal -l'òvul fertilitzat i trasplantat al ventre de la Verge, prescindint de la fertilització carnal?

20
The candles
Les espelmes

CANDLES ARE LIT for auspicious beginnings. Light a candle to light the way. Candles lit to placate the gods and remember the departed. Placed here in this imaginary exhibition, one hundred candles are situated halfway between the wax that made them and created their shape and mystique, and halfway to the the Daedalian light-house, their possible cumulative out-come. For centuries, architects have constructed lighthouses in the shape of candles. Let this set of one hundred flickering candles represent one hundred lighthouses. They are a remembrance and a guide.

LES ESPELMES S'ENCENEN per propiciar bons auguris. S'encén una espelma per il·luminar el camí. S'encenen per apaivagar els déus i recordar els qui ens han deixat. En aquesta exposició imaginària, les espelmes se situen a mig camí entre la cera que les ha fabricades i ha creat la seva forma i la seva mística, i el far dedalià, el seu resultat inevitable. Durant segles els arquitectes han construït fars en forma d'espelmes. Volem que aquest conjunt de cent espelmes enceses representin un centenar de fars. Són una evocació i una guia.

1. Church candlestand,
Barcelona
1. Lampadari d'església,
Barcelona

THERE IS A BRIGHT flashing light that manages, in some small part, to both dazzle and attract, to create deep shadows and sudden blindnesses. In these sudden blindnesses, we are afraid, just a little, for our feet, for the darkness has hidden them. The sudden brief oceans of bright light that illuminate this world of glass-reflections do not permit our eyes to get used to the gloom with any confidence. This dizzying sensation can be safely blamed on a lighthouse under water, sending out a bright flashing beam for a few seconds in every sixty.

Light under water is a dependable fascination. Experience certainly reminds us that light is hot and caused by fire, and fire and water do not mix, hence the unbelievable idea of volcanos under water and questions of sea phosphorescence and the unlikelihood of fish that submarinely glow and shine. But we have to believe these phenomena, we have the evidence. Even water and electricity can mix in the right conditions.

This underwater light reaches out across the submarine space, glinting and reflecting on all the glass-faceted surfaces, on all the multiple-reflecting panes. It is a cold-white bright light, both beckoning and warning, as is the nature of all lighthouse beacons.

HI HA UNA LLUM brillant i intermitent que, en alguna part reduïda, aconsegueix enlluernar i atraure, però també crear ombres profundes i encegaments sobtats. En aquests encegaments sobtats, ens mostrem una mica cautelosos respecte als nostres peus, perquè la foscor els ha ocultats, i els breus i sobtats oceans de llum brillant que il·luminen aquest món de reflexos sobre vidre no permeten que els nostres ulls s'acostumin prou a la foscor per adquirir confiança. Aquesta sensació vertiginosa deriva d'un far que hi ha sota l'aigua i envia un raig de llum brillant durant dos segons de cada seixanta.

La llum sota l'aigua exerceix una fascinació inevitable. La memòria popular serveix per recordar-nos que la llum és calenta i originada pel foc, i el foc i l'aigua no es barregen; d'aquí ve la idea increïble d'un volcà sota l'aigua, i de qüestions com la fosforescència del mar i la improbabilitat de peixos que brillin i fulgurin sota l'aigua. Però hi hem de creure, perquè en tenim proves. Fins i tot l'aigua i l'electricitat poden mesclar-se en les condicions adequades.

Aquesta llum subaquàtica ens arriba a través de l'espai subterrani i submarí, guspirejant i reflectint-se sobre totes les superfícies de vidre, sobre totes les facetes reflectores. És una llum brillant, blanca i freda, un senyal i alhora un advertiment, com és el cas de tots els fars de línia.

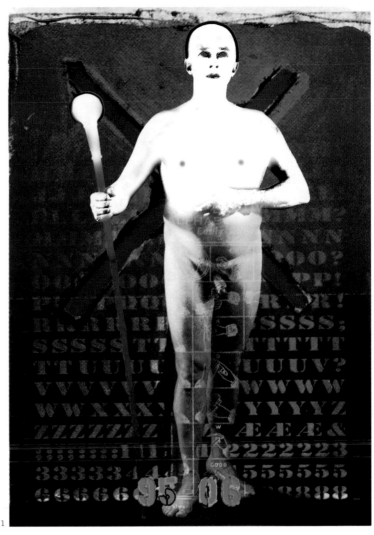

1

1. *Peter Greenaway*, Pharos – Allegory 95, 100 Allegories to Represent the World, *1996*
1. *Peter Greenaway*, Pharos – Al·legoria 95, 100 Allegories to Represent the World, *1996*

It is a cold-white bright light, both beckoning and warning, as is the nature of all lighthouse beacons.

És una llum brillant, blanca i freda, un senyal i alhora un advertiment, com és el cas de tots els fars de línia.

1

1. *Peter Greenaway,* Male corpse, 1990, *mixed media on card, from the film project* Death in the Seine
2. *Peter Greenaway,* Female corpse, 1990, *mixed media on card, from the film project* Death in the Seine
3. *Sue Fox ,* Open Hand, 1995, *photo*
4. *Feet of a feigned corpse from the film project* Death in the Seine

1. *Peter Greenaway,* Cadàver masculí, 1990, *tècnica mixta sobre cartolina, del projecte cinematogràfic* Death in the Seine
2. *Peter Greenaway,* Cadàver femení, 1990, *tècnica mixta sobre cartolina, del projecte cinematogràfic* Death in the Seine
3. *Sue Fox,* Mà oberta, 1995, *fotografia*
4. *Peus d'un cadàver fictici, del projecte cinematogràfic* Death in the Seine

WE NOW COME ACROSS the Icarine coffin. It is in a dark space, dimly lit. It is a white wooden, water-soaked, clamped-shut coffin. And it is oozing and bubbling water that runs down its sides where the wood is swollen with the perpetual soaking. The water constantly spills out between the coffin planking, dribbling down and over the metal edges of its pedestal into a metal trough. From this trough the water is conducted away down a dark damp conduit. This to an image of melodrama dimly lit. It might remind us of a flooded car or a drowned plane lifted from the deep water of a canal or river, or from the deep water of a harbour, the water sluicing out with a watching audience always knowing that the car's driver or the plane's pilot is still in the driving seat.

Here, the water never fails to stop sluicing out. The sluicing away is eternal, as a metaphor for the water in Icarus's lungs perpetually emptying. We can imagine the corpse inside, floating in the brine as it floated in the sea, the face pushed up against the coffin-lid, the limbs dangling in the cold water of that confined space.

I ARA ARRIBEM al taüt d'Ícar. Es troba en un espai fosc, escassament il·luminat. És un taüt de fusta blanca, amarat d'aigua i tancat amb armelles. Traspua una aigua bombollejant que corre pels costats, on la fusta s'ha inflat a conseqüència de l'amarament perpetu. L'aigua vessa constantment entre els taulons del taüt, goteja sobre els cantells metàl·lics del seu pedestal i va a parar en un bací de metall. Des d'aquí, l'aigua és transportada a través d'un conducte fosc i humit. És la imatge d'un melodrama tènuement il·luminat. Pot recordar-nos un cotxe o un petit avió rescatat amb una grua de les profunditats d'un canal o d'un riu, o del moll d'un port, amb l'aigua que regalima, i el públic que s'ho mira sabent que el conductor del cotxe o el pilot de l'avió és encara assegut a dins. Aquí, l'aigua no para mai de vessar. És un vessar etern, com una metàfora de l'aigua a l'interior dels pulmons d'Ícar que es buiden perpètuament. Podem imaginar el cadàver de l'interior flotant en la salmorra com flotava en el mar, amb la cara aixafada contra la tapa del taüt, i els membres penjant en aquell espai reduït.

2

The sluicing away is eternal, as a metaphor for the water in Icarus's lungs perpetually emptying

És un vessar etern, com una metàfora de l'aigua a l'interior dels pulmons d'Ícar que es buiden perpètuament

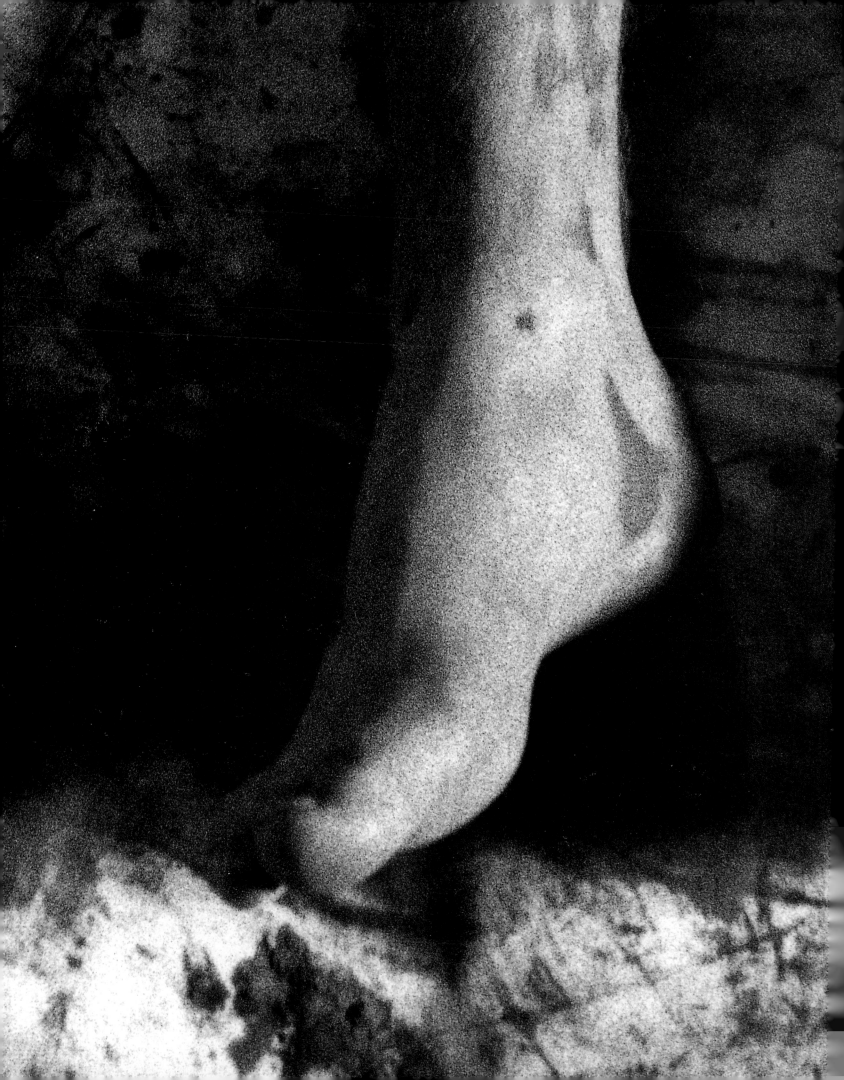

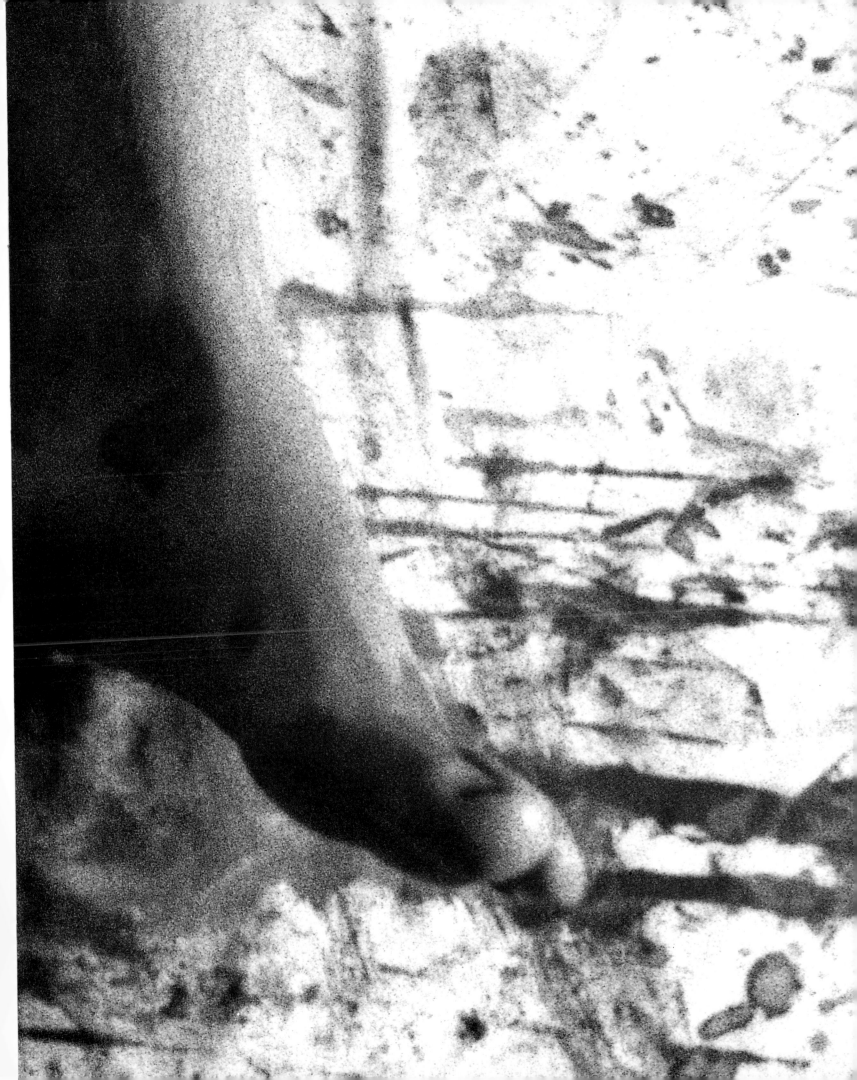

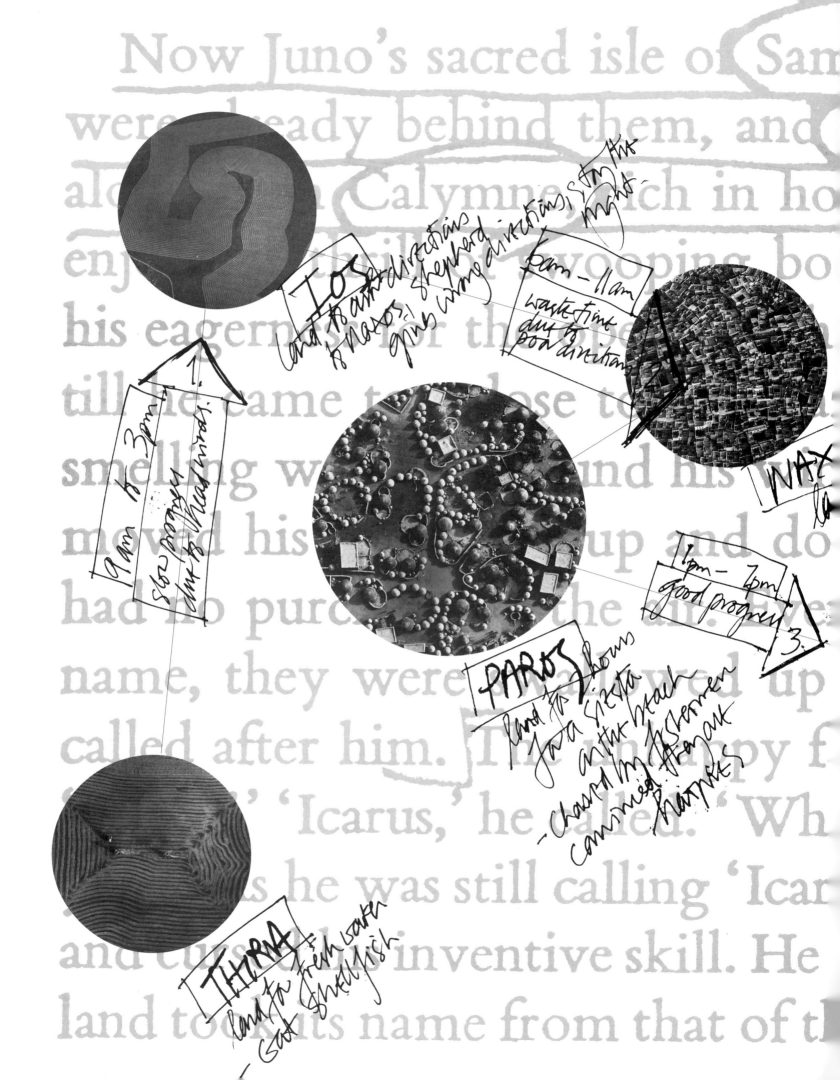

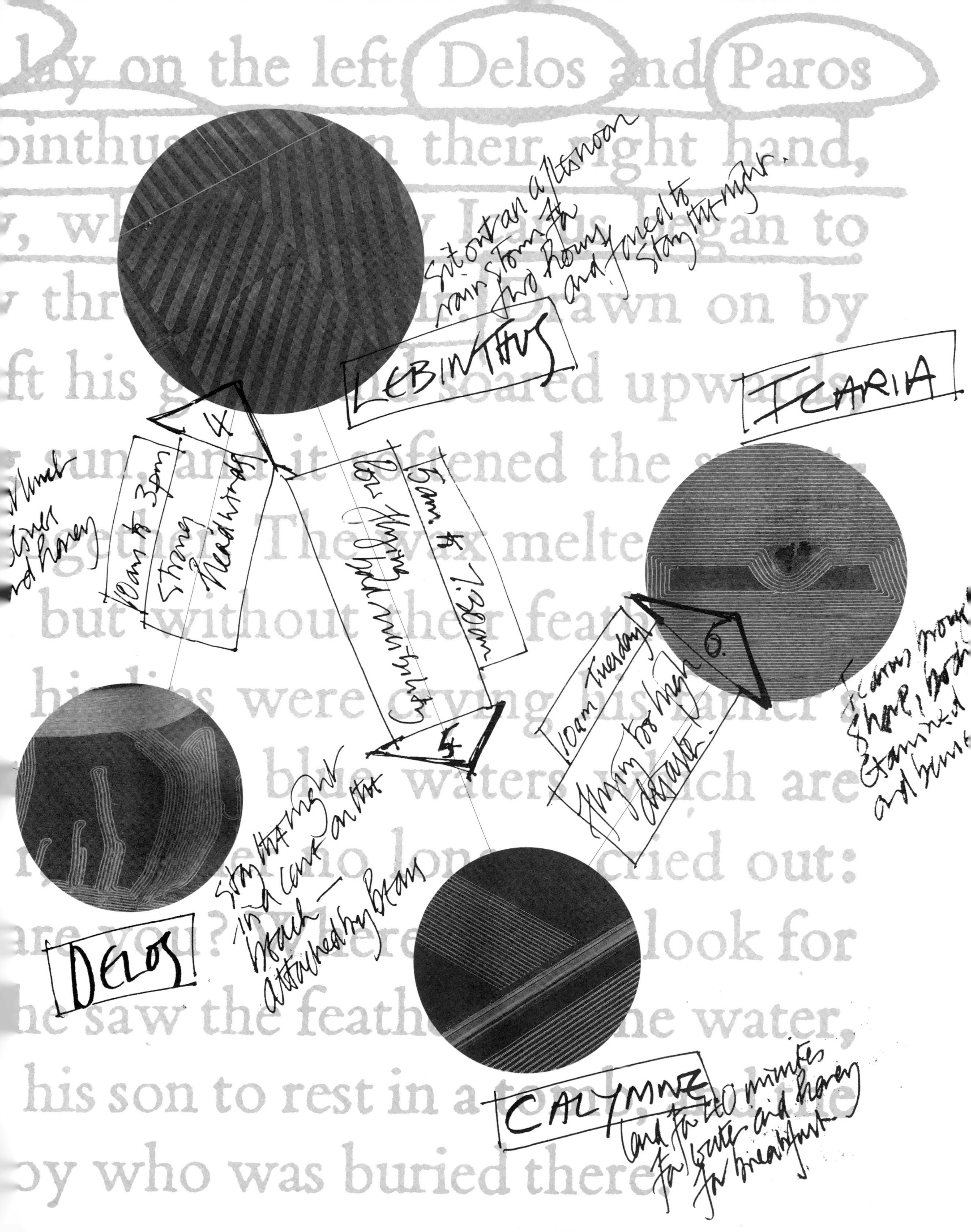

on the left Delos and Paros

on their right hand,

Drawn on by

ft his g   soared upwards

sun, and it softened the

together. The wax melted

but without their feath

birds were crying bits

blue waters which are

no longer cried out:

are you? Where   look for

he saw the feath   the water,

his son to rest in a tomb

by who was buried there

LEBINTHUS

ICARIA

DELOS

CALYMNE

Sit out an afternoon rainstorm and forced to stay the night

10am to 3pm strong headwind

6am to 7:30pm calm weather

stay the night in a cave on the beach — attached by beans

10am Tuesday too high too close

Icarus moved shore, body examined and buried

land for 20 minutes for water and honey for breakfast

24
The beating wings
Les ales bategants

WE ARE NOW STANDING in front of the highest and tallest exhibit we have witnessed so far. It is standing on the highest pedestal yet and it is lit with a pulsating beating light. It is a pair of wax-treated, white-feathered wings. They are Icarus-designed. Either we are in the future tense and they have not yet been worn in the grand flight, in which case we can regard them standing here as a public relations exercise of defiance to King Minos. Or they are in retirement, and we must view them as a requiem. However, at a closer look, the arm and torso leather-straps are loose, and they look worn and grease-stained, darkened with the sweat from between the shoulder blades and from under the arms.

The first thought is that they have been taken from the corpse of Icarus. But if the sun had melted the wax and the feathers were in total disarray, is this likely? Is it probable that the grief-stricken Daedalus had taken the trouble to reconstitute the wings? Ovid says that Daedalus only realized that his son had fallen because of the sight of the dismembered feathers floating on the sea's surface.

Perhaps they are the wings made for Ariadne, who declined to take up the invitation to escape from Crete and from her disappointment at being jilted by Theseus. At even longer odds, perhaps they were the wings designed for Icarus's mother who had also refused the opportunity to take to the air. She was a great swimmer, and flying is a sort of swimming in the air, and she knew that the opening and closing of the thighs for propulsion was indecorous, and she had no wish to attract the lewd up-turned eyes of shepherds and ploughmen idling on any hillside in Naxos or Paros or Delos.

Perhaps these wings are the wings of Daedalus, found neglected on a hillside outside Naples where Daedalus had abandoned them. Perhaps these are the wing prototypes, the very first wings, because surely Daedalus must have made wings first to test the possibilities, like any good designer, before considering that his son should risk his life.

ARA ENS TROBEM DAVANT de la peça més alta de totes les que hem vist. Descansa sobre el pedestal més alt que hem vist fins ara, i està il·luminada amb una llum de pulsacions bategants. Son dues ales de plomes blanques tractades amb cera. Van ser dissenjades per Ícar. Pot ser que ens trobem en un temps futur i les ales encara no s'hagin desgastat en el gran vol –i, en aquest cas, podem considerar-les com un exercici de relacions públiques per desafiar el rei Minos–, o bé ja han estat retirades i hem de considerar-les com un rèquiem. Vistes de més a prop, però, les corretges de pell dels braços i del tors estan afluixades, i es veuen desgastades i tacades de greix, enfosquides per la suor de l'esquena, entre els omòplats, i de les aixelles.

El primer que pensem és que han estat extretes del cadàver d'Ícar. Però, com pot ser, si el sol havia fos la cera i les plomes estaven totalment desgavellades? És probable que l'afligit Dèdal s'hagués pres la pena de reconstruir les ales? Ovidi diu que Dèdal no va saber que el seu fill s'havia ofegat fins que no va veure les plomes desmembrades surant a la superfície del mar.

Hi ha la remota possibilitat que siguin les ales fetes per a Ariadna, que va declinar la invitació de fugir de Creta i de la seva decepció perquè va ser rebutjada per Teseu. O bé –possibilitat encara més remota– que fossin les ales dissenyades per a la mare d'Ícar, que també havia declinat l'oferiment d'aixecar el vol indecorosament. Era una gran nedadora, i volar és una manera de nedar per l'aire, i sabia que la propulsió a base d'obrir i tancar les cuixes era indecorosa, i no tenia cap desig d'atraure les mirades impúdiques dels pastors i dels llauradors que vagarejaven pels vessants de les muntanyes de Naxos, de Paros o de Delos.

Potser, doncs, l'única conclusió encertada és que es tracta de les ales de Dèdal, que van ser trobades en el vessant d'algun turó dels afores de Nàpols, on Dèdal les havia abandonades. Podem estar segurs que són els prototips d'ales, les primeres ales, perquè sens dubte Dèdal devia fabricar les seves pròpies ales en primer lloc, per posar-ne a prova les possibilitats, com qualsevol pilot-dissenyador, abans de considerar que el seu fill pogués arriscar la vida.

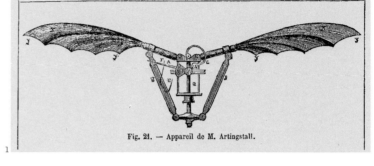

Fig. 21. — Appareil de M. Artingstall.

1

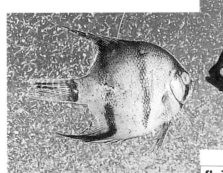

1. French experimental flying machine
2. Angel fish from the film, A Zed and Two Noughts, 1982
3. Richfeldt about to launch himself off the Eiffel Tower to his death
1. Màquina voladora experimental francesa
2. Peix àngel de la pel·lícula A Zed and Two Noughts, 1982
3. Richfeldt a punt de llançar-se des de dalt de la torre Eiffel i de matar-se

2

She was a great swimmer, and flying is a sort of swimming in the air **Era una gran nedadora, i volar és una manera de nedar per l'aire**

AFTER THE DISASTER, *post mortem*, there is to be an autopsy. The investigation is in secret. This is the second death of a boy that Daedalus has been associated with. And both deaths have been concerned with gravity. If Daedalus is a child-murderer then gravity is his trademark. The first death was that of his nephew hurled off the steep cliff of the Acropolis. Daedalus claimed it was an accident but everyone knew he was jealous of his sister's boy, who had invented the saw and the compasses and the potter's wheel.

Perhaps the original autopsy room for Icarus was on the island of Icaria in the Aegean where Daedalus brought the corpse fished from the sea. The body could not have been in the water very long. There would be no bloating, no swelling, no nibbling by fish, no bruising from smashing against the rocks. The body would have been laid on a slab, cold water trickled over the flesh to wash away the last of the wax that had melted and dribbled and then frozen brittle-hard again at the touch of the cold sea-water.

The autopsy room has limited entrance. We do not want all the world and his wife trickling through here gawping, gossiping, behaving like vultures at the victim of what Daedalus insists is a domestic accident. Boys drown. Their exuberance in the water, taking risks, showing off, behaving badly, trying it on, is well known. Daedalus keeps the flying aspects of the case very quiet. It is too difficult to explain, even to the forensic pathologist, certainly too difficult to explain to the presiding coroner.

There is the usual collection of furniture for such a place – the silver metal-slab the length of a human body, the crushed ice that is slowly melting on a silver tray. If we are very quiet we can hear the ice melting, dribbling a slow trickle of water away into a hidden drain. The ice is to keep the body fresh. The slab is to cradle the body while we pump the sea-water from its lungs.

There are the usual rubber coats, the rubber gloves, the aluminium buckets, three of them clean and spotless, the fourth containing a yellow-

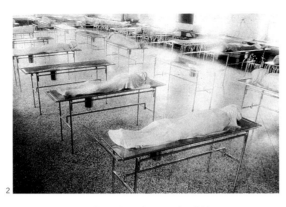

2

green, strong-smelling disinfectant, the fifth containing an ambiguous liquid – that could perhaps be … what? Diluted blood from the haemorrhaging head as it hit the water, or sea-water pumped from the stomach?

All other suggestive circumstantial evidence is provided by the light – light that reproduces the sea and the sky. At our feet and under them, the floor ripples and refracts with watery blue-green shadows, like a constant tide washing over the shallow rocky bottom of the sea. On the four walls and reaching high up above our heads, the pale-blue light of a sky is stippled, partially hidden at intervals by the shadows of clouds passing silently and blamelessly over the suggestion of sea at our feet.

DESPRÉS DE L'ACCIDENT, *post mortem*, hi ha d'haver una autòpsia. La investigació és secreta. Aquesta és la segona mort d'un nen amb qui Dèdal ha estat associat. I totes dues morts han estat relacionades amb la gravetat. Si Dèdal és un assassí de nens, aleshores la gravetat és el seu segell personal. La primera mort va ser la del seu nebot, llançat daltabaix de l'espadat de l'Acròpoli. Dèdal va dir que havia estat un accident, però tothom sabia que estava gelós del fill de la seva germana, que havia inventat la serra, el compàs i el torn de fer ceràmica.

Potser la sala d'autòpsies original d'Ícar era a l'illa d'Icària, a la mar Egea, on Dèdal va portar el cadàver rescatat del mar. El cos no podia haver estat gaire temps a l'aigua. No hi podia haver ni tumescència, ni inflor, ni mossegades de peixos, ni blaus causats pels cops contra les roques. El cos devia haver estat col·locat sobre una superfície metàl·lica, i devien haver ruixat la carn amb aigua freda per netejar-lo de l'última cera que s'havia fos i havia

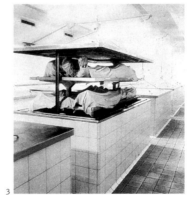

3

degotat, i després s'havia tornat a endurir en congelar-se amb el contacte fred de l'aigua del mar.

La sala d'autòpsies té una entrada limitada. No és qüestió que tothom vagi passant per aquí badoquejant, xafardejant, comportant-se com voltors davant la víctima d'allò que Dèdal insisteix a dir que va ser un accident domèstic. Hi ha molts nens que s'ofeguen. És prou sabuda la seva exuberància a l'aigua, la seva tendència a arriscar-se, a lluir-se, a portar-se malament, a posar-se a prova. Dèdal manté un silenci estricte sobre els aspectes del cas relacionats amb el vol. És massa difícil d'explicar-ho, fins i tot al patòleg forense, i sens dubte a l'oficial de justícia.

Hi ha l'habitual col·lecció de mobles per a un lloc així: la superfície platejada de la mateixa longitud que un cos humà, el gel trinxat que es va fonent a poc a poc en una safata platejada. Si estem en un silenci absolut podem sentir com es va fonent el gel, gotejant lentament en un desguàs ocult. El gel és per mantenir fresc el cos de l'absent. La superfície metàl·lica és perquè hi descansi el cos mentre li extraiem l'aigua marina dels pulmons.

Hi ha les bates de goma habituals, els guants de goma habituals, les galledes d'alumini…, tres de les quals són netes i impecables, i la quarta conté un desinfectant d'un verd groguenc que fa una olor molt forta, la cinquena conté un líquid ambigu que potser podria ser… què? Sang diluïda de l'hemorràgia del cap produïda en xocar contra l'aigua o aigua de mar extreta de l'estómac?

Totes les altres proves circumstancials suggeridores, les proporciona inconscientment la llum, una llum que reprodueix el mar i el cel. Als nostres peus i a sota d'ells, el terra s'arrissa i refracta amb unes ombres d'un blau-verd aquós, com una marea constant que renta el fons rocallós i poc profund del mar. Les quatre parets, fins molt per sobre dels nostres caps, estan puntejades amb la llum blava i pàl·lida d'un cel parcialment ocult a intervals per les ombres dels núvols que passen silenciosament i sense culpa sobre el mar que s'insinua als nostres peus.

1. Goya, Los Caprichos: 64 Buen Viaje, 1799, aquatint
2. Hans Danuser, Mortuary, 1984, black-and-white photograph, New York, The New Museum of Contemporary Art
3. Hans Danuser, Mortuary, 1984, black-and-white photograph, New York, The New Museum of Contemporary Art

1. Francisco de Goya, Los caprichos, 64, Buen viaje, 1799, aiguafort, aiguatinta i burí
2. Hans Danuser, Dipòsit de cadàvers, 1984, fotografia en blanc i negre, Nova York, The New Museum of Contemporary Art
3. Hans Danuser, Dipòsit de cadàvers, 1984, fotografia en blanc i negre, Nova York, The New Museum of Contemporary Art

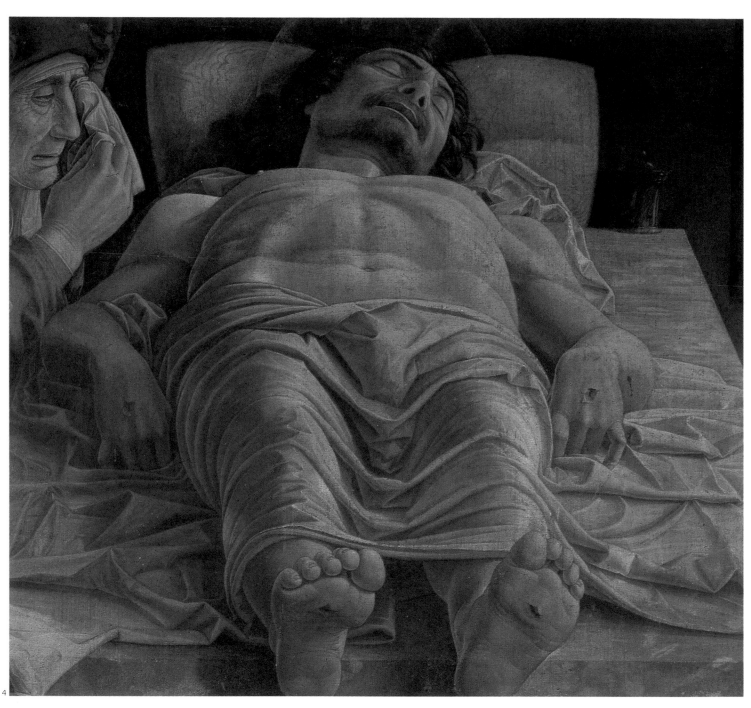

4

4. Mantegna, Body of
Christ, ca. 1500, oil on
panel, Milan, Brera
5. Bastienne Schmidt,
Untitled (Bogota,
Colombia, 1991), 1991,
Inside the morgue during an
autopsy with medical
students, black-and-white
photograph, New York,
The New Museum of
Contemporary Art
6. Still from the film Death
in the Seine, 1989
7. Jeffrey Silverthorne,
Listen ... beating victim,
1972-74, black-and-white
photograph, New York, The
New Museum of

Contemporary Art
8. Jeffrey Silverthorne, Listen
... the woman who died in
her sleep, 1972-74, black-and-
white photograph, New York,
The New Museum of
Contemporary Art
9. Hans Danuser, Medizin 1,
1984, black-and-white
photograph, New York, The
New Museum of
Contemporary Art
10. Hans Danuser, Medizin
1, 1984, black-and-white
photograph, New York, The
New Museum of
Contemporary Art

4. Andrea Mantegna, Crist
mort, ca. 1500, oli sobre
taula, Milà, Pinacoteca di
Brera
5. Bastienne Schmidt, Sense
títol (Bogotà, Colòmbia,
1991), 1991, "Al dipòsit de
cadàvers, durant una autòpsia
amb estudiants de medicina",
fotografia en blanc i negre,
Nova York, The New Museum
of Contemporary Art
6. Fotograma de la pel·lícula
Death in the Seine, 1989
7. Jeffrey Silverthorne,
Escolteu... víctima d'una
pallissa, 1972-74, fotografia
en blanc i negre, Nova York,
The New Museum of

Contemporary Art
8. Jeffrey Silverthorne,
Escolteu... la dona que va
morir mentre dormia, 1972-
74, fotografia en blanc i
negre, Nova York, The New
Museum of Contemporary
Art
9. Hans Danuser, Medicina 1,
1984, fotografia en blanc i
negre, Nova York, The New
Museum of Contemporary
Art
10. Hans Danuser, Medicina
1, 1984, fotografia en blanc i
negre, Nova York, The New
Museum of Contemporary
Art

5

6

7

8

9

10

DEATH BY FLYING
No doctor simply puts "death" as the cause of death on a death certificate. To a doctor it would seem there is no such thing as simply "death". What could Icarus have died of? Sunstroke from being too near the sun? Heart failure from excessive fright? Flesh burns from re-entering the earth's atmosphere at high speed? Concussion from hitting the sea surface from a great height?

MORT A CAUSA DE L'INTENT DE VOLAR
No hi ha cap metge que, en estendre un certificat de defunció, es limiti a posar la paraula "mort" com a causa de la mort d'una persona. Per un metge, sembla que la simple "mort" a seques no existeix. Què podia haver causat la mort d'Ícar? Una insolació per acostar-se massa al sol? Una aturada cardíaca ocasionada per un excés de por? Les cremades provocades en tornar a entrar en contacte amb l'atmosfera terrestre a alta velocitat? L'impacte contra la superfície de l'aigua, en caure al mar des d'una gran alçada?

DEATH BY DROWNING
Death by Drowning would be the simplest explanation, yet such a verdict takes no acknowledgement whatsoever of his achievement of flying. Anyway would it be true? Daedalus could have been at the sea-surface within seconds to rescue his son. The most suitable verdict is shame and disappointment, but these symptoms do not show up on a mortuary table. The most hospitable verdict would have to be Death by Falling. Everyone can feel sympathetic to such a decision. Without exception, we are all subject to gravity.

MORT PER OFEGAMENT
"Mort per ofegament" seria l'explicació més senzilla, però un veredicte com aquest no tindria en compte en absolut la proesa d'haver aconseguit volar. I, a més, fins a quin punt podria ser cert? Dèdal hauria pogut acudir a la superfície del mar en qüestió de segons per rescatar el seu fill. El veredicte més adequat és "vergonya i decepció", però aquests símptomes no es manifesten en una autòpsia. El veredicte més favorable hauria de ser "mort a causa d'una caiguda". Tothom pot mostrar-se comprensiu davant d'una decisió com aquesta. Sense excepció, tots estem subjectes a la força de la gravetat.

It took millions of years to turn a small dinosaur into a swallow, an albatross, a starling, a vulture, a hummingbird.

Van caldre milions d'anys per convertir un petit dinosaure en una oreneta, en un albatros, en un estornell, en un voltor, en un colibrí.

BIRD BONES. HERE stands a bird ossuary. One hundred birds perhaps are represented here, their skeletons bleached by brine and the sun, turned up on beaches, washed in from the sea, excavated from ploughed fields. When birds die, how many of them fall suddenly from the sky? This is a bird graveyard, evidence of that which once flew confidently, now is laid low, brought to earth.

Archaeopteryx. This is the cast of a primitive bird or, to put it more accurately, it is a recording in limestone of an animal that was half-reptile and half-bird. The reptiles did not fade away, they metamorphosed into birds. You can easily see, in the mind's eye, the scales and the small eyes, the clawed feet, the sharp-edged beak. But of course this change happened very very slowly indeed. It took millions of years to turn a small dinosaur into a swallow, an albatross, a starling, a vulture, a hummingbird. Is Icarus the pathetic attempt of man to repeat such a metamorphosis? How could man hope to complete such a wondrous change in one Greek afternoon?

OSSOS D'OCELLS. Això és una ossera d'ocells. Potser hi ha representats cent ocells, amb els esquelets blanquejats per la salmorra i pel sol, apareguts en platges, arrossegats des del mar fins a la costa, desenterrats de camps llaurats. Quan els ocells es moren, quants n'hi ha que cauen sobtadament del cel? Això és un cementiri d'ocells, la prova que aquell qui una vegada va volar confiat, ara ha tornat a la terra, on jeu sense vida.

L'arqueòpterix. Això és el motllo d'un ocell primitiu; o, per dir-ho més exactament, l'empremta en pedra calcària d'un animal que era mig rèptil i mig ocell. Els rèptils no van desaparèixer, sinó que es van metamorfosar en ocells. Podem veure fàcilment, amb l'ull de la ment, les escames i els petits ulls, les urpes de les potes, el bec esmolat. Però, naturalment, aquest canvi va ser lentíssim. Van caldre milions d'anys per convertir un petit dinosaure en una oreneta, en un albatros, en un estornell, en un voltor, en un colibrí. És Ícar l'intent patètic de l'home de repetir una metamorfosi d'aquest tipus? Com esperava l'home poder consumar un canvi tan prodigiós a Grècia, en una sola tarda?

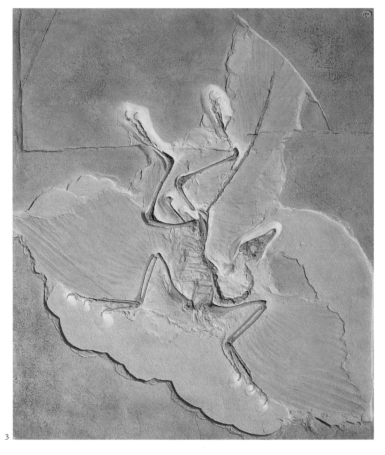

3

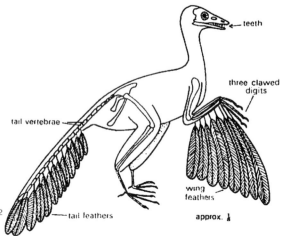

teeth

three clawed digits

tail vertebrae

wing feathers

tail feathers

approx. ⅓

2

1. This is an instruction package on the business of learning to fly complete with examples, directives, suggestions, nourishment and one or two in-flight jokes
2. Reconstruction of archaeopteryx
3. Fossil archaeopteryx
1. Això és un paquet d'instruccions per aprendre a volar. Inclou exemples, orientacions, suggeriments, pautes d'alimentació i un parell de bromes sobre vols
2. Reconstrucció d'un arqueòpterix
3. Fòssil d'arqueòpterix

27
The urine spill
El raig d'orina

THERE IS AN ISOLATED vitrine that presents us with something different, for inside, contained within the four glass walls, is a spiralling stream of urine, flipping and whipping, as the Icarine body, far overhead, falls forever without landing, wetting itself in endless incontinent and humiliating fright and panic.

This is a present-tense disaster-symptom perpetually signalling fear, as Rembrandt depicted with the infant Ganymede.

This is a thrashing snake of urine, wetting the glass in its random writhing, abusing us, the audience, for if it were not for the protective glass, we should indeed be unable to escape the spiralling lashings of the liquid, rich in the staining ammonia of fright.

HI HA UNA VITRINA aïllada que ens presenta una cosa diferent: en el seu interior, entre les quatre parets de vidre, hi ha un raig espiral d'orina que surt disparat, descontrolat, mentre el cos d'Ícar, molt per sobre dels nostres caps, cau per sempre sense aterrar, orinant-se a causa d'un temor i d'un pànic interminables, incontinents i humiliants.

És un símptoma de l'accident en temps present, que assenyala perpètuament la por, tal com ho va il·lustrar Rembrandt en l'infant Ganimedes.

Es tracta d'una serp d'orina fuetejant, que mulla el vidre en el seu retorçament atzarós i ens agredeix a nosaltres, el públic, perquè, si no fos pel vidre protector, sens dubte no podríem esquivar els flagells espirals del líquid, ple de l'amoníac maculant de la por.

HERE IS THE LAST LEG of Icarus. Set back from the death-splashes, away from the damp and wet, set on a pedestal and illuminated by a warm light, is a leg. A male limb from thigh to toe made in bronze. It is elegant and sensuous.

Preserved in green, sea-splashed, patinated bronze, it is the last-seen image of the young man disappearing into the salt water of the Aegean. It is the split-second, last photographic evidence of Icarus reworked in metal. Bruegel's last glimpse of an incipient hero. Our last glimpse of the first mortal hero who flew over water.

AQUÍ HI HA L'ÚLTIMA CAMA d'Ícar. Rescatada del xoc mortal contra l'aigua, lliure de la humitat i la mullena, sobre un pedestal i il·luminada per una llum càlida, hi ha una cama. Una extremitat masculina de bronze, des de la cuixa fins als dits dels peus. És elegant i sensual. És la cama d'Ícar.

Conservada en bronze amb una pàtina verdosa i erosionada pel mar, és l'última imatge que es veu del jove mentre desapareix entre l'aigua salada de la mar Egea. És l'última instantània fotogràfica d'Ícar reconstruïda en metall. L'última visió bruegeliana d'un heroi incipient. La nostra última visió del primer heroi mortal que va volar sobre l'aigua.

1. *Cornelius van Haarlem,* The Fall of Ixion, *1588, oil on canvas, Rotterdam, Boymans van Beuningen*
2. *Giulio Romano,* The Fall of Icarus, *ink and wash on paper, Paris, Musée du Louvre*
3. *Ballooning attacked*
4. *Cornelius van Haarlem,* The Four Disgraced: Tantalus, Icarus, Phaeton, Ixion, *1588, engraved by Goltzius, Rotterdam, Boymans van Beuningen*

1. *Cornelis van Haarlem,* La caiguda d'Ixió, *1588, oli sobre tela, Rotterdam, Museum Boymans van Beuningen*
2. *Giulio Romano,* La caiguda d'Ícar, *tinta i aiguada sobre paper, París, Musée du Louvre*
3. *Atac contra un globus*
4. *Cornelis van Haarlem,* Els quatre infortunats: Tàntal, Ícar, Faetont, Ixió, *1588, gravats per Goltzius, Rotterdam, Museum Boymans van Beuningen*

4

30
The welcoming frame
El marc de benvinguda

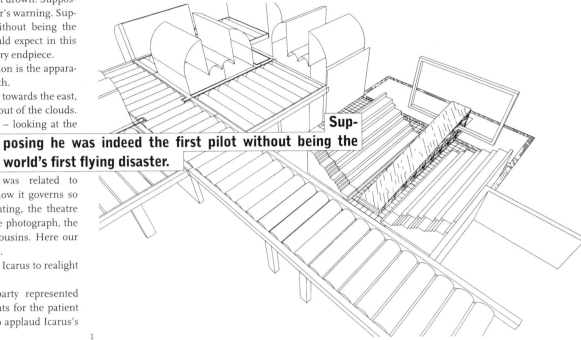

Supposing Icarus did not fall and did not drown. Supposing he did have the sense to obey his father's warning. Supposing he was indeed the first pilot without being the world's first flying disaster. Then we could expect in this exhibition an optimistic finale, a celebratory endpiece.

Out in the garden court of this exhibition is the apparatus for a triumphal return of Icarus to earth.

First there is a frame of the sky looking towards the east, towards Greece, to site his landing from out of the clouds. We may sit and wait for Icarus's return – looking at the rectangle of sky across the city. Rectangular frames in nature are very rare. The frame is an artificial device, developed in the Renaissance when it was related to the circumstances of architecture, and now it governs so many of the constructions of art – painting, the theatre with its rectangular proscenium arch, the photograph, the cinema and now television and all its cousins. Here our frame is used to sight the return of a hero.

Second, there is a landing platform for Icarus to realight on the earth after so long in the air.

And third, there is a welcoming party represented by one hundred seats, row on row of seats for the patient exhibition-visitor to sit and then finally to applaud Icarus's triumphant return.

Sup-posing he was indeed the first pilot without being the world's first flying disaster.

1

1 and 2. Computer simulation of Installation 30 – The Welcoming Frame – for the Courtyard of the Joan Miró Foundation, Barcelona
3. Icarus returns, an audience, dazzled by the bright light of the returning prodigal Icarus, are delighted to welcome him back to earth. (Audience watching a 3-D movie)
1 i 2. Simulació feta amb ordinador de la instal·lació 30, El marc de benvinguda, per al pati de la Fundació Joan Miró, Barcelona
3. Ícar torna. El públic, enlluernat per la llum intensa del retorn del pròdig Ícar, està encantat de poder donar-li la benvinguda a la terra. (Públic presenciant una pel·lícula en tres dimensions)

Suposem que Ícar no hagués caigut ni s'hagués ofegat. Suposem que hagués tingut el bon seny d'obeir l'advertiment del seu pare, i que hagués estat certament el primer pilot però no el primer accident aeri de la història de la humanitat. Aleshores podríem esperar que aquesta exposició tingués un final optimista, que acabés amb una rúbrica benèvola.

A fora, al jardí d'aquesta exposició, hi ha el muntatge per a un retorn triomfal d'Ícar a la terra.

Primer hi ha un tros de cel emmarcat mirant cap a l'est, cap a Grècia, per situar el seu amaratge des dels núvols. Podem seure a esperar el retorn d'Ícar, mentre mirem el rectangle de cel per damunt la ciutat. En la natura són molt insòlits –o potser inexistents– els marcs rectangulars. El nostre marc és un giny prou familiar perquè des de lluny sembli una zona d'aterratge preparada per a un helicòpter, una zona que ofereix un port de benvinguda, com en el cas dels coloms que tornen a casa. El marc és un giny artificial, creat durant el Renaixement en relació amb les circumstàncies de l'arquitectura, i actualment governa un gran nombre de construccions artístiques: la pintura, el teatre amb el seu prosceni rectangular, la fotografia, el cinema i ara la televisió i tots els seus cosins. Aquí s'utilitza per presenciar el retorn d'un heroi.

En segon lloc, hi ha una plataforma d'aterratge perquè Ícar torni a posar els peus a terra després d'haver passat tant de temps a l'aire.

I, en tercer lloc, hi ha un comitè de benvinguda representat per cent seients, files i files de seients perquè el pacient visitant de l'exposició pugui seure i finalment aplaudir el retorn d'Ícar.

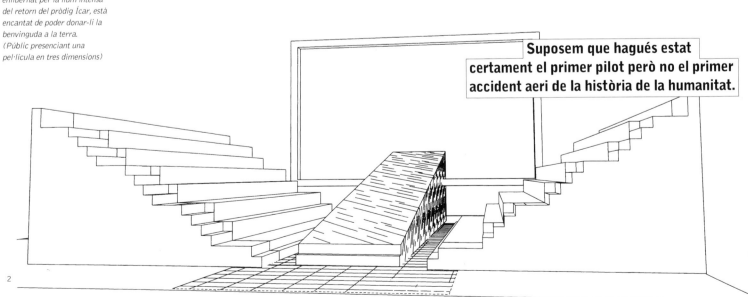

Suposem que hagués estat certament el primer pilot però no el primer accident aeri de la història de la humanitat.

2

in *The Draughtsman's Contract*, the first providing the structural mid point and the second the strategic ending of the film, and in their exact reprising, indicating exactly who was responsible for both murders. Intimations of these watery theatricals are often proclaimed in the water-stories told by the film's minor characters:

THE DRAUGHTSMAN'S CONTRACT

"Some years ago, two gentlemen went back to Amsterdam saying that Allhevinghay was just like home, there was so much water, so many ornamental **PONDS**, so many **CANALS**, so many **SINKS** and **BASINS**. There was even a wind-pump. What they had not realized was that my father had made his land into a pattern of reservoirs because he was terrified of fire. There was even a room under the front stairs that housed two hundred buckets, **all of them filled with water.** I know because whenever I was taken short, my brothers and I used to rush in there and use them. Those buckets were filled before my mother died. I expect them to be still there with the same water of thirty years ago, I shouldn't wonder, mixed with a little of myself of course. **I used to pee like a horse.** I still do."

10

In *The Draughtsman's Contract*, when plans for the draughtsman's downfall are being polished by the film's female protagonists, a new draughtsman is introduced, a Dutchman who has no doubt at all of what to do with the English landscape to cleanse and purify it (and the story) of all old associations.

11

THE DRAUGHTSMAN'S CONTRACT

MRS TALMAN: I was about to take Mr Van Hoyten to the river – he has plans to make a **dam** and **flood the lower fields**; MR NEVILLE: Flooded fields Madam? Do you plan to join your property to the **sea?**

The film *A Zed and Two Noughts* begins with a car crash caused by a low-flying swan smashing into a vehicle driven by a woman called Alba Bewick. From such a start, the swan's mythological, ornithological and literary associations – Leda, Jupiter, Castor and Pollux, twinship, a coward's white feathers, Swan and Swann's way – jump and dance throughout the story, sometimes lightly, sometimes portentously, hoping that such lucid hauntings meet up with associations way beyond the margins of the film.

The film *The Belly of an Architect* has been described as an essay in gravity. It tells of the ambitions of an architect to stage an architectural exhibition in Rome, and it is noticeably book-ended with incidents that revolve around an English banknote which in 1983 used to carry a portrait of Sir Isaac Newton. More than one commentator has suggested that Newton's celebrated discovery of gravity has legitimized the architect's profession. Stourley Kracklite, the American architect in question, toasts his Roman architectural friends who have made him a birthday cake in the shape of a building that celebrates Newton.

12

THE BELLY OF AN ARCHITECT

KRACKLITE: In England, architects are **respected.** Sir Christopher Wren appears on the English fifty-pound note. Architects are expensive. But **Sir Isaac Newton**, the subject of this cake, is in every Englishman's wallet – he's on the English pound-note. I always carry one on me for good luck. **A man who discovered gravity** and thus successfully secured our feet on the ground is a good companion. In fixing us to the earth he enabled us with equanimity to permit our heads to remain in the clouds.

A l'estiu li demanaven que es posés dreta sobre les clapes de la gespa del jardí."

Hi ha un estudi fílmic titulat *Shower* ('Dutxa'), una deliberació sobre el llibre extraordinàriament desinhibit d'Alexander Kira sobre l'ergonomia de la cambra de bany, que demostra, ben explícitament i amb una salacitat considerable, l'ordre exacte i l'equipament amb què la gent excreta i mictura, es dutxa, es renta, es banya i es renta les dents. Hi ha una pel·lícula titulada simplement *Water* ('Aigua'), que conté exactament mil imatges d'aigua, i es va rodar en els paisatges deliciosos dels Brecon Beacons de Gal·les –una lànguida i agradable experiència– per apreciar la complaença absolutament exuberant del sol sobre l'aigua.

La filmografia pública inclou *Water-Wrackets*, una irònica història antropològica d'animals mítics que colonitzen violentament una conca aquàtica autèntica de Wiltshire; *26 Bathrooms* ('26 cambres de bany'), una espècie de diccionari, aparentment arquitectònic, de les excentricitats dels anglesos a la cambra de bany, la segona habitació més petita d'una casa anglesa; *Death in the Seine* ('Mort al Sena'), una crònica de cadàvers rescatats del Sena just després de la Revolució Francesa, i *Making a Splash* ('Fer un capbussó'), un homenatge a la natació sincronitzada.

De manera accidental o deliberada, la preocupació per l'aigua continua amb un projecte actual commemoratiu del pont Erasmus de Rotterdam, recentment inaugurat, que curiosament uneix cel i aigua i constitueix un complement molt apropiat a aquesta exposició de Barcelona sobre Ícar, la inauguració de la qual coincidirà aproximadament amb l'estrena de la pel·lícula a Holanda.

Els llargmetratges narratius continuaven explotant les delícies i perills literals de l'aigua com a subjecte dramàtic, com a subtext metafòric i per la pura bellesa fotogènica que demostra de manera tan fàcil, eficaç i fiable.

Dos cossos ofegats són trets del fossat d'una mansió aristocràtica a *El contracte del dibuixant*: el primer proporciona el punt mig de l'estructura i el segon el final estratègic de la pel·lícula, i, en la seva *reprise* exacta, indiquen exactament qui era el responsable dels dos assassinats. Hi ha al·lusions a aquests efectes teatrals aquàtics proclamats sovint en les històries d'aigua explicades pels personatges secundaris de la pel·lícula.

"Fa uns quants anys dos senyors van tornar a Amsterdam dient que Allhevinghay era ben bé com el seu país, de tanta aigua, tants estanys ornamentals, tants canals, tantes aigüeres i tantes ribelles que hi havia. Hi havia fins i tot una bomba eòlica. Del que no s'havien adonat és que el meu pare havia omplert les seves terres de dipòsits d'aigua perquè el foc li produïa terror. Hi havia fins i tot una habitació sota les escales de davant que contenia dues-centes galledes, totes plenes d'aigua. Ho sé perquè, sempre que teníem una necessitat urgent, els meus germans i jo entràvem corrents allà dins i les fèiem servir. Aquelles galledes van ser omplertes abans de morir la meva mare. Suposo que encara hi són, amb la mateixa aigua de fa trenta anys –no m'estranyaria–, barrejades amb una mica de mi mateix, naturalment. Jo solia pixar com un cavall, i encara ho faig."

A *El contracte del dibuixant*, quan les protagonistes femenines de la pel·lícula acaben d'ultimar els plans per a la perdició del dibuixant, se'n presenta un altre, un dibuixant holandès que no té cap mena de dubte

Stourley Kracklite meets death by gravity. A heavy man, clutching his Newton currency, he makes a voluntary wingless fall from the top of the Victor Emmanuel building in Rome. Perhaps he, in turn, is fleshing out another story told in *The Draughtsman's Contract* – a variation of a tale often told of architects and their jealous clients, not least in the manufacture of the Taj Mahal, though here appropriately the story has watery connotations:

THE DRAUGHTSMAN'S CONTRACT

"It is said that the duc de Courcy invited his **water mechanic** to the top of an elaborate cascade he had built and asked him if he could build such a marvel for anyone else. The man, after offering various thanks and pleasantries, finally admitted that with sufficient patronage, he could. The duc de Courcy pushed him gently in the small of the back and **the wretched man fell to a WATERY death.**"

Kracklite's personal hero is Etienne-Louis Boullée, the heavy-builder, master of mass and gravity-conscious architecture, the admirer of Newton. And Kracklite's Road to Damascus conversion – a conversion that most painters saw as a fall from a horse – is a swift awareness of his own mortality, experienced, whilst he is bathing, naked and vulnerable, under a painted ceiling that features Phaethon. Phaethon dies by gravity. A symbol of hubris, he is hurled from Apollo's chariot for daring to think he can drive it across the dawn sky. Kracklite is frequently framed against a backdrop of fountains. He becomes drunkenly insane in a fountain basin, wildly splashing his pursuers, and he mockingly sustains thoughts of suicide in a domestic bath.

10. *Still from* The Draughtsman's Contract
11. *Still from* The Draughtsman's Contract
12. *Still from* The Belly of an Architect
13. *Still from* The Belly of an Architect
10. *Fotograma d'*El contracte del dibuixant
11. *Fotograma d'*El contracte del dibuixant
12. *Fotograma d'*El ventre d'un arquitecte
13. *Fotograma d'*El ventre d'un arquitecte

13

sobre què s'ha de fer per purificar i netejar aquell paisatge anglès (i els fets que s'hi desenvolupen) de tota antiga associació. (Senyora Talman: Estava a punt de dur el senyor Van Hoyten al riu; té planejat de construir una presa i inundar els camps inferiors; Senyor Neville: Camps inundats, senyora? Té intenció d'unir les seves propietats amb el mar?)

La pel·lícula *A Zed and Two Noughts* ('Una zeta i dos zeros') comença amb un accident automobilístic provocat per un cigne que vola baix i xoca contra un vehicle conduït per una dona que es diu Alba Bewick. Amb un començament així, les associacions mitològiques, ornitològiques i literàries del cigne –Leda, Júpiter, Càstor i Pòl·lux, el bessonatge, les plomes blanques d'un covard, el Cigne i el camí de Swann– salten i ballen al llarg de tota la història, de vegades amb lleugeresa, de vegades feixugament, esperant que unes obsessions tan lúcides puguin coincidir amb unes associacions que van molt més enllà dels límits de la pel·lícula.

La pel·lícula *El ventre d'un arquitecte* ha estat descrita com un assaig sobre la gravetat. Parla de les ambicions d'un arquitecte que vol muntar una exposició arquitectònica a Roma, i comença i acaba amb incidents que giren a l'entorn d'un bitllet de banc anglès del 1983, on figurava un retrat de Sir Isaac Newton. Més d'un comentarista ha suggerit que el cèlebre descobriment de la gravetat per part de Newton ha legitimat l'ofici d'arquitecte. Stourley Kracklite, l'arquitecte nord-americà en qüestió, brinda a la salut dels seus amics arquitectes romans que li han fet un pastís d'aniversari en forma d'un edifici en honor de Newton.

Kracklite: A Anglaterra, els arquitectes són molt respectats. Sir Christopher Wren apareix en els bitllets de cinquanta lliures. Els arquitectes són cars. Però Sir Isaac Newton, el tema d'aquest pastís, és a dins de la cartera de tots els anglesos: apareix en els bitllets d'una lliura. Jo sempre en duc un, perquè em porti sort. Un home que va descobrir la gravetat i d'aquesta manera va aconseguir afermar els nostres peus a terra és un bon company. En aferrar-nos a la terra, va permetre, amb equanimitat, que els nostres caps es mantinguessin als núvols.

Stourley Kracklite mor a causa de la gravetat. Home corpulent, aferrat al seu bitllet amb l'efígie de Newton, es llança voluntàriament, sense ales, des de dalt de l'edifici de Víctor Manuel, a Roma. Potser ell, al seu torn, enriqueix una altra història explicada a *El contracte del dibuixant*; una variant d'una història que s'explica sovint, sobre arquitectes i els seus gelosos mecenes –n'és un bon exemple la construcció del Taj Mahal–, si bé aquí, apropiadament, la història té connotacions aquàtiques:

Diuen que el duc de Courcy va convidar el seu mecànic hidràulic a pujar al capdamunt d'una elaborada cascada que havia construït, i li va preguntar si podria construir una meravella semblant per a qualsevol altra persona. L'home, després d'obsequiar-lo amb diversos regraciaments i compliments, va acabar reconeixent que, amb el mecenatge suficient, podria fer-ho. El duc de Courcy el va empènyer suaument per la regió lumbar i el pobre desgraciat va caure a l'aigua i es va ofegar.

L'heroi personal de Kracklite és Etienne-Louis Boullée, el "constructor robust", un arquitecte especialment conscient de la relació entre la massa

14

LOUISA: All right Kracklite – what are you doing?
KRACKLITE: Drowning.

Kracklite continues to splash about. When Louisa doesn't react any further, he stops splashing, and looks over the side of the bath at her. His hair is plastered to his forehead and water streams down his face.

KRACKLITE: [talking to himself but making sure that Louisa can hear] It's no good. Your body just won't let you do it. Nobody ever died by voluntarily ceasing to breathe. If you managed to stop breathing, you'd fall unconscious – and start breathing again …;

LOUISA: You could try slashing your wrists.

Considering her husband's hot-bath position, it is his wife who unsuspectingly gets the tradition of Roman suicide correct.

The title of the film *Drowning by Numbers* advertises its own water obsessions down to the fascinations of the games within it – like Sheep and Tides.

Sheep are especially sensitive to the exact moment of the **turn of the tide.** In this game, nine tethered sheep react, **pull** on the stakes, **jolt** the chairs and **rattle** the teacups. Bets are taken on the combined sensitivity of any line of sheep read vertically, horizontally or diagonally. Since there are normally three tide-turns every twenty-four hours, it is usual practice to take the best of three results. Reliable **clocks, calendars and time-tables** are used to determine the accuracy of the sheep's forecast.

These may explain the niceties of a young boy over-excited by games, but the water associations are not idle when he plays them against a background of bath-tubs, swimming-pools and the North Sea, places of painful drowning which the film's characters try to pretend are accidents but the audience knows full well are murders. Murder by water is perhaps the easiest murder to conceal.

In the film *The Cook, the Thief, his Wife and her Lover*, there are two sequences of hosing-down by water, arranged to complement one another; the first to cleanse away excrement and the humility of vulgar torture, the second to cleanse away putrefaction and the violence of a cuckolded husband. Both are dramatically powerful in their pathos. Both certainly emphasize literal and metaphorical cleansing. And both, back-lit and compositionally arranged to reprise one another, are exceedingly beautiful.

In the film *Prospero's Books*, the first volume of magic was *The Book of Water*.

This is a waterproof-covered book which has lost its colour by much contact with water. It is full of investigative drawings and exploratory texts written on many different thicknesses of paper. There are drawings of every conceivable watery association – **seas, tempests, rain, snow, clouds, lakes, waterfalls, streams, canals, water-mills, shipwrecks, floods and tears.** As the pages are turned, the watery elements are often animated. There are rippling waves and slanting storms. Rivers and cataracts flow and bubble. Plans of hydraulic machinery and maps of weather-forecasting flicker with **arrows, symbols and agitated diagrams.** The drawings are all made by one hand. Perhaps this is a lost collection of drawings by Da Vinci, bound into a book by the king of France at Amboise, and bought by the Milanese dukes to give to Prospero as a wedding present.

i la gravetat i admirador de Newton. I la conversió de Kracklite pel camí de Damasc (una conversió que la majoria de pintors veien com una caiguda d'un cavall) és una ràpida presa de consciència de la seva pròpia mortalitat, experimentada, mentre es banya, nu i vulnerable, sota un sostre pintat que representa Faetont. Faetont mor víctima de la gravetat. Com a símbol de la presumpció, és llançat daltabaix del carro d'Apol·lo perquè ha gosat pensar que podia conduir-lo a través del cel de l'alba.

Louisa: Està bé, Kracklite. Què fas?
Kracklite: M'ofego.

Kracklite continua capbussant-se. Quan Louisa deixa de reaccionar, ell s'atura i se la queda mirant des de la banyera. Té els cabells enganxats al front i li regalima aigua per la cara.

Kracklite:(parlant amb ell mateix, però procurant que Louisa ho senti) No t'hi escarrassis: el teu cos no et permetrà de fer-ho. No s'ha mort mai ningú per deixar de respirar voluntàriament. Si aconseguissis deixar de respirar, et quedaries inconscient... i tornaries a respirar...
Louisa: Podries provar de tallar-te les venes.

Tenint en compte la posició del seu marit, en una banyera d'aigua calenta, és la seva dona qui, sense sospitar-ho, interpreta correctament la tradició del suïcidi a la romana.

El títol de la pel·lícula *Drowning by Numbers* anuncia les seves pròpies obsessions per l'aigua i la fascinació pels jocs aquàtics, com ara el joc dels bens i les marees.

Els bens són especialment sensibles al moment exacte del canvi de la marea. En aquest joc, nou bens lligats a unes estaques reaccionen, arrenquen les estaques, claven una estrebada a les cadires i fan trontollar les tasses de te. Es fan apostes sobre la sensibilitat combinada de qualsevol filera de bens llegida verticalment, horitzontalment o en diagonal. Com que hi ha normalment tres canvis de marea cada vint-i-quatre hores, la pràctica habitual és agafar el millor dels tres resultats. S'utilitzen rellotges, calendaris i horaris fiables per determinar l'exactitud de la previsió del be.

Això pot explicar les subtileses d'un nen sobreexcitat pels jocs, però les associacions aquàtiques no són arbitràries quan juga contra un fons de banyeres, piscines i el mar del Nord, llocs d'ofegaments dolorosos que els personatges de la pel·lícula volen fer veure que són accidents però el públic sap perfectament que es tracta d'assassinats. L'assassinat amb aigua és potser el més fàcil d'ocultar.

A la pel·lícula *The Cook, the Thief, his Wife and her Lover,* hi ha dues seqüències d'irrigació amb mànegues, arranjades de tal manera que es complementen entre elles; la primera serveix per netejar els excrements i la humitat de la tortura vulgar, la segona per netejar la putrefacció i la violència d'un marit enganyat. Totes dues posseeixen un patetisme d'una gran força dramàtica. Totes dues, sens dubte, emfasitzen la neteja literal i metafòrica. I totes dues, il·luminades per darrere i arranjades composicionalment per *reprise* mútua, són extremament belles.

A la pel·lícula *Prospero's Books* ('Els llibres de Prospero'), el primer volum de màgia era el *Llibre de l'Aigua.*

Es tracta d'un llibre de tapes impermeables que s'ha descolorit pel contacte excessiu amb l'aigua. És ple de dibuixos experimentals i de textos exploratoris

Prospero's stage-island, located somewhere, according to both Prospero and Shakespeare, in the Bermudas, was milked for every possible watery reference, and appropriately the stage-sets were constructed around an excavated dry-dock inside an Amsterdam shipyard-hangar once used to build oil-tankers.

The film *The Pillow-Book* concerns itself with books, text, writing, and a consideration of the human body seen as a book. Yet the inks of writing are soluble, applied with a brush on washed skin, and conjuring the notion of the writing on water, the texts are washed, wiped, bathed, cleansed away by rain, steam, tears and the comforting warm water of the bath.

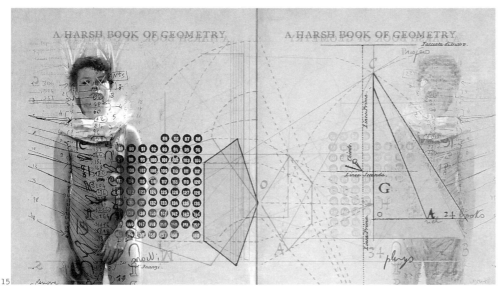

WATER AND SKY OFF THE SCREEN

The fascination with water as a pictorial excitement, as a metaphor and as an instrument of narrative has persisted outside its depiction on the screen. Various disenchantments with the nature of cinema plus a desire to associate cinematic language with the business of exhibitions and live performance have created various long-term projects.

The first, a cycle of operas called collectively *The Death of Webern and Others*, concerns a **conspiracy** against composers that seeks to make a connection between **the death of Anton Webern** and the **death of John Lennon** via the deaths of eight other composers in between. It is a series that hopes to place a mix of film and opera language together on stage. The first of these ten operas – number six in the series – called *Rosa*, with music by Louis Andriessen, was staged in the Amsterdam Opera House in 1994. The seventh opera, still to be realized with music, concerns Corntopia Felixchange, a Californian soprano **murdered in a San Francisco swimming-pool**.

In 1980 an opera project was conceived, to be called *The Massacre at the Baths*, in which ten anti-establishment theatrical companies in Santiago are rounded up at the time of the Pinochet coup in 1973 and dumped in an empty Olympic-style swimming-pool. Before the pool fills up and all participants drown, the actors and singers fortify themselves and taunt their jailers by enacting three heroic water-stories of self-sacrifice – Hero and Leander, Ophelia, and the Death of Virginia Woolf, with the help of a chorus of Synchronized Swimmers and a master of ceremonies called Marat.

14. *Still from* The Belly of an Architect
15. *Still from* Prospero's Books
14. *Fotograma d'*El ventre d'un arquitecte
15. *Fotograma d'*Els llibres de Prospero

escrits sobre paper de diversos gruixos. Hi ha dibuixos de totes les associacions aquàtiques concebibles: mars, tempestes, pluja, neu, núvols, llacs, cascades, rierols, canals, molins d'aigua, naufragis, inundacions i llàgrimes. A mesura que anem passant les pàgines, els elements aquosos sovint són animats. Hi ha ones arrissades i tempestes esbiaixades. Rius i cascades flueixen i bombollegen. Plànols de maquinària hidràulica i mapes meteorològics centellegen amb fletxes, símbols i diagrames agitats. Tots els dibuixos són fets de la mateixa mà. Potser es tracta d'una col·lecció perduda de dibuixos de Da Vinci relligada en un llibre pel rei de França a Amboise i comprada pels ducs milanesos per oferir-la a Prospero com a regal de noces.

L'illa teatral de Prospero, situada, tant segons Prospero com segons Shakespeare, en algun lloc de les Bermudes, va ser explotada per extreure'n totes les possibles referències a l'aigua, i, apropiadament, els escenaris es van construir al voltant d'un dic sec excavat dins un hangar d'una drassana d'Amsterdam que havia estat utilitzat per construir petroliers.

La pel·lícula *The Pillow book* ('El llibre de capçalera') tracta de llibres, de textos, d'escriptura, i és una consideració del cos humà vist com un llibre, i del llibre vist com un cos. Però les tintes del text són solubles, aplicades amb un pinzell sobre pell rentada, i evoquen la idea de l'escriptura sobre aigua; els textos són rentats, netejats, banyats, esborrats per la pluja, pel vapor, per les llàgrimes i per la recomfortant aigua tèbia de la banyera.

Aigua i cel fora de la pantalla

La fascinació per l'aigua és un estímul pictòric, com a metàfora i com a instrument narratiu, i ha persistit fora de la seva representació a la pantalla.

Diversos desenganys sobre la naturalesa del cinema, juntament amb un desig d'associar el llenguatge cinematogràfic amb les exposicions i les actuacions en directe, han creat uns quants projectes a llarg termini. El primer, un cicle d'òperes amb el títol col·lectiu de *The Death of Webern and Others* ('La mort de Webern i d'altres'), tracta d'una conspiració contra els compositors que pretén relacionar la mort d'Anton von Webern amb la de John Lennon, a través de la mort de vuit compositors més que ha tingut lloc entremig. És una sèrie que es proposa situar sobre un escenari una mescla de cinema i òpera. La primera d'aquestes deu òperes –la número sis de la sèrie–, titulada *Rosa*, amb música de Louis Andriessen, va ser representada a l'Òpera d'Amsterdam el 1994. La setena, a la qual encara s'ha de posar música, tracta de Corntopia Felixchange, una soprano californiana assassinada en una piscina de San Francisco.

El 1980 va ser escrit un projecte d'òpera titulat *The Massacre at the Baths* ('La matança als banys'), en què els membres de deu companyies teatrals anti-establishment de Santiago de Xile són detinguts durant el cop d'estat de Pinochet del 1973 i amuntegats en una piscina olímpica buida. Abans d'omplir-se la piscina i d'ofegar-se tots, els actors i cantants es confabulen i es burlen dels seus escarcellers representant tres històries heroiques d'aigua i d'autosacrifici: Hero i Leandre, Ofèlia i la Mort de Virginia Woolf, amb l'ajuda d'un cor de Nedadors Sincronitzats i d'un mestre de cerimònies que es diu Marat.

Hi ha hagut diverses exposicions que han intentat

There have been several curatorial exhibitions that have tried to combine standard curatorial practices with cinematic and theatrical languages.

The first, *The Physical Self* – in Rotterdam – considered the human body and its representation through five hundred years of painting, sculpture and design within the Boymans-Van Beuningen Museum. Here I saw for the first time prints of the Van Haarlem-Goltzius falling figures of Icarus, Ixion, Phaethon and Tantalus: Icarus who attempts and fails to fly, Ixion flung to earth for

his attempted rape on Juno, Phaethon thrust from the sky for stealing Apollo's chariot, and Tantalus thrown down into Hell for stealing ambrosia, the food of the gods.

The second was an exhibition of old and

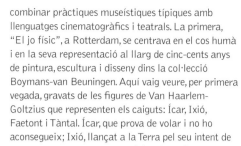

new master drawings in the Louvre, called *Flying out of this World*, that dealt with the impossible wish to fly. The third exhibition, in Vienna, *100 Objects to Represent the World*, drew up a shopping list of one hundred objects that would satisfy a stock-taking exercise of what remained to us as significant at the end of the second millennium. Included in the shopping list were a cloud, water, snow, one hundred umbrellas, a rainbow, wind, a crashed aircraft, a bath, ice, archaeopteryx, a rowing-boat, feathers, the domestic fly and the sun.

100 Allegories to Represent the World is a book of allegories manufactured in Strasbourg on new image-technology as computer-created collages – to find a state-of-the-art contemporary equivalent for the illuminated manuscripts of *Les Très Riches Heures* when the latest technology was the commital of gold leaf, cochineal and lapis lazuli to calfskin. The Strasbourg allegories complement and expand on the fascination with familiar characters from a universal flying and water encyclopaedia. Among the flyers are Icarus and Phaethon, and included as water-enthusiasts are the drowner and his victim, Ophelia, Marat, the survivors of the Raft of the Medusa, Hero and Leander, Noah and his wife, and Neptune and Charon.

The opera *Flying over water*, conceived as a project for the Strasbourg opera house but never realized, exists on paper for future consideration, possibly at Turin in 1998, and as material yet to be completed as a film-script to be shot hopefully at a major European airport. Its basic structure incorporates this present Description of an Imaginary Exhibition on the theme of The Icarus Adventure, seen as a reconstruction of the original classical mythology alongside a modern-day equivalent, substituting Germany for Crete, a modern aeronautics engineer for Daedalus, and a test-pilot for Icarus; and embracing old and new variations of Ariadne (as an air-stewardess), Pasiphaë, Theseus, Bacchus and the Minotaur.

16. Still from the exhibition 100 screens at the Marstal Theatre, Munich, 1995
17. Still from 100 Objects to Represent the World
18. Still from for the double figure of King Minos from the opera Flying over water. Design by Cathy Strub
16. Fotograma de l'exposició "100 pantalles" al teatre Marstal, Munic, 1955
17. Fotograma de "100 objectes per representar el món"
18. Fotograma de la doble figura del rei Minos de l'òpera Volar damunt l'aigua. Dibuix de Cathy Strub

combinar pràctiques museístiques típiques amb llenguatges cinematogràfics i teatrals. La primera, "El jo físic", a Rotterdam, se centrava en el cos humà i en la seva representació al llarg de cinc-cents anys de pintura, escultura i disseny dins la col·lecció Boymans-van Beuningen. Aquí vaig veure, per primera vegada, gravats de les figures de Van Haarlem-Goltzius que representen els caiguts: Ícar, Ixió, Faetont i Tàntal. Ícar, que prova de volar i no ho aconsegueix; Ixió, llançat a la Terra pel seu intent de violar Juno; Faetont llançat des del cel perquè ha robat el carro d'Apol·lo, i Tàntal llançat a l'Infern perquè ha robat l'ambrosia, l'aliment dels déus.

La segona era una exposició de dibuixos antics i nous del Louvre titulada "Volar fora d'aquest món", i tractava del desig impossible de volar. La tercera exposició, "100 objectes per a representar el món", celebrada a Viena, presentava una irònica llista de la compra amb cent objectes que podrien constituir un inventari d'allò que quedaria de nosaltres com a significatiu del final del segon mil·leni. A la llista de la compra, entre altres coses, hi havia un núvol, aigua, neu, cent paraigües, un arc de Sant Martí, vent, un avió estavellat, una banyera, gel, un arqueòpterix, una barca de rems, plomes, la mosca domèstica i el sol.

100 Allegories to Represent the World ('100 al·legories per a representar el món') és un llibre d'al·legories confeccionat a Estrasburg sobre la nova tecnologia de la imatge com a *collages* creats amb ordinador, per trobar l'equivalent més actual dels manuscrits il·luminats de *Les Très Riches Heures*, quan la tecnologia més recent era l'aplicació de pa d'or, cotxinilla i lapislàtzuli sobre pell de vedell. Les al·legories d'Estrasburg complementen i amplien el tema de la fascinació pels personatges familiars d'una enciclopèdia universal sobre el vol i l'aigua. Entre els voladors hi ha Ícar i Faetont, i, entre els entusiastes de l'aigua, hi ha l'Ofegador i la seva víctima, Ofèlia, Marat, els supervivents del rai de la Medusa, Hero i Leandre, Noè i la seva dona, Neptú i Caront.

L'òpera *Flying over water* ('Volar damunt l'aigua'), concebuda per a l'òpera d'Estrasburg però que no s'ha arribat a representar, existeix sobre el paper com un projecte susceptible de ser reconsiderat, possiblement a Torí el 1998, i com a material que encara s'ha de completar com a guió d'una pel·lícula que s'intentaria rodar en un important aeroport europeu. La seva estructura bàsica incorpora la present "Descripció d'una exposició imaginària sobre el tema de l'aventura d'Ícar", vista com una reconstrucció de la mitologia clàssica original juntament amb un equivalent de l'època actual, substituint Creta per Alemanya, Dèdal per un modern enginyer aeronàutic i Ícar per un pilot de proves, i abastant variants antigues i modernes d'Ariadna (com a hostessa), Pasífae, Teseu, Bacus i el minotaure.

18

Volar sobre el agua

Prefacio

Peter Greenaway es un cineasta con formación pictórica. Siempre ha sido escéptico respecto a los límites restringidos del cine, y no puede decirse que sus películas muestren una obsesión por las características tradicionales de este arte –un arte que es el resultado de cien años basados en el argumento, en la narración de historias, en la necesidad de una implicación emocional entre el público y la pantalla, en unos personajes de perfil psicológico... un cine que, mayoritariamente, puede describirse como la ilustración de unos textos. Algunos comentaristas han dicho que sus películas son el anticine, y que Greenaway no es en absoluto un cineasta. Puede que él mismo suscriba esta opinión, porque le inquieta la incapacidad del cine actual para ofrecernos toda la riqueza de posibilidades, establecer todas las innumerables conexiones y engendrar todas las emociones potenciales del mundo de finales del siglo XX. Ausencia de tacto, de olor, de temperatura, corta duración, públicos pasivos y sedentarios, ausencia de un auténtico diálogo con el público, instrucciones técnicas sobrecargadas en una arquitectura artificiosa y efectista, limitada a un solo encuadre únicamente visible en una dirección, deseo excesivo de realismo, escenarios efímeros, actores adiestrados para fingir, ilusiones anodinas, una escasa comprensión de la pantalla como tal, sumisión a los intereses económicos de unos inversores omnipotentes, a las tiranías del fotograma, del actor y del texto, a la tiranía de la cámara (la más inquietante de todas)... la lista de desencantos es muy larga. Greenaway no está solo ni mucho menos en estos puntos de vista. Su estrategia actual, para investigar y corregir lo que él ve como defectos, consiste en dedicar mucho tiempo a actividades extracinematográficas, aunque sólo sea con la esperanza de incorporar estas actividades al cine y encontrar nuevas formas de reinventarlo, porque la reinvención del cine es sin duda una tarea pendiente desde hace mucho tiempo, y enormemente necesaria. Un medio que no se reinvente constantemente está condenado a morir. Muchos dicen que el cine actual ya no tiene grandes inventores, porque han emigrado a otros campos, y quizás tengan razón.

Greenaway podría decir que todo producto cinematográfico es una forma de exhibición, que nos exhibe cosas, objetos, imágenes, hechos, ideas. Pero podría argüir que no nos muestra suficientes cosas, o que no nos las muestra durante el tiempo suficiente, o en suficiente profundidad, o desde puntos de vista lo bastante contrapuestos, o que no nos da, como público, la oportunidad de decidir o de agotar nuestro placer o nuestro interés por un hecho, un objeto o una idea durante todo el tiempo que tanto nosotros como él desearíamos.

Peter Greenaway ha utilizado la exposición como un recurso cinematográfico. Tanto *A Walk Through H* ('Un paseo por H') como *The Belly of an Architect* ('El vientre de un arquitecto') se centran en el tema de una exposición: en el primer caso, se tracta de una sala de exposiciones donde los mapas pintados constituyen la sustancia del filme; en el segundo, de la historia de un arquitecto obsesionado por montar una exposición de un popular héroe arquitectónico en Roma. Greenaway ha sido comisario de exposiciones de pintura –de obra propia y de otros pintores– a las que se han incorporado las posibilidades del vocabulario cinematográfico. Ha utilizado ideas cinematográficas de secuencia, narración y percepción fílmicas en exposiciones

de dibujos en el Louvre, de pinturas en Viena, de artefactos históricos en Ginebra, de arqueología industrial en Swansea, de retratos fotográficos en Cardiff y de luminotecnia en Venecia. Ha iniciado una serie de diez exposiciones, titulada "The Stairs" ('Las escaleras'), que utilizan amplios espacios urbanos –empezando por Ginebra y Munich–, cada una de las cuales abarcará un aspecto diferente del vocabulario cinematográfico: localización, iluminación, encuadre, público, accesorios, actores, texto, sonido, escala e ilusión. Ha iluminado cinematográficamente espacios arquitectónicos como la Piazza del Popolo de Roma, utilizando el *genius loci* de un espacio determinado para realzar su historia y su uso público.

Esta exposición-instalación, "Volar sobre el agua", se basa en estas experiencias y en cierto modo constituye un nuevo punto de partida, porque es una consideración dramática de una ficción; es una exposición sobre una ficción, una narración mitológica con muchos componentes intrigantes que han sido descompuestos para ser examinados y contemplados como objetos reales, objetos preparados o ilusiones. Se invita al público a comparar, confrontar y considerar todas las partes que se juntan para componer una exposición que lo mismo podría ser la preparación de una película que una exposición sobre la reconstrucción de un hecho histórico o de las reliquias de un periodo de la historia, o una combinación de las tres cosas. Esta exposición muestra lo real y lo imaginario, cosas encontradas y cosas reconstruidas, con objetos, escenarios, actores, attrezzo, textos, diagramas, proyecciones y documentación, para ofrecer una experiencia de múltiples facetas que, de hecho, está emparentada con la forma en que nuestra vida transcurre por este mundo: absorbiendo y aprendiendo a través de la observación casual, incidental o concreta, con la búsqueda consciente, a través de las opiniones de los demás, a través de la memoria estimulada, de la aceptación y el rechazo de información recibida y prejuicios desarrollados, y a través de la reinterpretación imaginativa y de los sueños aparentemente intrascendentes llevados hasta los límites del agotamiento.

El tema de la exposición es la dualidad volar/ahogarse, o aire/agua, o cielo/mar. Estos dos ámbitos imaginativos son, desde hace mucho tiempo, una característica de los intereses de Greenaway. Sus primeras películas, como *Windows* ('Ventanas'), *A Walk Through H* y *The Falls* ('Las caídas'), contienen referencias obsesivas a la caída, a los vuelos, a las aves, a la sabiduría popular sobre vuelos, a la tradición de los vuelos, a la historia de los vuelos, al misterio de los vuelos y al mito de los vuelos. Su filmografía está llena de títulos como *Making a Splash* ('Zambullirse'), *Water-Wrackets* ('Monstruos de agua'), *26 Bathrooms* ('26 cuartos de baño'), *Drowning by Numbers* ('Ahogamientos numerados', estrenada en España con el título de *Conspiración de mujeres*) y *Death in the Seine* ('Muerte en el Sena'). Sus exposiciones llevan títulos como "Watching Water" ('Observar el agua') o "Flying Out of This World" ('Huir volando de este mundo'), y uno de sus libros de autocomentario se titula *Fear of Drowning* ('Miedo a ahogarse'). A menudo sus protagonistas mueren en el agua, se arrojan o caen desde una ventana, hacen el amor en el agua, intentan suicidarse en el agua, se cuelgan de un árbol, son sacados de un río, se creen peces, sueñan con la balsa de la Medusa, naufragan en las Bermudas o se identifican con Marat, con Leda, con Ofelia, con Neptuno o con Hero y Leandro.

Para esta exposición, el nexo que empareja el aire y el agua, el vuelo y la natación, el cielo y el mar, es Ícaro, el héroe mitológico que simboliza el primer piloto y a la vez el primer accidente aéreo. El primer hombre que voló y después se ahogó, cayendo directamente del cielo al mar. La crónica más autorizada de la historia de Ícaro proviene de las *Metamorfosis* de Ovidio. Pintores como Giulio Romano, Rubens, Bruegel o Rembrandt se han basado en ella directamente. Existen, sin embargo, muchas variantes de esta historia. El material narrativo básico nos dice que Ícaro y su padre querían huir de la tiranía del rey Minos, en la isla de Creta, y consiguieron levantar el vuelo con unas alas hechas de plumas pegadas con cera. Entusiasmado con esta libertad y este placer recién descubiertos, Ícaro, desoyendo el consejo de su padre, se acercó demasiado al sol. La cera se derritió, las alas se desprendieron e Ícaro cayó y se ahogó en el mar que aún lleva su nombre. Es la historia de una arrogancia, de una ambición excesiva que termina en una tragedia en tres partes: la muerte de un joven, la pérdida de un hijo y el derrumbamiento de un ideal.

Los mitos propician tan fácilmente la realización de deseos universales, y son tan proclives a encarnar aspiraciones y deseos profundos en épocas y lugares distintos, que la figura de Ícaro, directa o indirectamente, representa muchas variantes del tema y emerge en muchos sistemas que se alejan del canon clásico. Otras tradiciones mitológicas anteriores y posteriores, con diferentes perspectivas y grados de sofisticación, también puede decirse que contienen figuras parecidas a Ícaro en el núcleo de sus diversas búsquedas de elevación física o espiritual, o en su representación de cielos ideales, o en su deseo de comunión con el cielo, o en su afán por alcanzar diversas manifestaciones del más allá. Los teólogos cristianos pueden ver, en la alegoría de Dédalo-padre e Ícaro-hijo, un paralelismo con Dios-padre-inventor que da alas espirituales a su Adán inventado, antes de la caída de éste, ocasionada por no haber hecho caso de la advertencia paterna. O como una variante del intento de Abraham de sacrificar a Isaac, o como una anticipación profética de la relación entre Dios Padre y Dios Hijo que abarca en detalle el mito de la resurrección. El material padre-hijo, inventor-inventado, maestro-alumno, hombre sabio-hijo inconsciente, es retomado constantemente con variantes que unas veces inclinan nuestras simpatías hacia Dédalo y otras hacia Ícaro.

¿Cuáles son los múltiples componentes de este mito? ¿Pueden ser analizados con relación a nuestros superiores conocimientos actuales sobre sistemas de volar con la ayuda de máquinas, sobre ingeniería, anatomía humana, meteorología, ornitología, entomología y física? ¿Hasta qué punto no es frívola nuestra ironía cuando pensamos en la cera de abejas y en el vuelo de Ícaro hacia el sol? Con relación a nuestra idea contemporánea del niño y del adolescente, ¿es interesante especular sobre la edad de Ícaro? ¿Cuántos años tenía? ¿Tres, seis, doce, dieciocho, veintiuno? Tanto la golondrina como el albatros son magníficos voladores; teniendo en cuenta nuestra experiencia actual en el campo del atletismo, y el estatus, el uso y el exhibicionismo de los juegos olímpicos, si tuviéramos que fabricar unas alas personalizadas, ¿cómo las construiríamos?; y ¿cuál sería el cuerpo ideal que debería tener el mejor volador: el físico de un velocista, de un corredor de fondo, de un saltador, de un buzo, de un nadador? Imaginemos una

medalla de oro olímpica para la especialidad de volar. Si hablamos de mitos-ave, ¿nos sirve el de Leda y el Cisne? ¿Murió Ícaro a causa del impacto contra el agua al caer de una altura de 25.000 m, de 60.000, de 120.000? ¿O quizás se ahogó en una profundidad de 10, de 100 o de 250 m de agua salada? ¿No es una ironía que se ahogara? Después de intentar volar y no conseguirlo, ¿tampoco fue capaz de nadar? Volar y nadar –dos formas de desafiar la fuerza de la gravedad sobre el cuerpo humano– pueden considerarse dos cosas análogas. ¿Deberíamos aprender a nadar antes de poder aprender a volar, del mismo modo que es más sensato aprender a conducir un automóvil antes de aprender a pilotar un avión?

¿Y si Ícaro no hubiese caído, sino que hubiese acompañado a Dédalo a Italia y a Nápoles? ¿Y si, sencillamente, se hubiese perdido? ¿No había cielo de sobra para perderse en él? ¿Y si Dédalo hubiese juzgado erróneamente la prueba de las plumas flotando sobre el agua? ¿Y si resulta que lo que había que hacer era construir una plataforma de aterrizaje para el Ícaro que aún tenía que regresar, y un marco para seccionar el cielo y anticipar el último tramo de su vuelo antes de aterrizar?

Como estos interrogantes pertenecen al terreno movedizo de la ficción, las posibilidades de especular son infinitas, y al mismo tiempo muy divertidas. Y seguramente hay más interrogantes y especulaciones que los que nos permite el espacio de una sola exposición; sin duda, esta exposición, como proyecto, ha visto –por lo menos en sus fases de planificación– más de una manifestación. Esperemos que pueda haber otras versiones en otros sitios, por eso Greenaway, en este catálogo, inventa una forma de exposición ideal sobre el tema de "Volar sobre el agua", y ello le proporciona un segundo título, "Descripción de una exposición", que también le da la oportunidad de debatir la experiencia de las exposiciones en general, y de establecer conexiones con otros medios, el principal de los cuales es, naturalmente, el cine. No es ningún secreto que Greenaway tiene en cartera una ópera y como mínimo un guión cinematográfico en alguna forma de preproducción que utilizan el mismo tema, o uno parecido. Quizás esta "Descripción de una exposición. La aventura de Ícaro", es un prólogo para posteriores investigaciones sobre el tema de "Volar sobre el agua".

La aventura de Ícaro

DESCRIPCIÓN DE UNA EXPOSICIÓN
Introducción

El deseo de volar es universal. Volar como un pájaro, volar como un espíritu, subir hasta el Cielo, vencer la gravedad, es una aspiración humana antigua y con un inmenso atractivo. Es una ambición que puede traducirse en cosas ornitológicas, espirituales, poéticas, religiosas y prácticas. Todas las culturas de todos los tiempos, tarde o temprano, abiertamente o de una forma encubierta, expresan este deseo. Incluso los trogloditas sienten el deseo de volar. Y, sin embargo, es un sueño imposible. Individualmente y sin ninguna ayuda, nosotros jamás podremos despegar, flotar por los aires y volar. La gravedad ha conformado nuestra anatomía para que tengamos los pies anclados en el suelo.

Ni las alas de Leonardo, ni el globo de

Montgolfier, ni los aeroplanos de los hermanos Wright, ni el helicóptero, ni el paracaídas, ni el Concorde, ni la misión espacial Apolo ni las alas delta son la solución. Son máquinas condenadas a volver tarde o temprano a la Tierra; máquinas temporales que se alimentan de una energía artificial, todas ellas limitadas y especializadas. Ningún ser humano podrá volar como una golondrina. Nadie puede volar como un albatros, como un aguilucho, como una mariposa, como una abeja o como un colibrí. El sueño más elevado, por lo tanto, es imposible. Hemos inventado los ángeles. Hemos inventado el cielo. Sempre nos ha sido muy fácil inventar cosas irrealizables.

La cultura europea ha mostrado una inventiva exuberante en lo que se refiere a crear mitos voladores: Perseo, Pegaso, la Esfinge, Cupido, Hermes, Faetón, los ángeles, los querubines, la ascensión de Cristo... Entre todos estos mitos destaca Ícaro, el primer piloto, el primer volador, el primer accidente aéreo. En él, y en su padre Dédalo, podemos ver reflejados a Blériot, Lindbergh, Gagarin, Amy Johnson..., la lista es larga, y podríamos añadir muchos fracasos: Glenn Miller, Buddy Holly...

Esta exposición trata de las esperanzas, las ambiciones, los breves éxitos apócrifos y el fracaso ubicuo y definitivo del sueño imposible de volar, reunidos alrededor de Ícaro, el primer piloto y el primer accidente aéreo.

Es una investigación sobre el mito de Ícaro y su sueño de volar. Examinamos los distintos candidatos a Ícaro para ver cuál reúne los rasgos más deseables para poder volar, examinamos las plumas de Ícaro, la cera que soldaba dichas plumas, los huevos puestos por los cisnes que proporcionaron las plumas, su estrategia de despegue, la sustancia del aire en el que voló, las condiciones meteorológicas, el agua donde cayó, los sistemas alternativos que podrían haber hecho que su vuelo tuviera más éxito... Analizamos su caída, el impacto sobre el agua que señaló su muerte. Sentimos curiosidad por conocer el peso de su cuerpo cuando cayó al fondo del mar, y los rasgos de arqueópterix de sus huesos en descomposición, petrificados bajo el agua. Observamos otros aspectos del mito para entender por qué fue necesaria una ambición de este tipo, por qué fue inevitable esta pretensión arrogante, y para ver qué otros sueños y qué otros mitos podría haber engendrado.

Y, desde la perspectiva de nuestra superior capacidad de juicio, construimos un marco del cielo y graderías de bienvenida y una plataforma de aterrizaje en espera de que regrese definitivamente y a salvo.

Todas estas cuestiones y curiosidades las analizamos desde una perspectiva contemporánea, y quizás, más pertinentemente, desde la perspectiva de las tecnologías contemporáneas que asociamos con la producción y disfrute del cine. No se nos pide que nos sentemos, pero la oscuridad nos resulta familiar. Podemos esperarnos una acción dramática, aunque no necesariamente de tipo narrativo. Pero, en generosa compensación, encontraremos una evolución secuencial en todas direcciones.

Es probable que, en esta exposición, lo que esperamos del cine nos provoque una cierta inquietud. Conociendo la temática habitual del cine, puede que esperemos encontrar sexo, peligro, sangre, alguna dosis de violencia y quizás algún dilema moral; o incluso humor (aunque esto siempre es incalculable). Aquí encontraremos la mayoría de los temas y características del cine: un artificio evidente, la típica obligación de dejar la incredulidad en suspenso, cambios de escala súbitos e imposibles, espectáculo, una mezcla de realidad y ficción, cambios de ritmo, unos cambios rápidos de escena, unos planos visuales cambiantes... y el concepto de montaje, entendido como el acto de construir ideas a partir de unas imágenes dispares tan estrechamente unidas que parecen indivisibles. Y encontraremos también algo que –desgraciadamente– raras veces consigue proporcionarnos el cine: la simultaneidad. En esta exposición, la acción simultánea está tan presente que parece como si todo ocurriera al mismo tiempo. Sin duda, el pasado y el presente conviven aquí junto con el *post mortem*, y con el proceso que hace que estos diversos estadios temporales puedan entremezclarse.

Esta exposición puede apuntarse fácilmente varias victorias sobre el cine. Podremos, sin duda, experimentar con el olfato y el tacto. Podremos experimentar directamente humedades y corrientes de aire, sensaciones que podríamos pensar que no siempre son ventajosas; pero, en una exposición sobre el martirio en el mar, el escurrirse insidioso de la humedad y la presencia de varec, neblina y niebla, son factores poderosos para dejar fácilmente la incredulidad en suspenso. Dado que el uso del espacio –y del marco temporal de este "filme tridimensional en la oscuridad"– pertenece al visitante y no al director, el visitante o espectador puede ser selectivo. Al presenciar una película en el cine, un espectador no tiene capacidad de decisión para reemfatizar los acontecimientos, no tiene la oportunidad de reexperimentar un incidente o revivir un hecho inmediatamente para contemplarlo desde otra perspectiva o investigarlo más a fondo. En una exposición, la atención del visitante es variable e infinitamente repetible, y le pertenece a él.

Y también está el texto. El cine nunca ha podido existir –a pesar de los que desearían que fuera de otra manera– sin un texto; un texto como origen, como método, como crítica, como descripción, incluso como título. Como casi toda la pintura, el cine es esclavo del texto hasta el punto de reducir la imaginería al papel de ilustración. Sin duda hay texto en esta exposición, y es un texto que realiza todas las funciones que acabo de nombrar.

Todas las cuales, he supuesto, sostienen las preocupaciones actuales por investigar una idea ampliada del cine... que incorpora acción viva en un filme muerto, que incorpora sonido vivo con un filme muerto, que relaciona a actores vivos con un filme muerto, que combina teatro y cine, que utiliza tiempo real, que investiga la simultaneidad, que permite una interacción con el público, en la medida en que sea posible conseguirla sin alienar la capacidad de elección del director, que convierte al público en algo más que espectadores pasivos, que siente curiosidad por la mezcla de distintos medios, que cree que el cine es ciertamente la herramienta altamente imaginativa que se creyó que era a principios del siglo XX, que ciertamente quiere creer en el enorme potencial de la nueva revolución Gutenberg en la educación visual que están desencadenando las nuevas tecnologías. Explorar el cine como una exposición y ampliar la exposición con el lenguaje y las expectativas del cine es permitir a ambos medios alcanzar alturas nuevas y reinventadas en esta antesala del próximo siglo. Quizás, con este entusiasmo y esta ambición, Ícaro podrá ciertamente aprender a volar.

1. El arco de plumas

La exposición se inicia con un arco de plumas para celebrar el éxito potencial de Ícaro. Con un muy necesario optimismo, los monumentos a los difuntos, así como las tumbas y las necrológicas, a menudo pueden prepararse antes del acontecimiento. Deberían erigirse varios arcos en las calles circundantes, en la plaza principal de la ciudad, en el puente más importante de la ciudad, a la entrada de la ciudad y sin duda en el aeropuerto, el lugar oficial y apropiado para el descenso de Ícaro en su regreso a la Tierra. Estos arcos deberían ser de vidrio y estar totalmente rellenos de plumas de un blanco puro, acompañadas del sonido del mar. Por la noche deberían iluminarse con una luz de un color azul acuoso que refulgiera y resplandeciera.

El arco es un símbolo arquitectónico tradicional que señala una entrada con estridentes letras públicas. Las ciudades amuralladas, las fortalezas, los lugares de culto, los exhiben y los sostienen. La mayoría de los arcos de triunfo erigidos aisladamente eran efímeros, se construían para una ocasión concreta y se derribaban poco después: arcos para la Reina del Primero de Mayo, para visitas de dignatarios, para el regreso de un héroe, construidos con materiales diversos, como madera, tela pintada, ramas de árboles, flores... Los modelos permanentes son famosos: el arco de Séptimo Severo es la puerta norte de acceso al foro romano, el arco de Constantino está delante del Coliseo, el arco de Triunfo de París es la puerta de entrada a los Campos Elíseos, pesado, enorme, macizo, trascendental, hecho con costosa piedra esculpida arrastrada desde grandes distancias, cubierto de símbolos gráficos de heroísmo, sacrificio, nacionalismo, muerte y poder... y promesas portentosas que ningún hombre ni ninguna nación puede cumplir.

Pasar por debajo de un arco ceremonial es como adquirir un compromiso, como franquear la puerta de acceso a un edificio oficial, como cruzar el umbral de una casa para una boda, como acceder a un recinto funerario, como atreverse a pasar por debajo de una escalera y tentar la mala suerte, como pasar por debajo de un yugo para sellar un acuerdo. Si el gran arco arquitectónico es una puerta triunfal –como el arco de Triunfo de París, como la puerta de Brandenburgo de Berlín–, también es el monumento tradicional a los muertos. Para Ícaro, sin duda, puede ser ambas cosas: un arco de triunfo –porque Ícaro es el segundo hombre que voló– y un arco conmemorativo de su muerte, porque Ícaro es también el primer aviador que se estrelló. Pero, como en el caso del foro romano y de l'Étoile, es posible no pasar por debajo del arco, esquivar su formalidad –aunque un desvío tan tímido como éste no nos permitirá vivir con plenitud la misma experiencia arquitectónica.

Parodiando los pesados arcos de piedra ceremoniales, triunfales y monumentales de Roma, París, Berlín y Londres, nuestro arco de triunfo, ceremonial y conmemorativo de la muerte de Ícaro, está hecho de vidrio para que podamos ver fácilmente su contenido, que consiste en plumas –el material más efímero e insustancial y que es la esencia de esta exposición. Este arco, en efecto, está totalmente relleno de material volador. No hay ninguna inscripción, ningún pesado ornamento simbólico: con las plumas hay bastante. La presunción irónica es deliberada, porque, ¿quién puede edificar un monumento a base de plumas? Es una entrada a la presencia del misterio del vuelo asociado a Ícaro. Una entrada conmovedora.

2. Los primeros textos sobre vuelos: los textos menores

Después de cruzar el arco de plumas nos hallamos enseguida ante un conjunto de textos, un primer conjunto de textos llamados Textos Menores, que están medio iluminados per la luz diurna de nuestra entrada y medio ocultos en las sombras que nos esperan. Este primer conjunto de textos es una introducción irónica a nuestro tema general. Es conveniente que los leamos. En nuestro mundo literario occidental hay mucho material visual que es en primer lugar una cuestión de texto, y en segundo lugar una cuestión de imagen. Deberíamos reconocer ese estado de cosas. Así es, por ejemplo, como se hace el cine.

Estos primeros textos están encerrados en vitrinas agrupadas de forma regular, como una pequeña tropa de soldados que protegen lo que hay más allá. El importante estatus de estos textos como introducción a esta exposición es confirmado por su presencia en vitrinas colocadas a la altura adecuada para poder ser leídos. Cada texto está iluminado desde abajo por una cálida luz móvil de color verde que evoca aguas dulces y poco profundas, como si anduviéramos por el sótano inundado de un fresco edificio, quizás incluso por el sótano del palacio de Cnosos, en Creta, antecámara del laberinto, que Dédalo construyó para el rey Minos con la finalidad de alojar al minotauro. Y –como una anticipación del futuro– dos textos, los dos últimos, se encuentran bajo el agua. Podría decirse que son submarinos. Hay que leer las palabras de estos textos a través del agua. Podríamos decir que estos dos textos están ahogados.

Los textos pueden consistir en lo siguiente:
1. Un periódico con la noticia de un accidente aéreo ocurrido en España en 1959.
2. Un texto en un libro abierto que explique cómo hacer volar una cometa.
3. Una página de diagramas de una revista de unas líneas aéreas que muestren el plano del aeropuerto de Medina Sidonia.
4. Una página de una novela sobre gemelos voladores.
5. Una página de instrucciones de un manual de vuelo.
6. El diario de vuelo de un piloto.
7. Una descripción de una gran ave pelágica.
8. Una descripción, hecha por un niño, de cómo se hace un avión de papel.
9. Manuales de natación, proezas natatorias, construcción de piscinas.
10. La crónica de un suicida que se arrojó desde lo alto de la Sagrada Familia.

3. La enciclopedia de muestras de agua

Después de los primeros textos, e instalados bajo una luz más brillante, centelleantes y chispeantes como la luz del sol sobre un mar gris, se encuentran unos treinta tarros de vidrio tapados, cada uno de los cuales contiene exactamente un litro de agua. Sólo agua. En general, el agua es muy límpida y clara. Tan límpida y clara, de hecho, que si no nos acercamos demasiado podemos pensar que por lo menos algunos de los tarros tapados están vacíos. Los tarros están colocados a una misma distancia el uno del otro, y todos ellos numerados y etiquetados. Las etiquetas indican el lugar y el momento en que fue encontrada y recogida el agua de cada tarro: agua de cierto riachuelo cercano, agua de un río cercano, agua de una bañera de un pueblo determinado, agua de cierta cascada, de cierto lago, estanque, charco, pozo, cisterna, gruta subterránea, río, riachuelo o acequia.

Sin duda, como visitantes, al principio nos sorprende un poco que haya tantos lugares donde se puede encontrar agua. Pero, al cabo de un rato, cuando la repetición de los recipientes se hace hipnotizante, nos damos cuenta del truismo. Al fin y al cabo, en el mundo hay una gran cantidad de agua, y en un sitio u otro tiene que estar. E Ícaro debió de caer, según el mito, en algún lugar donde hubiera agua. El agua es volátil, y su estado cambia constantemente: hielo, nieve, lluvia, vapor, condensación, espuma, agua dulce, agua salada, tibia, caliente, fría, helada. Y el agua, como tal, se mueve constantemente. Avanza y retrocede con las mareas. Sube y baja por las costas. Se alza del fondo del mar y vuelve hacia el fondo del mar. Se precipita en el Mediterráneo desde el Egeo. Entra arremolinada en el Mediterráneo desde el Atlántico, a través del estrecho de Gibraltar. Arrastrada por el viento, convertida en nubes, precipitada sobre las montañas, agrupada en corrientes, cayendo gota a gota sobre las rocas, permaneciendo cavernosa bajo tierra, absorbida por la esponja de la capa freática. ¿Agua nueva? ¿Agua vieja? ¿Puede el agua ser vieja? Dicen que una misma agua entra y sale del organismo de la reina de Inglaterra dos veces al año como mínimo. El agua en la que cayó Ícaro puede estar actualmente en cualquier lugar de la Tierra.

4. La primera hélice

Después de haber pasado por los primeros textos introductorios, ahora podemos acercarnos a una alta vitrina que contiene una hélice que gira en posición vertical, el tipo de hélice que mueve a un avión por el aire; la misma que, basándose en el mismo principio pero con un diseño y una configuración diferentes, hace que un barco avance por el agua.

Casi todo el rato hemos sido conscientes de la presencia de esta hélice porque su ala rotatoria ha estado proyectando una sombra de aspecto peligroso, que sobresale y centellea y gira a través del espacio de la exposición. La hélice produce un ruido que a ratos es como un zumbido y a ratos como un ronroneo. Unas veces recuerda el zumbir de las abejas en verano, otras veces una peonza, otras el chirrido de una fresa de dentista, o el "zzzzzzzz" que sale en las historietas para indicar la monotonía del sueño. Con los pies podemos notar la vibración del movimiento rotatorio de esta hélice. Si Ícaro hubiera tenido una hélice... Quizás la tenía; quizás la teoría de las alas hechas con plumas y cera es errónea. Este ala rotatoria es intimidante, porque nos han contado muchas veces –y lo hemos visto demostrado en las películas– que un objeto como éste puede partir a un hombre por la mitad, arrancarle la cabeza y lanzarla dando vueltas por los aires, por encima del asfalto y de los campos, hasta acabar en el agua.

5. Las marcas de un aeropuerto

Hay también dos nuevos fenómenos que habría que señalar. Ambos empiezan a nuestros pies, pero se extienden hacia delante, a derecha e izquierda, en la distancia; y se relacionan entre sí. El primero tiene que ver con una plétora de marcas en el suelo, y las asociaciones no nos resultan extrañas. Las marcas sugieren que caminamos sobre la pista de un aeropuerto, no necesariamente una pista de aterrizaje principal, sino más bien una pista de entrada o un aparcamiento. Éstas podrían ser nuestras líneas orientadoras. Puede ser que la frontalidad persistente de todas las vitrinas que hemos experimentado hasta ahora no tenga una

relación directa con estas marcas, porque parece que avanzan angularmente respecto al eje central de la evolución que seguimos en este momento. Se considera, por lo tanto, que las marcas de esta hipotética pista de aeropuerto están descentradas, lo cual, por supuesto, puede resultar una metáfora pertinente.

La mayoría de las marcas no son necesariamente nuevas. Algunas, ciertamente, son fragmentarias, como si hubieran sido trazadas por un ojo y una mano vacilantes, inseguros de cómo deben funcionar las instrucciones de la pista de un aeropuerto. Sin duda, el autor de estas marcas ha entendido que hay que poder verlas desde una altura considerable, la de un avión en movimiento.

Las líneas también nos sugieren una pista de despegue principal más allá, pero también hay desvíos, pistas de despegue secundarias con indicaciones de entrada restringida, flechas embotadas, figuras y cifras apenas perceptibles. Debido a la oscuridad, estas instrucciones en el suelo no son necesariamente fáciles de ver ni de leer. Ciertos segmentos son brillantes y claros como si estuvieran recién pintados, otros están medio borrados y desgastados por el caminar continuo de la gente y la abrasión constante de las ruedas, hay zonas donde se han vertido líquidos que podrían ser perfectamente ácidos... ¿o es algo que se ha quemado, o es que las marcas sugieren algo que quizás se ha descompuesto, quién sabe si un animal de gran tamaño que murió hace un año y medio y ha ido pudriéndose poco a poco sobre las instrucciones lineales, y finalmente ha sido retirado de forma brusca pero no demasiado pulcra? También hay marcas que no resultan fáciles de explicar, como si de pronto su autor hubiera desistido de volar, o hubiera pensado que la pretensión de volar era demasiado peligrosa, o demasiado absurda, o demasiado estúpida.

En cuanto al segundo fenómeno, hay luces en el suelo. Producen una luz mortecina, y a veces llegamos a dudar de que estén allí. Trazan un trayecto de varios caminos fragmentarios en líneas estrechas, como un surco, como un rastro de luz no más grueso que una cuerda. A veces se repiten y transcurren paralelas durante cortas distancias, o incluso en diagonal, y se entrecruzan como si dudaran antes de arrancar definitivamente. Sin duda no transcurren en simpatía con las otras marcas de la pista que hemos descrito. Estas líneas del suelo son de un color azul oscuro –casi negro–, pero más allá podemos ver ya como el color azul de la línea va haciéndose más claro y brillante y adopta una coloración púrpura, o incluso malva. Podría ser perfectamente que estas líneas de luz ofrecieran un camino especial a través del laberinto de vitrinas. En este momento, sin embargo, no hay ningún deseo ni urgencia particular de seguir dichas marcas. Es posible que no sean más que una alusión al hilo de Ariadna a través del laberinto de Creta, tal como fue ideado por Dédalo.

Hay unas figuras oscuras que caminan por encima del suelo. ¿Son empleados oscuros y silenciosos del aeropuerto, con unos auriculares que hacen que sus cabezas parezcan los ojos de una mosca gigantesca? ¿Y llevan monos manchados de petróleo y cascos iluminados y franjas reflectantes en los codos, y sobre el pecho, y en medio de la espalda?

Cuando estas figuras oscuras se nos acercan, podemos oír un ligerísimo rumor de voces: mensajes fragmentarios recibidos confusamente por sus auriculares, instrucciones sin duda llenas

de interferencias de las ondas aéreas, destinos que quizás nos son familiares y lugares de los que nunca hemos oído hablar, lugares inaccesibles, utopías, mapas a veces conocidos y a veces desconocidos, en el interior del cuerpo, bajo la tierra que hay bajo el mar... y bajo el mar hay una gran cantidad de tierra. Vivimos en un planeta muy bien provisto de agua.

Pero estas figuras oscuras se alejan de nosotros a medida que nos vamos acercando: han sido instruidas para mantenerse a una distancia prudente de los visitantes, y sólo les interesa mirar al cielo para buscar aviones que se acercan, criaturas voladoras, dirigibles, hombres cayendo, plumas que flotan.

Las marcas del suelo –tal como las vemos en la semipenumbra– ahora están dibujadas o estarcidas con más nitidez. Ahora están asociadas con letras y cifras de gran tamaño. Quizás nos encontramos al principio de una pista de aterrizaje, en el comienzo mismo de una plataforma de lanzamiento de un viejo aeropuerto, cuyo final está a cuatro kilómetros de distancia. Es aquí donde, en otros tiempos, los dirigibles no vistos hacían su carrera previa al intento de despegar.

Se oyen voces. Voces que leen, susurrantes, el segundo grupo de textos. No hay ningún interés especial en que entendamos totalmente todas y cada una de las palabras de estos textos: sólo hay la constatación suficiente de que están siendo leídos. Oímos palabras en latín y en griego, y sin duda en inglés y en catalán: estas lenguas del mundo occidental que, en un momento u otro, se han visto obligadas a realizar servicios internacionales en la diplomacia, discursos sobre el arte, la astronomía, la física, y ciertamente, para nuestro propósito actual, a transmitir las instrucciones necesarias entre torres de control de distintos aeropuertos.

Podemos estar seguros de que cada palabra de los textos expuestos que pueda resultarnos pertinente ha sido grabada en las cintas magnetofónicas. Pero la cinta total no es muy larga: dura sólo diez minutos. Un visitante con mucha paciencia, aunque no pueda descifrar todas las palabras, podrá estar seguro de que cada palabra de nuestros textos se encuentra allí.

6. Los segundos textos sobre vuelos: los textos mayores

Pasando cautelosamente junto a la hélice vibrante y percusora, el visitante se encuentra ahora ante un segundo grupo de textos dentro de unas vitrinas colocadas sobre pedestales. En este caso, los textos están iluminados por una luz vacilante, más azulada que verde, un color con reminiscencias de aguas más profundas y frías, y de extensiones más antiguas de mar y de océano. Este segundo grupo de textos son los Textos Mayores. Son más augustos y venerables, probablemente más autorizados que los del primer grupo. Tienen un pedigrí más antiguo. Aquí el visitante encontrará:

11. Una venerable edición española del Antiguo Testamento –abierta por la parte del Génesis–, con ilustraciones que muestran a Dios creando los océanos del mundo.

12 y 13. Dos relatos del diluvio del Antiguo Testamento judío, uno en hebreo y el otro en griego.

14 y 15. Dos versiones del mito de Ícaro, provenientes de las *Metamorfosis* de Ovidio, la primera en latín y la segunda en español. Aparte de la Biblia, seguramente no hay otra fuente de inspiración en el arte occidental que haya sido tan utilizada por escritores y pintores como las

Metamorfosis de Ovidio. Bruegel se basó en ellas en una representación muy precisa y descriptiva, como también lo hicieron Dante –aunque más libremente–, Giulio Romano, Daumier y Rauschenberg, lord Leighton y Rodin.

16. Una representación gótica catalana de la ascensión de Cristo.
17. Un libro antiguo de historia natural con ilustraciones de aves volando y peces nadando.
18. Un libro antiguo de "Historias de viajeros", ilustrado con una progenie de peces-ave.
19. Crónicas ilustradas de navegación, de batallas navales, de irrigación, de hidráulica.
20. Venerables libros ilustrados donde pueden aparecer sirenas, monstruos marinos, ahogamientos, Neptuno, la caída de Faetón, la caída de los ángeles.
21. Venerables libros ilustrados con grabados que representan las máquinas voladoras de Da Vinci, submarinos, defensas navales, diseño de canales, irrigación, el tornillo de Arquímedes.
22. Un libro sobre ángeles.
23. Un libro de grabados que representan el *Pterodáctilo con el guante* de Max Klinger, de la serie sobre *La violación del guante*.

7. Los acuarios

Pasando a través del Arco de Plumas, leyendo los textos Menores y Mayores, contemplando los distintos tipos de agua, reconociendo las señales y mapas del suelo bajo sus pies, el visitante ha adquirido un compromiso y ahora se enfrenta al agua en estado puro: el agua, la enemiga y el bálsamo.

Agua. Sólo agua. Agua recluida en una hilera de grandes acuarios de cristal situados por encima del nivel de los ojos e iluminados con un estimulante programa de luz controlada... simplemente, agua.

Se nos recuerda el efecto de la luz solar sobre el agua, del ahogamiento, de la tregua del calor del sol, de la amenaza de peces peligrosos, de cadáveres que flotan y se hunden en el mar.

El agua ocupa las cuatro quintas partes de la Tierra y constituye las nueve décimas partes del cuerpo humano. El agua es la vida de la Tierra. Cualquier animal o planta que no viva en el agua está obligado a transportar agua en su interior a dondequiera que vaya. El agua representa el acto de beber, de lavarse, la lubricación, la orina, la limpieza, la sed saciada y el ahogamiento confirmado. Podemos sumergir fácilmente la cabeza de un hombre en cada uno de estos recipientes llenos de agua. El agua está limpia, clara y fría. La luz es conducida a través de estos acuarios y se solidifica en estos bloques de agua fríos y cúbicos.

Sabemos que el agua es pesada, y ver el agua en esta posición elevada, sobre esta especie de podios, resulta preocupante. Si los acuarios reventaran, seríamos sepultados por una lluvia de cristales y un alud de agua fría.

No hay la menor duda de que esta agua podría ser perfectamente el medio posible de un desastre.

8. Las alas y el corazón mecánico

Después de haber leído los textos, de haber sido intimidados por la hélice rotatoria y de haber ponderado la ambigüedad de las marcas en el suelo y la presencia inquietante de los observadores del aire con sus auriculares, esta exposición de pruebas de la primera, última y definitiva aventura aérea de Ícaro es particularizada y centrada temáticamente.

Ante nosotros hay dos objectos. El primero, el más pequeño, es una máquina sumergida que centellea debido a unes luces ocultas que iluminan el agua fría de su alrededor. Es una máquina que ha sufrido un accidente. Es un amontonamiento de metal. Tiene todos sus componentes retorcidos y destruidos, sus miembros metálicos han sido cortados en redondo, sus tuberías han sido fracturadas. Se puede describir antropomórficamente como una máquina con un corazón de metal. Presenta rastros de una aorta y de un ventrículo. Quizás bombea lentamente. Es una reliquia, una máquina metálica de un antiguo accidente aeronáutico, un accidente arqueológico, pero su potencia, como si de criptonita se tratara, hace que todavía brille, como un vestigio volcánico en el fondo de un mar profundo.

A su lado hay un ala magullada. Es, como mínimo, un objeto en forma de ala, lo bastante prototípico como para ser genérico. Es casi cierto que había volado, que había volado arqueológicamente. No hay duda de que el corazón-máquina y el corazón-ala podrían estar relacionados. Y es evidente que ahora, en cierto modo, funcionan al unísono. El ala tiene unas luces a babor y a estribor que centellean rítmicamente, y acompasadas con las pulsaciones del corazón-máquina. La relación no es sencilla. Quizás cinco latidos del centelleo del corazón de metal se corresponden a dos pulsaciones de luz de la proto-ala. Y, si el ala está vacía, entonces también hay luces en su interior. Es curioso que el agua de la sumersión del ala pueda ser protectora. Como un feto separado del líquido amniótico, si la máquina se separa del agua que la rodea, su vida puede extinguirse. Quizás el agua no es realmente agua, sino algún tipo de espíritu conductor, como alcohol, álcali, ácido, agua de áloes, agua de almendras... todos ellos fluidos importantes, y que empiezan por la letra a.

Quizás este corazón y estas alas son el centro de poder de la exposición. Nos recuerdan que cualquier cosa nueva está probablemente hecha a imagen de otra muy antigua, arqueológicamente antigua. Quizás son reliquias de una época dorada de los vuelos, y eso las convierte en artefactos venerados que han inspirado esta tentativa.

9. Los aspirantes a Ícaro

Hay una serie de vitrinas que contienen a los aspirantes a asumir el papel de Ícaro. No sabemos cuántos años tenía Ícaro cuando realizó su primer vuelo iniciático. Cuanto más jovencito hubiera sido, menos habría pesado y menos le habría costado sostenerse en el aire, pero por otro lado también habría tenido menos fuerza en los brazos para maniobrar las alas. Si Ovidio es nuestra fuente de información, entonces nos podemos inclinar por la hipótesis de que Ícaro todavía era un niño, digamos que de unos diez u once años, una edad como para hacer caso de la advertencia de su padre de no acercarse demasiado al sol, pero también lo bastante impetuoso y olvidadizo como para hacerle caso omiso. Otras fuentes, tanto visuales como literarias, presentan a un Ícaro mayor. Estos hombres jóvenes que se presentan para el papel de Ícaro se dividen básicamente en dos grupos. El primer grupo de candidatos son seis jóvenes que creen que una complexión fibrosa y una anatomía angular son características idóneas para un vuelo de largo recorrido. Están sentados a la espera de ser evaluados por los visitantes, y son los candidatos que muestran una mayor capacidad de asumir el papel de Ícaro como atleta capaz de cubrir largas distancias.

Ésta es una lista hipotética de candidatos:

1. El primero es un joven nervioso. Está delgado y lleva una ropa indefinida, quizás una camisa blanca de cuello abierto y un pantalón blanco sucio. Calza botas. Está sentado con las manos entre las rodillas y con los pies muy juntos.
2. El segundo candidato tiene tantas ganas de convencernos de su aptitud para el papel, que va completamente desnudo y su cuerpo blanco tiene un aspecto poco saludable bajo la luz intensa que lo ilumina desde arriba. Con sus hombros encorvados parece un pollo desplumado, porque no le resulta fácil exhibirse en público totalmente desnudo.
3. El tercer joven, con la intención de copiar a su vecino, también se quitó toda la ropa, pero se dejó puestos unos calzoncillos blancos. Lleva bigote. ¿Ícaro llevaba bigote? Durante la Segunda Guerra Mundial, en Inglaterra, era tradicional que los aviadores llevaran bigote. ¿Es posible que los bigotes, peinados a derecha e izquierda por encima del labio, fueran un símbolo o emblema de las alas?
4. El cuarto joven es un soldado. Lleva uniforme de camuflaje y se ha quitado los calcetines y las botas, como si estuviera dispuesto a caer en el mar pero no a ahogarse en él.
5. El quinto candidato lleva un bañador azul, consciente de que acentúa y realza su sexo. Se le ve bien dispuesto, pero tiene frío y lleva puesta una camiseta corta de color negro que deja su ombligo al descubierto. Le convendría cortarse las uñas de los pies.
6. El sexto está desnudo de cintura para arriba, y lleva unos tirantes rojos que le sostienen un pantalón de cheviot con muestra de espiga; su cintura es insignificante. Quizás piensa que los tirantes son una ayuda para la propulsión. También va descalzo.

El segundo grupo de candidatos a Ícaro, iluminados desde arriba con la misma intensidad que sus compañeros más delgados, creen que su musculatura les mantendrá en el aire y les ayudará a combatir la fatiga del vuelo. Creen que el exceso de peso quedará equilibrado por los músculos. Han estado desarrollando su musculatura, y ahora quieren mostrar sus músculos para impresionar al público. Están sentados en unas actitudes que demuestran el convencimiento de que sus músculos son aptos para volar y dignos de ser exhibidos.

7. El primer joven es un candidato ancho de pecho, con un traje de una sola pieza muy ceñido al torso. Su peso, sin duda, le hará caer.
8. El segundo va pulcramente vestido, con camisa blanca y esmoquin, como si tuviera el éxito asegurado e Ícaro ya hubiera llegado a la cena de celebración posterior a su vuelo, en las afueras de una ciudad llamada Nápoles, que su padre había fundado por el solo hecho de aterrizar en aquel lugar.
9. El siguiente candidato se ha quitado toda la ropa, y está sentado en actitud indolente. No está tan bien dispuesto a asumir el papel, pero no cabe duda de que le gusta mucho la autopublicidad. Se ha informado debidamente, y ha descubierto que todos los héroes clásicos iban extravagantemente desnudos y afeitados. Se ha afeitado el pecho y las piernas, y se ha recortado los pelos del pubis al estilo de un héroe griego.
10. El cuarto cantidato se ha bronceado la piel para tener un aspecto mediterráneo, pero el bronceado termina en la cintura y sus nalgas son de una blancura norteeuropea.

11. El quinto es un nadador y saltador de complexión fuerte. Puede que crea que volar es lo mismo que nadar, y que, si no es posible nadar por los aires, entonces, cuando la cera se derrita, podrá por lo menos efectuar un salto perfecto en el agua. Lleva uno de esos curiosos bañadores masculinos holgados, que cubren el cuerpo desde el pecho hasta las rodillas.

12. El sexto candidato del segundo grupo lleva un sombrero de alas por si se pone a llover sobre el Mediterráneo. El sombrero da sombra sobre su cara, y no podemos ver la expresión de sus ojos ante la aventura que le espera. Lleva un pantalón corto de color blanco.

13. El séptimo está convencido de que Ícaro es ya un cadáver. Ha pintado su cuerpo desnudo de un verde cadavérico, y tiene el regazo lleno de algas marinas.

Idealmente tenemos una lista de trece hombres jóvenes que están sentados cara a cara y se observan mutuamente, cada uno evaluando las posibilidades del otro de ser elegido para el papel de Ícaro.Esperan pacientemente que los visitantes hagan su selección. Componen un equipo de doce, más uno de reserva. Trece sacrificios como los trece jóvenes atenienses que se requerían periódicamente para ser ofrecidos al minotauro, en Creta. ¿Cómo es posible que unos toros vegetarianos necesitasen carne? ¿O es que el minotauro poseía una cabeza humana y seguía una dieta omnívora?

Una luz blanca y cálida, que nos recuerda el sol mediterráneo que derritió la cera, ilumina intensamente desde arriba a estos aspirantes a Ícaro, blanquea sus carnes y les forma unas profundas sombras en las cuencas de los ojos y bajo el mentón, y bajo los músculos pectorales si es que los tienen.

Usted, el visitante, puede hacer la selección. ¿Cuál de estos jóvenes cree usted que es el más idóneo para encarnar el sueño y la locura de un Ícaro?

10. Cera
Dédalo maldijo a las abejas por haber proporcionado la cera que soldó las alas causantes de la muerte de su hijo.

Hay tres muestras de cera relacionadas con la historia de Ícaro, en tres vitrinas. La cera –al margen de lo que Dédalo pensara posteriormente– es un material del sueño de Ícaro. Y es más: con la cera, el hombre puede producir luz en la oscuridad. Las abejas son portadoras de luz –*post tenebras lux*–, y la cristiandad adoptó a Ícaro como recordatorio del Cristo que ascendió, voló y cayó para la redención del hombre.

En la exposición hay un espacio en penumbra reservado al producto de la industria de las abejas, aunque la cera de abeja ya no es la fuente primaria para la fabricación de velas; los sucedáneos son más asequibles, más baratos, producen un olor más extraño y explotan menos a este industrioso insecto.

1. Una vitrina contiene cera de vela derretida, vertida dentro de la vitrina para que se solidifique lentamente. La cera blanca se pega al interior del cristal. Es cera pura, aún no modelada en la forma fálica de las velas.

2. Una segunda vitrina contiene un alto montón de velas, con sus extremos tocándose, como cartuchos de dinamita horizontales, y formando un edificio triangular. Las velas tienen un tacto pegajoso, huelen a grasa manufacturada y su brillo recuerda un poco al sudor en la tenue luz del día que entra por las ventanas cubiertas con una gasa de color crema.

3. En la tercera vitrina, las velas están amontonadas en forma de cubo y apretadas contra el cristal. Aquí también, los pábilos de las velas son como mechas cortas a punto de iluminar el mundo con una explosión.

11. Las abejas
En un jardín cercano a la sala donde está expuesta la cera hay catorce colmenas pintadas de blanco y llenas de abejas vivas, las suministradoras originales de luz por medio de la cera que fabrican. En verano, una colmena está arrimada a una ventana de cristal para que el visitante de la exposición pueda observar la actividad de las abejas mientras fabrican la cera.

12. Las plumas para el vuelo
¿Dónde se originaría la idea de los humanos volando con alas de plumas? El origen de los centauros pudo haber sido la observación de un jinete tan diestro que dejó la incredulidad en suspenso hasta hacer creer que jinete y caballo eran una misma cosa. Quizás, para los inocentes y los ignorantes, desde una cierta distancia, el fenómeno era del todo convincente. Se dice que los primeros indios norteamericanos estaban convencidos de que los jinetes españoles eran una prolongación de sus caballos. ¿Y el minotauro? ¿Es posible que, en los juegos cretenses en que se utilizaban toros para montarlos y torearlos, se percibiera una fusión del hombre y el toro? ¿Es Ícaro una continuación de la misma idea basada en una observación de la abducción de un niño por un águila, que condujo a la idea del Ganimedes abducido, niño y ave tan íntimamente identificados que el niño lleva las alas y el ave está ausente?

¿O es que todos los híbridos de caballo y toro son fantasías sexuales, la expresión de un deseo, un sueño pornográfico del macho humano, que se excita sexualmente con la contemplación de la humillación sexual de las mujeres al ser violadas por un animal? En la mayoría de hibridaciones, la hembra humana es la víctima pasiva o colaboradora. En el canon mitológico griego no hay ninguna bestia hembra que seduzca a un hombre.

¿O es que esta interpretación es errónea, y en el centro de la fantasía está la idea de la unión de una sensibilidad, una conciencia y una inteligencia humanas con las fuerzas poderosas y deseables del animal? El biomorfismo contemporáneo sustituye el animal por una máquina, pero, en otros tiempos, el hombre deseaba y soñaba una comunión entre él y la velocidad y elegancia de un caballo, la potencia y la fuerza de un toro, la belleza y el vuelo de un cisne.

¿Tienen los cisnes algún papel en el caso de Ícaro? En las *Metamorfosis* de Ovidio, la fabricación de las alas diseñadas por Dédalo es imprecisa. Ningún ingeniero podría sacar gran cosa de esta singular explicación para poder reproducir unas alas de este tipo. No hay medidas, ni detalles sobre cómo se soldaron, se pegaron, se solidificaron. No se menciona ninguna cantidad, ni se hace ninguna descripción del tipo de plumas necesario, ni del ave de la cual procedían. No hay ningún comentario sobre aeronáutica ni aerodinámica. Dédalo, como maestro artesano, trabajó en solitario, e Ícaro no puede ser descrito como un alumno, ni como un aprendiz ni como un ayudante.

¿Cuál podía ser, con más probabilidad, el ave que, voluntariamente o de mala gana, hubiera cedido sus plumas para que el hombre pudiese volar? El candidato ideal habría sido el cisne, sobre todo desde la perspectiva europea. Tanto metafórica como físicamente, el cisne es un animal fuerte. Las plumas blancas indican inocencia, pureza, limpieza, el alma ideal. La fuerza del cisne es legendaria. Un golpe de sus alas puede romper una pierna o unas costillas y causar graves lesiones internas en órganos sensibles. Las plumas de las alas son largas, y sus cañones son rígidos. Un cisne adulto pesa poco más de seis kilos, y un hombre joven de complexión media pesa aproximadamente sesenta y cinco. Se precisarían las plumas de siete cisnes para levantar a un hombre, las de cuatro para levantar a un niño y las de dos para levantar a un bebé de pocos meses.

El cisne, sin embargo, ¿es un animal muy corriente en el Mediterráneo? ¿En Creta? Del mito de Leda podríamos deducir que los cisnes no eran excesivamente exóticos. El cisne es monógamo: tradicionalmente tiene una sola pareja para toda la vida. En Inglaterra, el cisne es un ave real –un ave heráldica, que también se come–, protegida por la corte real. ¿Podría ser que el tiránico rey Minos, como el tiránico Enrique VIII, hubiera criado cisnes en Cnosos?

¿Y las ocas? Tradicionalmente, las ocas son ruidosas aves guardianas: en los claustros de la catedral de Barcelona se utilizaban para custodiar el oro de los gremios. ¿Tenía ocas el rey Minos? La pastora de ocas es el más humilde de los seres que aparecen en las leyendas populares. ¿Es posible que Dédalo pidiera, tomara prestadas o robara las plumas caídas a una pastora de ocas? ¿Ariadna, la hija del rey Minos, disfrazada de princesa María Antonieta guardando ocas? ¿Es posible que Dédalo cebara una oca para matarla y satisfacer su deseo de volar? ¿Realizó estos actos en secreto, resguardado de miradas indiscretas? ¿Fue acumulando plumas en la cabaña de una pastora de ocas hasta tener las suficientes para fabricar unas alas? La oca no es tan elegante ni tan regia como el cisne, pero sus alas son lo bastante fuertes y potentes como para recorrer grandes distancias, para hacer unas migraciones impresionantes. Pero también es un ave belicosa, una voraz devoradora de hierba, y no resulta una buena metáfora.

¿Y las aves del norte de África? La costa norteafricana no está excesivamente lejos de Creta. El avestruz es un símbolo pobre porque no vuela; las plumas rudimentarias de sus alas son un desastre para el vuelo, las pequeñas plumas de su pecho son una excusa para adornar sombreros. Los buitres están bien dotados para elevarse en el aire caliente –sus plumas anchas y rígidas pueden resistir los incrementos térmicos–, pero la mayor parte de sus plumas son de color negro, y el buitre, tradicionalmente, es un ave altamente malévola que se alimenta de carroña, de carne putrefacta; es rapaz y maliciosa, y busca rastros de muerte con ojos penetrantes desde largas distancias.

Quizás el ingenio de Dédalo era de otro tipo, más clandestino. Quizás no le interesaban las plumas obviamente anchas y grandes, sino otras más pequeñas, mucho más modestas, y sacrificó, por ejemplo, a miles de millares de pequeños pájaros cantores: tordos, petirrojos, ruiseñores, alondras... El símbolo es apropiado. Los pájaros cantores cantan para la elevación del espíritu. Puede que Ícaro volara con alas multicolores.

13. La sala de las plumas
Hay una sala pequeña y claustrofóbica con cien plumas que cuelgan del techo. La sala es observable detrás de unas gruesas cortinas. Se trata de las plumas de las alas y de las colas de cisnes blancos adultos, y cada una de ellas está atada a un cordón

invisible que cuelga de un techo oscuro y oculto. Cada pluma está discretamente etiquetada con un número. Existe la posibilidad de que las plumas estén ordenadas según su tamaño, su longitud, su fuerza o alguna otra cualidad. La corriente de aire más ligera hace mover las plumas. La instalación está iluminada por la luz del sol de finales de verano, que entra a través de los postigos de unos ventanales cerrados. En la pared del fondo, donde alternan la penumbra y la luz del sol, se proyecta una diapositiva, un primer término, en blanco y negro sucio y manchado, de la pluma con la que escribía Marat; y, proyectada sobre ella, aparece una cita de las *Metamorfosis* de Ovidio escrita a mano.

Quizás esta sala representa uno de los cobertizos de secado del taller de Dédalo. Las plumas están colgadas para que se sequen, para que maduren, engrasadas y enceradas, a punto para ser utilizadas, aunque es difícil imaginar que pueda mejorarse la calidad de una pluma de cisne recién obtenida.

14. La purificación: la bebida y la bendición
También hay dos objetos –uno antiguo y el otro nuevo– que representan la preparación para un viaje: uno es espiritual y supersticioso; el otro es práctico, y quizás también supersticioso. Los dos tienen que ver con el agua. El primero es una pila de agua bendita, una jofaina de piedra llena de agua para que el visitante pueda sumergir el dedo y, con el dedo mojado, humedecerse la frente, o quizás los labios, o cualquier otra parte del cuerpo que crea apropiada para ungirse, como gesto sagrado en demanda de protección y seguridad en el viaje.

El segundo es una fuente de aluminio de donde sale un chorro minúsculo de agua burbujeante, después de aplicar el dedo o el puño sobre un grifo que funciona a presión. La boca se sitúa muy cerca del chorro de agua, y es muy difícil recibir y retener toda el agua dentro de la boca con una precisión perfecta. El visitante puede elegir entre beber un sorbo de agua fría para refrescarse el paladar o mojarse las manos para refrescarse la cara o la nuca. La aplicación práctica es evidente por sí sola, pero muchos usan la fuente sin tener una necesidad real, como si fuera el gesto de un hombre que se acerca a un desierto y no sabe dónde ni cuándo tendrá la oportunidad de volver a refrescarse.

15. Las tres hélices
Si la primera hélice, al principio de la exposición, representaba el más fuerte de los vientos mediterráneos, el viento del oeste, aquí hay otras tres hélices que nos recuerdan los otros tres puntos cardinales: el este, el sur y el norte. Ícaro y Dédalo habrían necesitado conocer la dirección de los vientos principales, y habrían hecho un minucioso escrutinio de sus distintas fuerzas. Estas tres hélices están situadas en direcciones distintas, de acuerdo con los tres vientos que representan.

16. Las bañeras
Hay un grupo de tres bañeras domésticas de hierro fundido, las tres con agua corriente que sale de unos grifos metálicos. El nivel del agua es siempre el mismo en las tres bañeras: se mantiene constante gracias a un movimiento de afluencia y desagüe que proporciona un equilibrio hidráulico. El ruido del agua que entra y sale tan cómodamente de las bañeras es amplificado, llena el espacio circundante y conjura las incomodidades domésticas. Agua tibia para el cuerpo desnudo. Sumersión plácida. Sin embargo aquí, en este oscuro espacio público, hay un ambiente de incertidumbre: ¿quién entraría aquí

desnudo para tomar un baño? Quizás están en juego varios presagios. Quizás aquí, en este agua, no es posible la relajación soporífera, el descanso en agua tibia: sólo una rápida inmersión del cuerpo desnudo, para lavarlo antes de emprender el vuelo. Como el baño de agua fría que quizás tomaron Ícaro y Dédalo antes del vuelo, para purificarse.

Hay también otras resonancias. Quizás, en otros tiempos, las bañeras habían contenido cera diluida o grasa tibia. Sabemos que los nadadores de larga distancia se cubren el cuerpo con grasa para mantener la temperatura corporal y combatir la irritación que produce el agua del mar.

Quizás fue en un baño de agua caliente donde Dédalo forjó sus ideas inventivas. Dicen que las ideas sobreviven a los que se tumban y sueñan dentro de una bañera. Pensemos, por ejemplo, en Arquímedes: "Un cuerpo total o parcialmente sumergido en un fluido es afectado por una fuerza ascensional igual al peso del fluido desalojado".

Y ¿por qué tres bañeras? ¿Había un tercer volador? ¿Era quizás la decepcionada Ariadna, abandonada por Teseo después de haberlo guiado con éxito a través del laberinto para poder matar al minotauro? Ariadna fue seducida y posteriormente abandonada por Teseo, y finalmente fue recogida por Baco. Pero, ¿y durante el tiempo transcurrido entre una cosa y la otra? ¿Es posible que Ariadna pensara en la posibilidad de huir volando de Creta y de toda su infelicidad? ¿O quizás la tercera bañera estaba destinada a la madre de Ícaro, la esposa de Dédalo, a quien la mitología griega no asigna ningún nombre? Si una mujer hubiera previsto acompañar a Dédalo y a Ícaro, ¿le habría resultado más difícil volar que a un hombre? Quizás tenía menos fuerza, pero también un cuerpo más ligero. ¿Marca alguna diferencia la anatomía femenina? ¿Justifica un cálculo distinto la redistribución del peso en las nalgas, los muslos y los pechos? ¿Es quizás una cuestión de reequilibrio? Los nadadores contemporáneos se afeitan el cuerpo para aumentar su rendimiento aeronáutico: esto, en todo caso, sería una prioridad menor para una mujer.

Y aún cabe hacer otra consideración. Existía el rumor de que Dédalo había matado a su tiránico jefe, el rey Minos, en una bañera de agua hirviendo. Quizás una de estas bañeras sea el arma homicida.

17. Los vientos
En un rincón pequeño y oscuro se encuentra la despensa de los vientos, el espacio donde los vientos incuban hasta alcanzar la madurez. Están los vientos en estado de crisálida, reconocidos por la actividad de cien ventiladores eléctricos que dan vueltas, zumban, ronronean y producen aire en todas direcciones.

Los hombres-pájaro Dédalo e Ícaro habrían necesitado estos pequeños servicios meteorológicos, las variantes térmicas temporales, la elevación provocada por las rocas calientes y la propulsión del aire sobre los mares fríos, la turbulencia desigual del interior de las nubes, las corrientes de viento seco que se originan entre los archipiélagos de rocas y las islas, las súbitas brisas que siguen a las corrientes, las corrientes de aire cálido y húmedo que menguan y crecen con cada pequeña marea mediterránea.

18. Hielo
La historia de Ícaro se basa en un mito poético que sería imposible refutar en los tiempos en que la observación corriente nos decía que, cuanto más nos acercábamos a una fuente de luz, más

aumentaba el calor. La luz y el calor eran necesariamente inseparables. Si nos acercáramos al sol, nos abrasaríamos. ¿Es posible que Dédalo creyera que la luna era una fuente de calor? ¿Es posible que el espíritu de indagación por el que era célebre le indujera a escalar una alta montaña para experimentar cómo el frío aumentaba a medida que él iba subiendo?

Aquí hay dos bloques cúbicos de hielo, uno para cada volador, dos cubos de agua helada, que se derriten lentamente en unas bandejas de zinc que sólo son un poco más anchas que cada bloque de hielo. Se oye el chapoteo del agua que va derritiéndose, gota a gota, dentro del barreño de zinc que está debajo. Son dos centinelas de temperatura cero: bloques de agua congelada, evocadores de los vuelos que se acercan demasiado al polo, o de la impenetrabilidad del agua, o de la hipotermia. Si Ícaro deseaba el extremo opuesto al sol ardiente que derritió sus alas, el hielo podía ser igualmente destructivo: podía congelar la cera hasta que se volviera quebradiza y se desprendiera de las plumas.

19. Huevos
Si sentís el deseo de volar y de que se os asocie con las aves, y no queréis depender de un caballo volador o de la Esfinge, probablemente sujeta al suelo, hay tres potentes caminos mitológicos que podéis seguir. Fabricad unas alas con plumas, igual que Dédalo. Montad encima de un águila, como Ganimedes. O acoplaos con un cisne, tened paciencia y esperad los huevos. Igual que Leda.

Quizás Dédalo consideró esta última opción. No era ajeno a las uniones sexuales atípicas, si tenemos en cuenta su ingeniosa asistencia a Pasífae. ¿Cuántos huevos habría necesitado para criar el número de aves necesario para producir la cantidad adecuada de plumas? Los años de cautividad en Creta le podrían haber dado tiempo suficiente para hacer los cálculos necesarios y convertirse en criador de pollos. Su habilidad verbal habría convencido a Minos de que estaba llevando a cabo un cierto programa de investigación en beneficio de toda Creta, posiblemente en el ámbito militar.

Previendo que Dédalo hubiera podido considerar la posibilidad de utilizar los huevos como solución a su problema, y en honor de Leda, que puso dos huevos blancos en su lecho, aquí hay mil huevos de color blanco (el color de la pureza, el color de las alas de cisne, aunque es dudoso, naturalmente, que esto sean huevos de cisne). Están todos cuidadosamente alineados en dos grandes vitrinas. Quinientos a la izquierda, quinientos a la derecha. Quinientos huevos blancos que se sostienen sobre la parte redondeada más larga, cada uno a la misma distancia de su vecino, quinientos huevos blancos que se sostienen sobre la parte redondeada más corta –al estilo del huevo de Colón–, y también cada uno a la misma distancia de su vecino. Esto plantea dos interrogantes: ¿se puede determinar el sexo de los huevos antes de ser incubados, suponiendo que los huevos que Dédalo quería utilizar tuvieran que ser todos de un mismo sexo? Y el otro interrogante lo plantea la dificultad de describir la geometría de un huevo.

20. Las velas
Las velas se encienden para propiciar buenos augurios. Se enciende una vela para alumbrar el camino. Se encienden para aplacar a los dioses y recordar a los que nos han dejado. En esta exposición imaginaria, las velas se sitúan a medio

camino entre la cera que las ha fabricado y ha creado su forma, su mística y el faro dedaliano, su resultado inevitable. Durante siglos, los arquitectos han construido faros en forma de velas. Queremos que este conjunto de cien velas encendidas representen un centenar de faros. Son una evocación y una guía.

21. El faro

Hay una luz brillante e intermitente que, en alguna parte reducida, consigue deslumbrar y atraer, pero también crear sombras profundas y cegueras repentinas. En estas cegueras repentinas nos mostramos un poco cautelosos respecto a nuestros pies, porque la oscuridad los ha ocultado, y los breves y repentinos océanos de luz brillante que iluminan este mundo de reflejos sobre cristal no permiten que nuestros ojos se acostumbren lo bastante a la oscuridad como para adquirir confianza. Esta sensación vertiginosa deriva de un faro que está bajo el agua y envía un rayo de luz brillante durante dos segundos de cada sesenta.

La luz bajo el agua ejerce una fascinación inevitable. La memoria popular sirve para recordarnos que la luz es caliente y originada por el fuego, y el fuego y el agua no se mezclan; de aquí la idea increíble de un volcán bajo el agua, y de cuestiones como la fosforescencia del mar y la improbabilidad de peces que brillen y fulguren bajo el agua. Pero debemos creer en ello, porque tenemos pruebas. Incluso el agua y la electricidad pueden mezclarse en las condiciones adecuadas.

Esta luz subacuática nos llega a través del espacio subterráneo y submarino, chispeando y reflejándose sobre todas las superficies de cristal; sobre todas las facetas reflectoras. Es una luz brillante, blanca y fría, una señal y al mismo tiempo una advertencia, como todos los faros de línea.

22. El ataúd

Y ahora llegamos al ataúd de Ícaro. Se encuentra en un espacio oscuro, escasamente iluminado. Es un ataúd de madera blanca, empapado de agua y cerrado con armellas. Rezuma un agua burbujeante que corre por sus lados, donde la madera está hinchada a consecuencia del empapamiento perpetuo. El agua mana constantemente por entre los tablones del ataúd, gotea sobre los cantos metálicos de su pedestal y va a parar a un bacín de metal. Desde aquí, el agua es transportada a través de un conducto oscuro y húmedo. Es una imagen de melodrama tenuemente iluminada. Puede recordarnos un automóvil o un pequeño avión rescatado con una grúa de las profundidades de un canal o de un río, o del muelle de un puerto, con el agua que chorrea y el público que lo observa sabiendo que el conductor del automóvil o el piloto del avión sigue sentado en su interior. Aquí, el agua no para nunca de chorrear. Es un chorrear eterno, como una metáfora del agua en el interior de los pulmones de Ícaro que se vacían perpetuamente. Podemos imaginar el cadáver del interior flotando en la salmuera como flotaba en el mar, con su cara pegada contra la tapa del ataúd y sus miembros colgando en aquel espacio reducido.

23. Los cielos

Hay una panorámica del cielo mediterráneo que se extiende desde Sicilia hasta Chipre, desde la tierra hasta la estratosfera superior. Y en este espacio de cielo se proyectan el viento y la meteorología, las tormentas, los rayos, las nubes, la lluvia y los cielos claros y nítidos, desde el azul más oscuro hasta el

más pálido. El movimiento rápido y lento de las nubes, los bancos ondulados de vapor de agua, la condensación moviéndose en forma de comadrejas, de camellos, de ciudades en el cielo, de caballos, de ejércitos, de visiones del futuro, de imágenes del pasado. Cirros, cúmulos, cielos tormentosos, nubes altivas, algodonadas... el cielo rojizo matinal es una advertencia para los pastores, el cielo rojizo nocturno es la delicia de los pastores.

No tenemos la menor idea de los planes de Dédalo, de la hora de su partida, de sus conocimientos de meteorología, de si era consciente de su destinación ni de la duración de su vuelo. El único estímulo era alejarse de Creta, y quizás todo lo demás se explicaría en función de este hecho. Si tenía unos planes concretos, podemos suponer que eran secretos porque no le convenía poner en guardia al rey Minos ni a sus cómplices. Quizás Pasífae sabía cuándo Dédalo había abandonado Creta, acompañado de su hija Ariadna. Hay quien dice que Ariadna sentía afecto por Ícaro, y quizás Ícaro, por lo tanto, se resistía a irse.

No hay, pues, constancia ni del año ni del momento del día o de la noche en que el grupo volador huyó de Creta. Y, en cuanto a la caída de Ícaro, cualquier hora, desde las últimas luces del alba hasta las primeras sombras del crepúsculo, habría sido adecuada para aquel accidente.

El cielo mediterráneo es más constante que los cielos de más al norte, y su famoso color azul está bien documentado. Pero el color azul es un engaño. En realidad el cielo no es azul: es un espejismo, una ilusión, una refracción de la luz. Y el mar refleja el cielo y crea una ilusión combinada que podría haber deslumbrado y embrujado a Ícaro. Rodeado de esta ilusión de azul compuesto, por encima y por debajo, no es extraño que su entusiasmo se intensificara hasta conducirle a la destrucción.

24. Las alas batientes

Ahora nos encontramos ante la pieza más alta de cuantas hemos visto. Descansa sobre el pedestal más alto que hemos visto hasta ahora, y está iluminada con una luz de pulsacions latientes. Son dos alas de plumas blancas tratadas con cera. Fueron diseñadas por Ícaro. Puede que nos encontremos en un tiempo futuro y las alas todavía no se hayan desgastado en el gran vuelo –y, en este caso, podemos considerarlas como un ejercicio de relaciones públicas para desafiar al rey Minos–, o puede que ya estén retiradas y debamos considerarlas como un réquiem. Vistas más de cerca, sin embargo, las correas de piel de los brazos y del torso están aflojadas, y se ven desgastadas y manchadas de grasa, oscurecidas por el sudor de la espalda, entre los omóplatos y las axilas.

Lo primero que pensamos es que han sido extraídas del cadáver de Ícaro. Pero ¿cómo es posible, si el sol había derretido la cera y las plumas se hallaban en un desorden total? ¿Es probable que el afligido Dédalo se hubiera tomado la molestia de reconstruir las alas? Ovidio dice que Dédalo no supo que su hijo se había ahogado hasta que vio las plumas desmembradas flotando en la superficie del mar.

Existe la remota posibilidad de que sean las alas hechas para Ariadna, que declinó la invitación de huir de Creta y de su decepción por haber sido rechazada por Teseo. O bien –posibilidad aún más remota– que fueran las alas diseñadas para la madre de Ícaro, que también había declinado la oferta de levantar el vuelo indecorosamente. Era una gran nadadora, y volar es una forma de nadar por los

aires, y sabía que la propulsión a base de abrir y cerrar los muslos era indecorosa, y no tenía ningún deseo de atraer las miradas impúdicas de los pastores y los labradores que ganduleaban por las laderas de Naxos, de Paros o de Delos.

Quizás, entonces, la única conclusión acertada es que se trata de las alas de Dédalo, que fueron encontradas en la ladera de alguna colina de las afueras de Nápoles, donde Dédalo las había abandonado. Sin embargo, aquí podemos experimentar auténticamente la presencia de la tragedia y de la gloria de Ícaro en la contemplación de estas alas de plumas. Podemos estar seguros de que son los prototipos de alas, las primeras alas, porque sin duda Dédalo debió de fabricar sus propias alas en primer lugar, para poner a prueba sus posibilidades, como cualquier piloto-diseñador, antes de considerar que su hijo pudiera jugarse la vida.

25. La sala de autopsias

Después del accidente, *post mortem*, tiene que haber una autopsia. La investigación es secreta. Esta es la segunda muerte de un niño con quien Dédalo ha sido asociado. Y ambas muertes han estado relacionadas con la gravedad. Si Dédalo es un asesino de niños, entonces la gravedad es su sello personal. La primera muerte fue la de su sobrino, arrojado desde lo alto del precipicio de la Acrópolis. Dédalo dijo que había sido un accidente, pero todo el mundo sabía que estaba celoso del hijo de su hermana, que había inventado la sierra, el compás y el torno de cerámica.

Quizás la sala de autopsias original de Ícaro estaba en la isla de Icaria, en el mar Egeo, donde Dédalo llevó el cadáver rescatado del mar. El cuerpo no podía haber estado mucho tiempo en el agua. No podía haber tumescencia, ni hinchazón, ni mordiscos de peces, ni cardenales causados por los golpes contra las rocas. El cuerpo debió de haber sido colocado sobre una superficie metálica, y su carne rociada con agua fría para limpiarlo de la última cera que se había derretido y había goteado, para endurecerse de nuevo al congelarse con el contacto frío del agua del mar.

La sala de autopsias tiene una entrada limitada. No es cuestión de que todo el mundo vaya pasando por aquí fisgando, husmeando, comportándose como buitres ante la víctima de lo que Dédalo insiste que fue un accidente doméstico. Hay muchos niños que se ahogan. Es de sobra conocida su exuberancia en el agua, su tendencia a arriesgarse, a lucirse, a portarse mal, a ponerse a prueba. Dédalo mantiene un silencio estricto sobre los aspectos de esas cosas relacionados con el vuelo. Es demasiado difícil de explicar, incluso al patólogo forense, y sin duda al oficial de justicia.

Está la habitual colección de muebles para un sitio así: la superficie plateada de la misma longitud que un cuerpo humano, el hielo triturado que va derritiéndose poco a poco en una bandeja de plata. Si guardamos un silencio absoluto podemos oír como el hielo va derritiéndose, goteando lentamente en un desagüe oculto. El hielo es para conservar fresco el cuerpo del ausente. La superficie metálica es para que el cuerpo descanse sobre ella mientras extraemos el agua marina de sus pulmones.

Están las batas de goma habituales, los guantes de goma habituales, los cubos de aluminio... tres de los cuales están limpios e impecables, y el cuarto contiene un desinfectante de un verde amarillento que desprende un olor muy fuerte, el quinto contiene un líquido ambiguo que quizás podría ser... ¿qué? ¿Sangre diluida de la hemorragia de la cabeza al chocar contra el agua o agua de mar extraída del estómago?

Todas las demás pruebas circunstanciales sugerentes las proporciona inconscientemente la luz, una luz que reproduce el mar y el cielo. A nuestros pies y debajo de ellos, el suelo se riza y refracta con unas sombras de un verde-azul acuoso, como una marea constante que lava el fondo rocoso y poco profundo del mar. Las cuatro paredes, hasta muy por encima de nuestras cabezas, están punteadas con la luz azul y pálida de un cielo parcialmente oculto a intervalos por las sombras de las nubes que pasan silenciosamente y sin culpa por encima del mar que se insinúa a nuestros pies.

26. Los huesos de aves

Huesos de aves. Esto es un osario de aves. Quizás están representadas diez mil aves, con sus esqueletos blanqueados por la salmuera y por el sol, aparecidos en playas, arrastrados desde el mar hasta la costa, desenterrados de campos labrados. Cuando las aves mueren, ¿cuántas de ellas caen súbitamente del cielo? Esto es un cementerio de aves, la prueba de que quien una vez voló confiado, ahora ha regresado a la tierra, donde yace sin vida.

El arqueópterix. Ese es el molde de un ave primitiva; o, por decirlo más exactamente, la huella en piedra calcárea de un animal que era mitad reptil y mitad pájaro. Los reptiles no desaparecieron, sino que se metamorfosearon en aves. Podemos ver fácilmente, con el ojo de la mente, las escamas y los pequeños ojos, las garras de las patas, el pico afilado. Pero, naturalmente, este cambio fue lentísimo. Hicieron falta millones de años para convertir un pequeño dinosaurio en una golondrina, en un albatros, en un estornino, en un buitre, en un colibrí. ¿Es Ícaro el patético intento del hombre de repetir una metamorfosis de este tipo? ¿Cómo esperaba el hombre poder consumar un cambio tan prodigioso en Grecia, en una sola tarde?

27. El chorro de orina

Hay una vitrina aislada que nos presenta algo distinto: en su interior, entre las cuatro paredes de cristal, un chorro espiral de orina sale disparado, descontrolado, mientras el cuerpo de Ícaro, muy por encima de nuestras cabezas, cae para siempre sin aterrizar, orinándose a causa de un temor y un pánico interminables, incontinentes y humillantes.

Es un síntoma del accidente en tiempo presente, que señala perpetuamente el miedo, tal como lo ilustró Rembrandt en el niño Ganimedes, un hecho propenso a darnos una idea del vuelo voluntario.

Se trata de una serpiente de orina flagelante, que moja el cristal en su retorcimiento azaroso y nos agrede a nosotros, el público, porque, a no ser por el cristal protector, sin duda no podríamos esquivar los azotes espirales del líquido, lleno del amoníaco maculante del miedo.

28. La última pierna

Aquí está la última pierna de Ícaro. Una pierna rescatada del choque mortal contra el agua, libre de la humedad y del empapamiento, sobre un pedestal de mármol e iluminada por una luz cálida. Una extremidad masculina de bronce, desde el muslo hasta los dedos de los pies. Es elegante y sensual. Una magnífica pierna de bronce procedente de la colección de bronces clásicos del Louvre. Es la pierna de Ícaro.

Conservada en bronce con una pátina verdosa y erosionada por el mar, es la última imagen que

se ve del joven mientras desaparece entre las aguas saladas del mar Egeo. Es la última instantánea fotográfica de Ícaro reconstruida en metal. La última visión bruegeliana de un héroe incipiente. Nuestra última visión del primer héroe mortal que voló sobre el agua.

29. La gran zambullida

Para ofrecer la penúltima prueba de la historia de Ícaro, aquí nos encontramos con la gran zambullida que indica la entrada de Ícaro en el mar.

¿Qué es lo que podemos recrear de la muerte de Ícaro? ¿Algún tipo de investigación fraudulenta de "hombre-al-agua" sin un cadáver, y sólo con litros y litros de agua de mar? No hay mucho que reconstruir. Pero podemos medir su muerte a partir del impacto de un cuerpo sobre el agua. Podemos intentar medir su choque mortal. Bruegel lo hizo, y le pareció insuficiente.

Hay un espacio oscuro, una especie de galería o callejón trasero donde se reconstruye la fatalidad de Ícaro. Es una zona oscura centrada en un acuario tenebroso de grandes dimensiones. El suelo de cemento está mojado. Aquí sería posible torturar delfines, o matar ballenas, o arrancar los caparazones a tortugas vivas, o, como mínimo, tener cangrejos con las pinzas atadas con alambres, más muertos que vivos y preparados para ser escaldados sobre los fogones de la cocina. Nos llega el olor del vapor de hervir los cangrejos. Podemos sentir la peligrosa combinación de agua y electricidad, quizás la electricidad de la energía estática, de la fricción entre un cuerpo desnudo y el aire, mientras Ícaro cae a gran velocidad a través del cielo egeo, como un meteorito que se quema antes de la zambullida final en medio de espuma y vapor.

Intentaremos recrear la enorme zambullida de Ícaro al entrar en el mar vacío. Con un movimiento súbito e irregular, saliendo de la oscuridad, las aguas se remueven violentamente, chorros de agua blanca suben por los altos costados de un acuario oscuro y cuadrado... unos chorros iluminados sincronizadamente con luz blanca.

Y cada uno es registrado y contabilizado para comparaciones posteriores.

Este es un territorio hockneyano, pero las zambullidas de Hockney estaban controladas dentro de los límites de una piscina. Sus zambullidas eran las de unos hombres jóvenes que controlaban su caída y su entrada en el agua, y al mismo tiempo buscaban el éxtasis; sus zambullidas no eran sólo a cámara lenta, sino en imágenes separadas e inmovilizadas que proporcionaban una evidencia imposible de conocer y de comprobar antes de la invención de la fotografía. La gran zambullida de la caída de Ícaro pintada por Bruegel y la de la fotografía de 1911 del joven Lartigue son muy parecidas: la única prueba del cuerpo rompiendo contra la superficie del agua, en ambos casos, son dos piernas y dos pies desnudos rodeados de agua burbujeante y espumosa. Y con eso ya hay bastante.

Nunca puede haber dos zambullidas idénticas. Pensemos en cuántas ha habido en la historia de los mares y los lagos y los ríos de la Tierra, y limitemos este número al de las ocasionadas por la caída de un cuerpo humano. Limitémonos aún más a las zambullidas de un cuerpo masculino. Dejemos a un lado a Safo cayendo al mar Egeo y a Hero cayendo en el Helesponto, a Ofelia cayendo dentro del Avon y a Virginia Woolf cayendo dentro del Ouse. ¿Puede determinarse el sexo de una zambullida? Y aún quedan decenas de millares de zambullidas por considerar. Las de los hijos de Medea dentro del

Egeo, la de Pedro en el mar de Galilea, la de César en el Rubicón, la de Barbarroja en su pequeño riachuelo, la de Clarence dentro de su barril de malvasía, las de los esclavos arrojados al Caribe, las de los amantes desesperados que se han arrojado al Sena desde el Pont Neuf, la de Shelley ahogándose en el mar, cerca de Leghorn, las de los judíos empujados al Danubio helado desde el puente colgante de Budapest.

Así, volando hacia el noroeste desde Creta, los dos hombres, o el hombre y el niño, según la edad que decidamos asignar a Ícaro, vuelan por encima de Samos, probablemente por encima de los árboles y los campos de Delos y de los pueblos de Paros, sus sombras duales ya sobre el océano, ya sobre la tierra. En algún lugar sobre el mar, cerca de la isla que después tomó su nombre, Ícaro, disfrutando plenamente del placer de la altura, de sentirse superior a las pequeñas figuras sobre la tierra –como Orson Welles en *El tercer hombre*–, deleitándose en el poder de observar el mundo en miniatura, una posición tan sólo adivinada en la antigua Grecia, porque, ¿quién había podido observar la tierra hasta entonces desde aquella altura?... Ícaro desobedeció a su padre, se acercó demasiado al sol y la cera se derritió, y las plumas se despegaron y finalmente se desprendieron. Y cayó.

¿Cayó a la tierra en picado, en línea recta, o en una trayectoria curva causada por la combinación de la gravedad con su movimiento previo hacia delante? ¿Cayó al mar de cabeza, o dando una violenta panzada de una altura tan impresionante? ¿O es que realmente cayó de cabeza, como si en el último momento, como un gato que cae con dignidad, hubiese podido romper la superficie del agua entrando primero la cabeza y las manos para hacer un último gesto humano de elegancia? ¿Una magnífica zambullida final de categoría olímpica?

En esta exposición están las posibles zambullidas de Ícaro al chocar contra el mar de Icaria. Si sólo ofreciéramos una, ¿cómo podríamos incluir la posibilidad de una zambullida que pudiera coincidir con la original? Pero las podemos ofrecer inmovilizadas. Cada zambullida simulada por un cuerpo que cae y pesa sesenta kilos, el peso medio de un europeo de diecisiete años, choca repetidamente contra el agua. Y cada vez podemos inmovilizar el contacto. Creamos un gran número de zambullidas para que el visitante decida cuál es la más probable gran zambullida final de Ícaro. Cada zambullida es diferente. Cada una es otra candidata posible a reproducir la zambullida original de Ícaro, la que puso fin a la primera aventura aérea del hombre.

30. El marco de bienvenida

Supongamos que Ícaro no hubiese caído ni se hubiese ahogado. Supongamos que hubiese tenido el buen sentido de obedecer la advertencia de su padre, y que hubiera sido ciertamente el primer piloto pero no el primer accidente aéreo de la historia de la humanidad. Entonces podríamos esperar que esta exposición tuviera un final optimista, que acabara con una rúbrica benévola.

En el exterior, en el jardín de esta exposición, se encuentra el montaje para un regreso triunfal de Ícaro a la tierra.

Primero hay un pedazo de cielo enmarcado mirando hacia el este, hacia Grecia, para situar su amerizaje desde las nubes. Podemos sentarnos a esperar el regreso de Ícaro, mientras miramos el rectángulo de cielo por encima de la ciudad. En la naturaleza son muy insólitos –o quizás inexistentes– los marcos rectangulares. Nuestro marco es un ingenio lo bastante familiar como para que desde lejos parezca una zona de aterrizaje preparada para un helicóptero, una zona que ofrece un puerto de bienvenida, como en el caso de las palomas que vuelven a casa. El marco es un ingenio artificial, creado durante el Renacimiento en relación con las circunstancias de la arquitectura, y actualmente gobierna un gran número de construcciones artísticas: la pintura, el teatro con su proscenio rectangular, la fotografía, el cine y ahora la televisión y todos sus primos. Aquí se utiliza para presenciar el regreso de un héroe.

En segundo lugar hay una plataforma de aterrizaje, para que Ícaro ponga de nuevo los pies en el suelo después de haber pasado tanto tiempo en el aire.

Y en tercer lugar hay un comité de bienvenida representado por cien asientos, filas y filas de asientos para que el paciente visitante de la exposición pueda sentarse y finalmente aplaudir el regreso de Ícaro.

Epílogo

UNA HISTORIA PERSONAL DEL CIELO Y DEL AGUA

La primera experiencia aérea que recuerdo es dramática, pero sólo retrospectivamente. Yo tenía ocho años, y el acontecimiento fue un accidente de avión. Era una exhibición aérea, con un cielo de tarde lleno de surcos de humo azul, blanco y rosado que salían de unos aviones que volaban a poca altura. El hecho de que un reactor nuevo y muy rápido echara un humo negro no pareció ningún mal presagio. El piloto de pruebas cayó después de haber volado muy bajo por encima de las cabezas de la gente. ¿Exhibición o accidente? La opinión general fue que el piloto había querido lucirse. Quizás era un veredicto inventado sólo para mí. Muchos años después, supe que dos pilotos se habían matado. El aeródromo era uno de los varios centenares que habían sido construidos precipitadamente durante la guerra en el sur y el este de Inglaterra; ése, concretamente, estaba en North Weald (Essex), a unos cincuenta kilómetros de Londres. El noventa por ciento de estos aeoródromos han sido reconvertidos en tierras de pasto y en campos de cultivo de trigo o de colza, y hace ya tiempo que han perdido la capacidad de producir terror o emoción. Los hangares, las naves y la torre de control de North Weald se alquilan para rodar películas. *The Cook, the Thief, His Wife and her Lover* ('El cocinero, el ladrón, su mujer y su amante') casi fue rodada allí.

Probablemente, la primera imagen fabricada de Ícaro que recuerdo es el *Ícaro* de Michael Ayrton, en la Tate Gallery de Londres. Yo tenía doce años, y era a mediados de los cincuenta. Este Ícaro era más un relieve que una pintura. Estaba protegido tras un cristal y era muy frágil, y estaba hecho con espinas de pescado y cera blanca. La fragilidad subrayaba la moraleja de la historia: las espinas sugerían huesos de reptiles y, como yo era un niño muy aficionado a los dinosaurios y mi padre tenía una auténtica obsesión por la ornitología, nos encontramos en terreno común alrededor del fósil de arqueópterix, que se suponía que era el animal de transición entre el reptil y el pájaro, posteriormente considerado

ideal para las metamorfosis ovidianas. Reconociendo con ironía la fascinación que sentía por el fósil, se convirtió en una fijación para el personaje de Agostina Fallmut, en la Biografía 71 de la película *The Falls*, de 1978.

Antes de la aparición del Hecho Violento Desconocido que es la base de *The Falls*, Agostina Fallmut había empezado su carrera en la investigación ornitológica como biógrafa oficial del doctor Friedrich Karl Haberlein, el oficial médico del distrito de Pappenheim. Haberlein era el famoso descubridor de los primeros restos fosilizados del primitivo pájaro reptil arqueópterix. En la primera página de la biografía de Haberlein, Agostina había escrito:

"¿Cuál de los dos objetos siguientes fue impelido y después ahogado en un vendaval en el lago Solnhoffen: el doctor Friedrich Haberlein o el arqueópterix?"

La fijación continuaba en 1992, cuando fue posible incluir uno de los tres fósiles de arqueópterix austríacos originales en la exposición del Hofburg vienés "Cien objetos para representar al mundo".

Este fósil puede representar a todos los fósiles, puede representar a la transición evolutiva, la paleontología y la metamorfosis, la revolucionaria teoría de Darwin sobre la transmutación, toda la ornitología y las ciencias biológicas investigadoras. Puede representar a todos los restos fosilizados que configuran la historia regional del mundo, una gota de agua en una inundación. Puede representar al tiempo mismo y a la disminución de la autoestima en el hombre. Es ciertamente una imagen potente del carácter efímero de cualquier especie.

Un arqueópterix e Ícaro coincidieron en Viena, en una exposición conjunta donde se instalaron cien cuadros de las colecciones vienesas en un orden sugerido por la iconografía de la concepción, el nacimiento, el matrimonio y la muerte, en un tratamiento inusual de la asociación entre Ícaro y Dédalo que se centraba más en el aspecto paterno-filial que en el drama del vuelo.

Mientras daba a Ícaro las instrucciones sobre la forma de volar, Dédalo, al mismo tiempo, ataba las alas recién construidas a los hombros de su hijo. Mientras trabajaba y hablaba, las mejillas del viejo se llenaban de lágrimas, y el afecto paterno hacía temblar sus manos. Besó a su hijo, a quien no volvería a ver nunca más. Esta relación paterno-filial de orgullo, de culpa y de dolor planea a lo largo de toda la exposición, y originó el guión de una ópera representada en Estrasburgo en 1994.

Volviendo a la escultura de Michael Ayrton en la Tate Gallery, las espinas de pescado incrustadas en la cera con las que se construyó eren elegantemente autoreflexivas, pues era precisamente la cera derretida lo que había provocado la caída de Ícaro, y, habiendo descubierto la versión ovidiana del mito de Ícaro un tiempo después, vi claramente que Ayrton había asociado los materiales no sólo con Ícaro sino con la muerte, en manos de Dédalo, de su sobrino y rival por haber inventado la sierra después de observar la espina de un pez.

Mientras Dédalo enterraba el cuerpo de Ícaro, una avefría gorjeante agitaba sus alas y cacareaba de alegría. En aquella época era el único pájaro de su especie, y nunca se había visto otro igual. La transformación se había

producido recientemente, y era un reproche perdurable dirigido a Dédalo; porque su hermana había enviado a su hijo, un chico inteligente de doce años, a aprender todo lo que Dédalo pudiera enseñarle. Este niño, observando la espina de un pez y adoptándolo como modelo, melló una serie de dientes en una hoja de hierro afilada e inventó la sierra. Fue también el primero que juntó dos brazos de hierro de tal forma que, mientras se mantenían equidistantes, un brazo quedaba inmóvil y el otro describía un círculo a su alrededor. Dédalo, celoso, había arrojado a su sobrino desde lo alto del precipicio de la Acrópolis, y después difundió la falsa noticia de que el chico se había caído. Pero Palas lo recogió mientras caía, lo convirtió en un pájaro y lo vistió con plumas mientras estaba suspendido en el vacío. La agilidad intelectual que demostrado hasta entonces fue reemplazada por la agilidad en las alas y en los pies. Conservó el mismo nombre de antes. Este pájaro, sin embargo, no acaba de levantar el vuelo ni anida en las ramas de las copas de los árboles: más bien aletea a ras de suelo y pone sus huevos en las vallas de los prados, porque recuerda su caída en el pasado y le dan miedo las alturas.

A través de Ayrton, un erudito griego también obsesivamente fascinado por el minotauro, descubrí la obra del escultor francés César. Yo era un estudiante de arte recién licenciado, interesado por la soldadura de los metales. Admiraba los Ícaros de metal oxidado de César e intenté imitarlos. Hace poco vi uno en Hong Kong, durante el rodaje de *The Pillow Book* ('El libro de cabecera'), bajo un sol de justicia que hacía que el metal de la única ala se calentara tanto que, como suele decirse, allí se podía freír un huevo, y sin duda derretir una vela, una auténtica demostración asociativa de la humilde fragilidad de la cera de abeja bajo la acción del sol.

Al célebre Ícaro de Bruegel debí de verlo poco después, en los Musées Royaux des Beaux-Arts de Bruselas. Las *Ways of Seeing* ('Maneras de ver') de John Berger realzaban el carácter efímero de la caída de Ícaro, y –quizás lo más importante para mí, porque me angustiaba la idea decepcionante de que el noventa por ciento de todas las pinturas fueran ilustraciones de textos– subrayaba inequívocamente la influencia directa que Ovidio ha tenido en la imaginación de los pintores; el Ícaro de Bruegel es una transposición ilustrativa exacta del texto de Ovidio, línea por línea, imagen por imagen. ... Un pescador, quizás, sosteniendo su caña temblorosa, un pastor apoyado en su bastón, o un campesino inclinado sobre el mango de su arado, les vieron pasar volando.

Más adelante vino la imagen icariana de Herbert Draper, que convertía el mito en un drama sentimentalizado y en una fantasía victoriana, pero aquí, por primera vez, quizás puede verse, en una imagen idealizada, una interpretación visual del tamaño de alas necesario para considerar mínimamente posible que los humanos podamos volar, y eso puede hacernos pensar en el ingenio que se necesita para fabricar unas alas. También sugería la posibilidad de que Ícaro no se hubiera ahogado, sino que hubiera caído sobre unas rocas. Podría haber muerto a causa del impacto contra el agua. Podría haber muerto a causa de la contusión, y no porque sus pulmones se hubieran llenado de agua. Es concebible que la imagen de Draper sugiriera que el cadáver había sido arrastrado hasta la playa por una subida de la marea. A la imagen de Draper, yo, por lo menos, le agradecí que no hubiera transpuesto servilmente a Ovidio una vez más.

El interés por el mito de Ícaro se hizo extensivo a otras aventuras exactamente coincidentes con la fascinación de Ovidio por la metamorfosis. Primero se centró ornitológicamente en la pasión de Leda por Júpiter-cisne y en los productos incubados por Leda –Cástor y Pólux, Helena y Clitemestra–, y después, más generalmente, en ideas ovidianas más amplias sobre metamorfosis de proles de progenitores mezclados creadas por aparente bestialidad para concebir la Esfinge, el centauro, la sirena, la quimera, las arpías y la gorgona y adiciones más recientes, como el hombre-lobo y el vampiro, y también Batman y Spiderman. ¿Se trata de fantasías masculinas universales de violaciones en las que la madre del bastardo es siempre la hembra humana, o está ciertamente más en consonancia con el deseo del hombre de adquirir la fuerza, las cualidades y las características del padre animal? La imaginación contemporánea, sobre todo en el cine, se ha desplazado, en general, de la paternidad animal a la paternidad tecnológica, en una raza muy variada de híbridos robóticos hombre-máquina en los que la poderosa inteligencia mecánica de la computadora y la enorme fuerza de las máquinas de metal, en cierto modo, cohabitan con los humanos. Pero, incluso después de películas como *Alien*, *Hal*, *Judge Dred* y *Terminator*, quizás no hay nada todavía que provoque una mezcla tan horrible de atracción y culpa respecto a estas uniones entre especies distintas como la criatura de otra parte de la mitología Dédalo-Ícaro: el minotauro, monstruo carnívoro, caníbal, de enorme falo y devorador de vírgenes que vive en el eterno sótano laberíntico, el hijo de Pasífae y del toro cretense por medio de un disfraz de vaca hecho por el alcahuete Dédalo. Quizás no deberíamos olvidar que no se trata de un accidente tan aislado como pueda parecer, porque el marido de Pasífae, el mismo rey Minos, era el producto de la violación de Europa por un toro que era Júpiter disfrazado con unos cuernos y unos atributos sexuales apropiados para este acto concreto de lascivia. Es curioso que Pasífae hubiera intentado emular a su suegra.

La mayor parte de mis conocimientos sobre aves auténticas procede de las pasiones ornitológicas de mi padre. De niño creía que todo el mundo sabía tanto de aves como él, y me sorprendía que hubiera gente incapaz de reconocer a un pájaro por su forma de cantar, o de distinguir a una foja de una polla de agua. Yo me resistía directamente a la insistencia de los conocimientos de mi padre, pero asimilé la información incluso de forma involuntaria. Cuando murió y vi hasta qué punto su aguda capacidad de observación había muerto con él (no era un erudito tradicional, y registraba sus observaciones básicamente en la memoria y sólo muy de vez en cuando en los márgenes de libros de ornitología), hice primero la película *A Walk Through H* y después *The Falls*, las dos, sin duda, compendios de saber popular sobre aves al servicio de conspiraciones teóricas y de una excentricidad general. *The Falls* está llena de imágenes voladoras: la ambición de volar, aves, plumas, aeronáutica..., y constata muchas figuras icarianas. Hay una, sobre todo, que ejerció en mí una fascinación muy superior a todas las demás: la trágica y patética figura de Richfeldt, el sastre bajito que cosió unas alas-paracaídas y se lanzó a una muerte segura desde la torre Eiffel. Le filmaron mientras caía, y los tres minutos resultantes de la filmación son

un ejemplo conmovedor de un hombre fachendoso hasta el límite, que se obliga a sí mismo a ser valiente ante la cámara. No podía rajarse. Finalmente salta, y naturalmente, a pesar del movimiento frenético de sus brazos, cae en picado hasta los pies de la torre y hace un hoyo de un metro y medio de largo en la grava del Campo de Marte.

En *The Falls* se llevaron a cabo varias investigaciones de conspiraciones de aves a base de analizar el pobre y poco satisfactorio final de la película *Los pájaros*, de Hitchcock. Y había interpretaciones cabalísticas de diversas enumeraciones de aves en el cine. La lista es muy larga, y entre otras figurarían *The Raven* ('El cuervo'), *Kes*, *The Two-Headed Eagle* ('El águila de dos cabezas'), *Only Angels Have Wings* ('Sólo los ángeles tienen alas'), *Caged Heat* ('Calor enjaulado', estrenada en España con el título de *Cárcel caliente*), *Blackbird* ('El mirlo', estrenada en España con el título de *Maldad encubierta*), *Sparrows Can't Sing* ('Los gorriones no pueden cantar'), *Three Days of the Condor*, ('Los tres días del cóndor'), *Jonathan Livingstone Seagull* ('Juan Salvador Gaviota'), *Birdie*, *The Owl and the Pussycat* ('La gatita y el búho'), *Where Eagles Dare* ('Donde sólo llegan las águilas', estrenada en España con el título de *El desafío de las águilas*), *The Yellow Canary* ('El canario amarillo'), *Birdman of Alcatraz* ('El hombre-pájaro de Alcatraz', estrenada en España con el título de *El hombre de Alcatraz*), *The Four Feathers* ('Las cuatro plumas') y *The Maltese Falcon* ('El halcón maltés'). También se ha buscado una significación especial en nombres botánicos regionales: *bird's-foot trefoil* (lit. 'trébol de pie de pájaro'), *henbane* (beleño, lit. 'veneno de gallina'), *chickweed* (hierba pajarera), *sparrowgrass* (lit. 'hierba de gorrión'), etc. Audubon tenía que ser uno de los protagonistas de esta película. Y ciertamente, las criaturas voladoras, desde Ganimedes y Faetón hasta los hermanos Wright, Yuri Gagarin, Montgolfier, Amy Johnson, Lindbergh y Saint-Exupéry, tenían que ser iconos. Había otros muchos intereses obsesivos menores, como una fascinación por ciertos proverbios, chistes, lenguaje infantil, títulos de canciones y juegos de palabras en general de la lengua inglesa: "*A bird in the hand is worth two in the bush*" ('Más vale pájaro en mano que ciento volando'), "*One shallow doesn't make a summer*" (lit. 'Una golondrina no hace verano'), "*Why did the chicken cross the road*" (lit. 'Por qué cruzó el camino el pollo'), "*Who killed cock-robin*" (lit. 'Quién mató al petirrojo'), "*Bye-bye blackbird*" (lit. 'Adiós mirlo'), *cock-a-hoop* (lit. 'saltar como un gallo'), *hen-pecked* (lit. 'pico de gallina'), *cock of the roost* (lit. 'el gallo del gallinero'). Se reservó un lugar especial a la pluma que sostiene en su mano el Marat muerto del cuadro de David, para evocar las ambigüedades del dicho inglés "*the pen is mightier than the sword*" ('la pluma es más poderosa que la espada') y desarrollarlo con adivinanzas de cosecha propia para realzar la supremacía de las aves: "Si la pluma sirve para escribir, ¿es más poderosa la pluma que la espada?".

Para mí, *The Falls* fue un punto decisivo en mi trayectoria: contenía numerosos hechos, ideas, conceptos y ambiciones que desde entonces he expandido y desarrollado. La estructura consiste en 92 biografías fílmicas enlazadas, y el contenido es el análisis de un Hecho Violento Desconocido que afecta a unos trece millones de personas de la Europa noroccidental y las metamorfosea, como mínimo, de 92 formas distintas. Las conclusiones se dejan deliberadamente abiertas, pero hay pruebas suficientes para poder relacionar el hecho con las

aves y con la pretenciosa ambición de volar. Pero la película es también un análisis irónico de todas las maneras en que podría acabarse el mundo, y no es del todo irrelevante que el 92 sea el número atómico del uranio. Cuando se hizo la película, entre 1978 y 1980, había un total convencimiento de que la bomba atómica podía ser lanzada –y posiblemente lo sería– desde el aire el día más inesperado, y que las agresiones de la guerra fría, los antagonismos de la carrera espacial y el coste descomunal de la defensa agresiva se materializarían en la solución final de un desastre que vendría del cielo.

Agua, nadar y ahogarse

La otra referencia potente, la otra imagen que siempre se repite en muchos de mis proyectos cinematográficos de los últimos veinte años, es el agua.

Así como hubo un accidente aéreo dramático presenciado personalmente cuando tenía pocos años, también hubo una asociación con un ahogamiento dramático. Pero, al igual que antes, no puedo decir que el hecho participara directamente en la creación de una obsesión continuada. El ahogamiento tuvo lugar en el estanque de Eagle Park (el parque del Águila) –un nombre que no deja de tener sus resonancias aéreas–, en Wanstead, al este de Londres, cuando un amigo de la escuela flotaba en el lago sobre una puerta de madera barnizada, con su pomo, su cerradura e incluso su buzón. La puerta se dio la vuelta y él se ahogó. Tenía once años. Durante mucho tiempo, cada vez que yo tocaba una puerta barnizada lo hacía con una veneración especial.

Aunque hay unas seis películas anteriores a ésta, la primera película pública que aún sigo dispuesto a exhibir con entusiasmo es *Intervals*, un experimento formal sobre la operación de contar, las *reprises* y las repeticiones, y en el que se construye una banda sonora con una serie de imágenes idénticas. Las imágenes son de Venecia, la ciudad que estoy seguro que representa, en el pensamiento, la memoria y la imaginación de casi todo el mundo, la vida sobre el agua y la ciudad en el mar; pero en esta película, perversamente, no hay ni una sola imagen de agua, aunque su presencia e influencia son constantes fuera de la pantalla.

Hay un filme inacabado que se titula *The Sea* ('El mar'), estrechamente vinculado al *Gesang der Jugend* de Stockhausen; un filme terminado sobre la erosión costera titulado simplemente *Erosion*, rodado en la costa de Cork; un filme completado titulado *Five Postcards from Capital Cities* ('Cinco postales desde varias capitales'), en el que aparecen cinco puertos –todos muy distintos entre sí–: el de Rotterdam, el de Amsterdam, el de Goole, el de Londres y el de Newport; un documental titulado *Coastline* ('Línea costera'), realizado por encargo del COI, y muchos proyectos relacionados con el agua en diversos estadios de realización, algunos de los cuales vieron brevemente la luz pública porque eran citados en *The Falls*. *Dreams of Water* ('Sueños de agua') intentaba, de un modo extremo y con técnicas del absurdo, hacer un estudio estadístico de lo efímero, categorizar los sueños de agua de la gente. *The Water-Woman* ('La mujer de agua') era un filme que parodiaba los intentos de Millais de pintar a su amante en el papel de Ofelia dentro de una bañera, en el jardín trasero de su casa. Parte del material escrito para esta idea fue elaborado en la Biografía 18 de *The Falls*, la biografía de Aptesia Fallarme.

Tulse Luper, un personaje de la película, con su imparcialidad habitual, ha dejado escrito que

Aptesia era "una cascada humana", y Majority Powels, otro personaje, ha escrito una afectuosa monografía que tiene más de ficción que de realidad. Dice Powels:

"Aptesia es una criatura ideada para prestar los servicios de un oasis. Con la producción de sus glándulas podría llenar una bañera templada de porcelana en veinte minutos. Si la bañera es de hojalata se tarda un poco más. Llenar una bañera fría de hojalata en menos de una hora requiere algunos incentivos, como una vista del mar, o pensar en una vaca mientras la están ordeñando, o ver a diez hombres anchos de pecho expectorando".

Y Leo-dee-nine dice:

"Cuando ella estaba excitada, el agua chorreaba por su piel, por las comisuras de la boca, por la nariz. En cuanto a los orificios más especializados en la expulsión de agua, el público no solía quedar decepcionado... y, en los pequeños cuartos de baño de los barrios periféricos, el agua se derramaba sobre la moqueta. La gente aplaudía y echaba monedas en la bañera. En verano, le pedían que se pusiera de pie sobre los claros del césped del jardín".

Hay un estudio fílmico titulado *Shower* ('Ducha'), una deliberación sobre el libro extraordinariamente desinhibido de Alexander Kira sobre la ergonomía del cuarto de baño, que demuestra, muy explícitamente y con una salacidad considerable, el orden exacto y el equipamiento con el que la gente excreta y mictura, se ducha, se limpia, se baña y se cepilla los dientes. Hay una película titulada simplemente *Water* ('Agua') que contiene exactamente mil imágenes de agua, y fue rodada en los deliciosos paisajes de los Brecon Beacons de Gales –una lánguida y agradable experiencia– para apreciar la complacencia absolutamente exuberante del sol sobre el agua.

La filmografía pública incluye *Water-Wrackets*, una irónica historia antropológica de animales míticos que colonizan violentamente una cuenca acuática auténtica de Wiltshire; *26 Bathrooms* ('26 cuartos de baño'), una especie de diccionario, aparentemente arquitectónico, de las excentricidades de los ingleses en el cuarto de baño, la segunda habitación más pequeña de una casa inglesa; *Death in the Seine* ('Muerte en el Sena'), una crónica de cadáveres rescatados del Sena justo después de la Revolución Francesa, y *Making a Splash* ('Zambullirse'), un homenaje a la natación sincronizada.

De forma accidental o deliberada, la preocupación por el agua continúa con un proyecto actual commemorativo del recién inaugurado puente Erasmus de Rotterdam, que curiosamente une cielo y agua y constituye un complemento muy apropiado a esta exposición de Barcelona sobre Ícaro, cuya inauguración coincidirá aproximadamente con el estreno de la película en Holanda.

Los largometrajes narrativos seguían explotando las delicias y peligros literales del agua como tema dramático, como subtexto metafórico y por la pura belleza fotogénica que demuestra de forma tan fácil, eficaz y fiable.

Dos cuerpos ahogados son sacados del foso de una mansión aristocrática en *El contrato del dibujante*: el primero proporciona el punto medio de la estructura y el segundo el final estratégico de la película, y, en su *reprise* exacta, indican exactamente quién era el responsable de los dos asesinatos. Hay alusiones a estos efectos teatrales acuáticos que

se proclaman a menudo en las historias de agua contadas por los personajes secundarios de la película.

"Hace unos cuantos años, dos señores regresaron a Amsterdam diciendo que Allhevinghay era igual que su país, por la gran cantidad de agua, estanques ornamentales, canales, fregaderos y jofainas que había. Incluso había una bomba eólica. Lo que les pasó por alto fue que mi padre había llenado sus tierras de depósitos de agua porque el fuego le producía terror. Había incluso una habitación bajo las escaleras de la entrada que contenía doscientos cubos, todos llenos de agua. Lo sé porque, siempre que teníamos una necesidad urgente, mis hermanos y yo entrábamos allí corriendo y los utilizábamos. Aquellos cubos fueron llenados antes de que muriera mi madre. Supongo que aún siguen allí, con la misma agua de hace treinta años –no me extrañaría–, mezclada con un poco de mí mismo, naturalmente. Yo solía mear como un caballo, y aún sigo haciéndolo."

En *El contrato del dibujante*, cuando las protagonistas femeninas de la película acaban de ultimar los planes para la perdición del dibujante, aparece otro, un dibujante holandés que no tiene la menor duda sobre lo que hay que hacer para purificar y limpiar aquel paisaje inglés (y los hechos que en él se desarrollan) de toda antigua asociación.

Señora Talman: Estaba a punto de llevar al señor Van Hoyten al río; tiene planeado construir una presa e inundar los campos inferiores.

Señor Neville: ¿Campos inundados, señora? ¿Tiene intención de unir sus propiedades con el mar?

La película *A Zed and Two Noughts* ('Una zeta y dos ceros') empieza con un accidente automovilístico provocado por un cisne que vuela bajo y choca contra un vehículo conducido por una mujer llamada Alba Bewick. Con un comienzo así, las asociaciones mitológicas, ornitológicas y literarias del cisne –Leda, Júpiter, Cástor y Pólux, los gemelos, las plumas blancas de un cobarde, Swan (cisne) y el Camino de Swann– saltan y bailan a lo largo de toda la historia, a veces con ligereza, a veces pesadamente, esperando que unas obsesiones tan lúcidas puedan coincidir con unas asociaciones que van mucho más allá de los límites de la película.

La película *El vientre de un arquitecto* ha sido descrita como un ensayo sobre la gravedad. Habla de las ambiciones de un arquitecto que quiere montar una exposición arquitectónica en Roma, y empieza y acaba con incidentes que giran alrededor de un billete de banco inglés de 1983, en el que figuraba un retrato de Sir Isaac Newton. Más de un comentarista ha sugerido que el célebre descubrimiento de la gravedad por parte de Newton ha legitimado el oficio de arquitecto. Stourley Kracklite, el arquitecto norteamericano en cuestión, brinda a la salud de sus amigos arquitectos romanos que le han hecho un pastel de cumpleaños en forma de un edificio en honor de Newton.

Kracklite:

"En Inglaterra, los arquitectos son muy respetados. Sir Christopher Wren aparece en los billetes de cincuenta libras. Los arquitectos son caros. Pero Sir Isaac Newton, el tema de este pastel, está en la cartera de todos los ingleses: aparece en los billetes de una libra. Yo siempre llevo uno, para que me traiga suerte. Un hombre que descubrió la gravedad

y de esta forma consiguió afianzar nuestros pies en el suelo es un buen compañero. Al sujetarnos al suelo permitió, con ecuanimidad, que nuestras cabezas se mantuvieran en las nubes."

Stourley Kracklite muere a causa de la gravedad. Hombre corpulento, aferrado a su billete con la efigie de Newton, se lanza voluntariamente, sin alas, desde lo alto del edificio de Víctor Manuel, en Roma. Quizás él, a su vez, enriquece otra historia contada en *El contrato del dibujante*; una variante de una historia que se cuenta a menudo, sobre arquitectos y sus celosos mecenas –un buen ejemplo de ello es la construcción del Taj Mahal–, aunque aquí, apropiadamente, la historia tiene connotaciones acuáticas:

"Dicen que el duque de Courcy invitó a su mecánico hidráulico a subir hasta lo alto de una elaborada cascada que había construido, y le preguntó si podría construir una maravilla parecida para cualquier otra persona. El hombre, después de obsequiarle con varios agradecimientos y cumplidos, acabó reconociendo que, con el mecenazgo suficiente, podría hacerlo. El duque de Courcy le empujó suavemente por la región lumbar, y el pobre desgraciado cayó al agua y se ahogó."

El héroe personal de Kracklite es Etienne-Louis Boullée, el "constructor robusto", un arquitecto especialmente consciente de la relación entre la masa y la gravedad y admirador de Newton. Y la conversión de Kracklite en el camino de Damasco (una conversión que la mayoría de los pintores ve como una caída de un caballo) es una rápida toma de conciencia de su propia mortalidad, experimentada, mientras está bañándose, desnudo y vulnerable, bajo un techo pintado que representa a Faetón. Faetón muere víctima de la gravedad. Como símbolo de la presunción, es arrojado del carro de Apolo por haberse atrevido a creer que podía conducirlo a través del cielo del amanecer.

Kracklite aparece a menudo enmarcado sobre un fondo de fuentes. Se emborracha hasta el delirio en la taza de una fuente, salpica desenfrenadamente a sus perseguidores y finge tener ideas suicidas en una bañera doméstica.

En el cuarto de baño de la suite-apartamento de Kracklite hay un gran chapoteo y zambullidas en el agua. El agua se derrama sobre el mosaico de mármol. La bañera está muy llena. Alguien está ahogándose. Es Kracklite. No está ahogándose: sólo lo está fingiendo. Louisa, su mujer, no le hace el menor caso y está preparándose para salir a cenar. Camina por la suite, entra en el cuarto de baño y vuelve a entrar en el dormitorio. Tiene el pelo mojado. Las cosas de Kracklite –sus libros, sus papeles, etc.– están arrinconadas en su lado del dormitorio. Están amontonadas alrededor de su cama, como un montón de basura. Exasperada, Louisa accede finalmente a hacerle caso, que es lo que Kracklite deseaba desde el principio.

Louisa: Está bien, Kracklite. ¿Qué estás haciendo?

Kracklite: Me estoy ahogando.

Kracklite sigue zambullendo su cabeza en el agua. Cuando Louisa deja de reaccionar, él se detiene y se queda mirándola desde la bañera. Tiene el pelo pegado a la frente y el agua chorreando por su cara.

Kracklite: (hablando consigo mismo, pero procurando que Louisa le oiga) No te esfuerces: tu cuerpo no te permitirá hacerlo. Nunca se ha muerto nadie por dejar de respirar voluntariamente. Si consiguieras dejar de respirar quedarías inconsciente... y volverías a respirar...

Louisa: Podrías intentar cortarte las venas.

Teniendo en cuenta la posición de su marido, en una bañera de agua caliente, es su mujer quien, sin sospecharlo, interpreta correctamente la tradición del suicidio a la romana.

El título de la película *Drowning by Numbers* anuncia sus propias obsesiones por el agua y la fascinación por los juegos acuáticos, como el de las ovejas y las mareas.

Las ovejas son especialmente sensibles al momento exacto del cambio de la marea. En este juego, nueve ovejas atadas a unas estacas reaccionan, arrancan las estacas, pegan un tirón a las sillas y hacen tambalearse las tazas de té. Se hacen apuestas sobre la sensibilidad combinada de cualquier hilera de ovejas leída verticalmente, horizontalmente o en diagonal. Al haber normalmente tres cambios de marea cada veinticuatro horas, la práctica habitual es coger el mejor de los tres resultados. Se utilizan relojes, calendarios y horarios fiables para determinar la exactitud de la previsión de la oveja.

Esto puede explicar las sutilezas de un niño sobreexcitado por los juegos, pero las asociaciones acuáticas no son arbitrarias cuando juega contra un fondo de bañeras, piscinas y el mar del Norte, lugares de ahogamientos dolorosos que los personajes de la película quieren hacer pasar por accidentes pero el público sabe perfectamente que se trata de asesinatos. El asesinato con agua es quizás el más fácil de ocultar.

En la película *El cocinero, el ladrón, su mujer y su amante* hay dos secuencias de riego con mangueras, dispuestas de tal forma que se complementan entre sí; la primera sirve para limpiar los excrementos y la humedad de la tortura vulgar, la segunda para limpiar la putrefacción y la violencia de un marido engañado. Ambas poseen un patetismo de una gran fuerza dramática. Ambas, sin duda, enfatizan la limpieza literal y metafórica. Y ambas, iluminadas por detrás y dispuestas composicionalmente por *reprise* mutua, son extremadamente bellas.

En la película *Prospero's Books* ('Los libros de Próspero'), el primer volumen de magia era el Libro del Agua. Se trata de un libro de tapas impermeables que se ha descolorido por el contacto excesivo con el agua. Está lleno de dibujos experimentales y textos exploratorios escritos sobre papel de grosor variable. Hay dibujos de todas las asociaciones acuáticas concebibles: mares, tormentas, lluvia, nieve, nubes, lagos, cascadas, riachuelos, canales, molinos de agua, naufragios, inundaciones y lágrimas. Según vamos pasando las páginas, los elementos acuosos a menudo están animados. Hay olas rizadas y tempestades sesgadas. Ríos y cascadas fluyen y burbujean. Planos de maquinaria hidráulica y mapas meteorológicos centellean con flechas, símbolos y diagramas agitados. Todos los dibujos están hechos por la misma mano. Quizás se trata de una colección perdida de dibujos de Da Vinci religada en un libro por el rey de Francia en Amboise y comprada por los duques milaneses para ofrecérsela a Próspero como regalo de boda.

La isla teatral de Próspero, situada, tanto según Próspero como según Shakespeare, en algún lugar de las Bermudas, fue explotada para extraer de ella todas las posibles referencias al agua, y,

apropiadamente, los escenarios se construyeron alrededor de un dique seco excavado dentro de un hangar de un astillero de Amsterdam que había sido utilizado para construir petroleros.

La película *The Pillow Book* trata de libros, de textos, de escritura, y es una consideración del cuerpo humano visto como un libro, y del libro visto como un cuerpo. Pero las tintas del texto son solubles, aplicadas con un pincel sobre piel lavada, y evocan la idea de la escritura sobre papel; los textos son lavados, limpiados, bañados, borrados por la lluvia, por el vapor, por las lágrimas y por la reconfortante agua tibia de la bañera.

Agua y cielo fuera de la pantalla

La fascinación por el agua es un estímulo pictórico, como metáfora y como instrumento narrativo, y ha persistido fuera de su representación en la pantalla.

Varios desengaños sobre la naturaleza del cine, junto con un deseo de asociar el lenguaje cinematográfico a las proyecciones y las actuaciones en directo, han creado varios proyectos a largo plazo. El primero, un ciclo de óperas con el título colectivo de *The Death of Webern and Others* ('La muerte de Webern y otros'), trata de una conspiración contra los compositores que pretende relacionar la muerte de Anton von Webern con la de John Lennon, a través de las muertes de otros ocho compositores que se han producido en el ínterin. Es una serie que se propone situar sobre un escenario una mezcla de cine y ópera. La primera de estas diez óperas –la número seis de la serie–, titulada *Rosa*, con música de Louis Andriessen, fue representada en la Ópera de Amsterdam en 1994. La séptima, a la que todavía hay que poner música, trata de Corntopia Felixchange, una soprano californiana asesinada en una piscina de San Francisco.

En 1980 se escribió un proyecto de ópera titulado *The Massacre at the Baths* ('La masacre en los baños'), en que los miembros de diez compañías teatrales anti-*establishment* de Santiago de Chile son detenidos durante el golpe de estado de Pinochet de 1973 y amontonados en una piscina olímpica vacía. Antes de que se llene la piscina y se ahoguen todos, los actores y cantantes se confabulan y se burlan de sus carceleros representando tres historias heroicas de agua y de autosacrificio: Hero y Leandro, Ofelia y la Muerte de Virginia Woolf, con la ayuda de un coro de Nadadores Sincronizados y de un maestro de ceremonias llamado Marat.

El segundo proyecto importante a largo plazo, titulado "The Stairs" ('Las escaleras'), pretende montar diez exposiciones en grandes ciudades de todo el mundo, para demostrar, analizar y debatir el carácter del cine y de las artes que con él se relacionan. Cada una de estas exposiciones se centra en un aspecto diferente: iluminación, encuadre, localización, escala, texto, ilusión...

Dos de estas diez exposiciones –localización e iluminación– se han montado en Ginebra y Munich en 1994 y 1996.

Ha habido varias exposiciones que han intentado combinar prácticas museísticas típicas con lenguajes cinematográficos y teatrales. La primera, "The Physical Self" ('El yo físico'), en Rotterdam, se centraba en el cuerpo humano y su representación a lo largo de quinientos años de pintura, escultura y diseño dentro de la colección Boymans-van Beuningen. Ahí vi por primera vez grabados de las figuras de Van Haarlem-Goltzius que representan a los caídos: Ícaro, Ixión, Faetón y Tántalo. Ícaro, que intenta volar y no lo consigue; Ixión, arrojado a la tierra por su intento de violar a Juno; Faetón

arrojado desde el cielo por haber robado el carro de Apolo, y Tántalo arrojado al Infierno por haber robado la ambrosía, el alimento de los dioses.

La segunda era una exposición de dibujos antiguos y modernos del Louvre titulada "Volar fuera de este mundo", y trataba del deseo imposible de volar. La tercera exposición, "100 objetos para representar al mundo", celebrada en Viena, presentaba una irónica lista de la compra con cien objetos que podrían constituir un inventario de lo que quedaría de nosotros como significativo del final del segundo milenio. En la lista de la compra, entre otras cosas, había una nube, agua, nieve, cien paraguas, un arco iris, viento, un avión estrellado, una bañera, hielo, un arqueópterix, una barca de remos, plumas, la mosca doméstica y el sol.

100 Allegories to Represent the World ('100 alegorías para representar el mundo') es un libro de alegorías confeccionado en Estrasburgo sobre la nueva tecnología de la imagen como *collages* creados por ordenador, para encontrar el equivalente más actual de los manuscritos iluminados de *Les Très Riches Heures*, cuando la tecnología más reciente era la aplicación de pan de oro, cochinilla y lapislázuli sobre piel de becerro. Las alegorías de Estrasburgo complementan y amplían el tema de la fascinación por los personajes familiares de una enciclopedia sobre vuelos universales y agua. Entre los voladores están Ícaro y Faetón, y, entre los entusiastas del agua, están el Ahogador y su víctima, Ofelia, Marat, los supervivientes de la balsa de la Medusa, Hero y Leandro, Noé y su mujer, Neptuno y Caronte.

La ópera *Flying over Water* ('Volar sobre el agua'), que fue concebida para la Ópera de Estrasburgo pero no ha llegado a representarse, existe sobre el papel como un proyecto susceptible de ser reconsiderado, posiblemente en Turín en 1998, y como material aún por completar como guión de una película que se intentaría rodar en un importante aeropuerto europeo. Su estructura básica incorpora la presente "Descripción de una exposición imaginaria sobre el tema de la aventura de Ícaro", vista como una reconstrucción de la mitología clásica original junto con un equivalente de la época actual, sustituyendo Creta por Alemania, a Dédalo por un moderno ingeniero aeronáutico y a Ícaro por un piloto de pruebas, y abarcando variantes antiguas y modernas de Ariadna (como azafata), Pasífae, Teseo, Baco y el minotauro.

La Fundació Joan Miró rep el suport continuat de les institucions següents:
Ajuntament de Barcelona
Generalitat de Catalunya
Diputació de Barcelona
Banco Bilbao Vizcaya

A més, la Fundació rep la col·laboració permanent dels Amics de la Fundació Joan Miró.

Protectors institucionals
Marc Bachs, Embalatges
Caixa d'Estalvis i Pensions de Barcelona
Canon España, S.A.
Col·legi d'Arquitectes de Catalunya
Edicions 62, S.A.
Editorial Gustavo Gili, S.A.
ENHER
FCC, S.A.
Hoechst Ibérica, S.A.
IBM
La Polígrafa, S.L.
Minas de Almadén y Arrayanes

Protectors distingits
Frederic Amat
Joan Badosa i Marco
Oriol Bohigas i Guardiola
Catalina Cisneros
August Ferrer
Josep Laporte Salas
Jordi Madern
Antoni Martí Carrasco
Josep Martorell
Josep Ramon Morera Balada
André Ricart
Josep Suñol i Soler

Concept and Art Direction/Concepció i direcció artística
Peter Greenaway

Director
Rosa Maria Malet

Coordination/Coordinació
Victòria Izquierdo Brichs

Registrar/Registre
Jordi Juncosa
Imma Carballés

Locating Materials/Recerca de materials
Helena Cordón

Press and Public Relations/Comunicació
Anna Noëlle

London Coordination/Coordinació a Londres
Eliza Poklewski-Koziell

Lighting Design/Disseny de la il·luminació
Reinier van Brummelen

Installation Design/Disseny del muntatge
Maarten Piersma
Reinier van Brummelen

Installation Manufacture/Producció del muntatge
Calidoscopi
Maarten Piersma
Rob Duiker
Constance de Vos
Marco Schürmann

Coffin & Wings/Taüt i ales
Henri de Maar

Lighting/Il·luminació
Arcoiris

Sound/Sonorització
IRCAM
Jean-Baptiste Barrière
Gilbert Nouno
David Poissonnier
Red Service

Insurance/Assegurances
AON Iberia Correduría de Seguros, S.A.

Transport/Transports
SIT Transportes Internacionales, S.A.

Photographs/Fotografies

Arxiu Històric de la Ciutat. Barcelona
Bildarchiv Preussischer Kulturbesitz, Berlin
Jaume Blassi
The Bridgeman Art Library, London
Caja de Ahorros de la Inmaculada, Zaragoza
The Conway Library, Courtauld Institute of Art, London
Hans Danuser
J.R. Eyerman, Life Magazine
Sue Fox
Gaumont Cinémathèque, Paris
Tom Haartsen
Hamburger Kunsthalle
Bettina Jacot-Descombes
Kunsthistorisches Museum, Wien
Jacques-Henri Lartigue
Musée d'art et d'histoire, Genève
Musée du Louvre, Paris
Musée d'Orsay, Paris
Musées royaux des Beaux-Arts de Belgique
Museum Boimans Van Beuningen, Rotterdam
The Natural History Museum, London
The New Museum of Contemporary Art, New York
Pere Pratdesaba
Réunion de Musées Nationaux, Paris
Nick Rogers
Bastienne Schmidt
Jeffrey Silverthorne
Speltdoorn et Fils
Staatliche Graphische Sammlung, München
Staatliche Kunstsammlungen Dresden
Statens Konstmuseer, Stockholm
Université des Sciences Humaines de Strasbourg en association avec Andromaque
Tate Gallery, London
Elke Walford
Weegee